PRAISE FOR NERO WOLFE . . .

"It is always a treat to read a Nero Wolfe mystery. The man has entered our folklore; he is part of the psyche of anybody who has ever turned over the pages of a mystery novel. Like Sherlock Holmes . . . he looms larger than life and, in some ways, is much more satisfactory."
—*The New York Times Book Review*

"The most interesting great detective of them all."
—Kingsley Amis, author of *Lucky Jim*

"The worst thorn in the flesh I know of."
—Inspector L. T. Cramer, Manhattan South

"Nero Wolfe is one of the master creations."
—James M. Cain, author of
The Postman Always Rings Twice

"(Wolfe) . . . is the best of them all."
—Supreme Court Justice Oliver Wendell Holmes

"My favorite fatty."
—Archie Goodwin

D0456609

ARCHIE GOODWIN . . .

"Archie is a splendid character."

—Dame Agatha Christie

"The most damn contrary pest within my knowledge."

—Inspector L. T. Cramer, Manhattan South

"Stout's supreme triumph was the creation of Archie Goodwin."

—P. G. Wodehouse

"I do nothing without Mr. Goodwin."

—Nero Wolfe

"If he had done nothing more than to create Archie Goodwin, Rex Stout would deserve the gratitude of whatever assessors watch over the prosperity of American literature . . . Archie is the lineal descendant of Huck Finn."

—Jacques Barzun

Bantam Books by Rex Stout
Ask your bookseller for the books you have missed

AND BE A VILLAIN
BAD FOR BUSINESS
THE BLACK MOUNTAIN
THE BROKEN VASE
DEATH OF A DOXY
DEATH OF A DUDE
THE DOORBELL RANG
DOUBLE FOR DEATH
A FAMILY AFFAIR
THE FATHER HUNT
FER-DE-LANCE
THE GOLDEN SPIDERS
THE HAND IN THE GLOVE
HOMICIDE TRINITY
IF DEATH EVER SLEPT
IN THE BEST OF FAMILIES
MIGHT AS WELL BE DEAD
THE MOUNTAIN CAT MURDERS
NOT QUITE DEAD ENOUGH
OVER MY DEAD BODY
PLEASE PASS THE GUILT
THE PRESIDENT VANISHES
PRISONER'S BASE
THE RED BOX
A RIGHT TO DIE
THE SILENT SPEAKER
THE SOUND OF MURDER
THREE AT WOLFE'S DOOR
TOO MANY COOKS
TRIPLE JEOPARDY
TROUBLE IN TRIPLICATE

Fer-de-Lance

by Rex Stout

A Nero Wolfe Mystery

Nero Wolfe: A Retrospective
by John McAleer

BANTAM BOOKS
TORONTO • NEW YORK • LONDON • SYDNEY • AUCKLAND

FER-DE-LANCE

*A Bantam Book / published by arrangement with
the author*

PRINTING HISTORY

Farrar & Rinehart edition published 1934

Bantam edition / March 1983
2nd printing . . . November 1984

ISBN 0-553-24918-5

Published simultaneously in the United States and Canada

PRINTED IN THE UNITED STATES OF AMERICA

O   11   10   9   8   7   6   5   4   3   2

Sometime in the 1950s I graduated from Nancy Drew to Nero Wolfe. The transition was a natural one for me, a third generation Wolfe reader; many of the yellowing paperback editions in my collection originally belonged to my grandfather or my father (one appears to have originally belonged to the Ridgewood, New Jersey, Public Library, where it was due on November 15, 1966, and I certainly hope they won't come after me for it now). But it has been only in the past six years, since The Wolfe Pack was founded, that I've made the acquaintance of literally hundreds of Wolfe fans.

It's a diverse group, The Wolfe Pack: teenagers and nonagenarians; collectors and casual readers; aficionados of the mystery genre and people who've never read a mystery except for the Wolfe corpus. A fair number confess to being madly in love with Archie Goodwin; a few even confess to being madly in love with Nero Wolfe. But all share an affection bordering on fanaticism for that remarkable household on West Thirty-fifth Street that sprang to life fully realized fifty years ago, on October 24, 1934, with the publication of Fer-de-Lance.

Of course, there have been some changes through the years. Mr. Wolfe's contact at the Gazette in 1934 was Harry Foster, not Lon Cohen; his lawyer, Henry Barber rather than Nathaniel Parker. And Inspector Cramer doesn't show up in Wolfe's office during Fer-de-Lance, as the murder in Fer-de-Lance was committed in Westchester. But the essential elements were all there: Mr. Wolfe in his office, consuming six quarts of beer a day, with Archie needling him into action; Fritz in the kitchen preparing the best food in the city (except possibly at Rusterman's); Theodore in the plant rooms tending the orchids; and Saul and Fred and Orrie free-lancing for Mr. Wolfe.

Visitors to London can actually go to 221B Baker Street. If you were to make a pilgrimage to West Thirty-fifth Street in New York—assuming you were able to decide which of the *various street numbers the house has had through the years is the real one—you would not be able to find Mr. Wolfe's brownstone. But no matter. You don't have to climb up the steps to the front stoop, ring the doorbell, and wait for Archie to look through the one-way glass panel and then admit you to the front room to await Mr. Wolfe's descent from the plant rooms. You can step into Mr. Wolfe's world simply by opening any of the thirty-three novels or thirty-nine short stories chronicling his illustrious career. And what better place to start than with his first recorded case, Fer-de-Lance. It is, to bestow upon it the highest imaginable praise, very satisfactory.*

Ellen E. Krieger
WEROWANCE
The Wolfe Pack

Nero Wolfe:
A Retrospective
by John McAleer

When in 1934, at the age of ninety-three, Justice Oliver Wendell Holmes read Rex Stout's *Fer-de-Lance*, he wrote on the margin of the last page, "This fellow is the best of them all." Holmes did not live to see his judgment vindicated over and over again, but others who shared his enthusiasm at the time survived to confirm his astuteness. Forty years later, when Rex Stout, at eighty-nine, published his seventy-second and final Nero Wolfe story, *A Family Affair* (1975), novelist Walter D. Edmonds declared: "I shall never forget my excitement on reading *Fer-de-Lance*, sprung like Athena perfect from the Jovian brow, fresh and new and at the same time with enough plain familiar things in scene and setting to put any reader at his ease. That in my mind is Rex Stout's secret, and with each new Nero Wolfe it has jelled more perfectly."

From its first appearance *Fer-de-Lance* has been recognized as one of the cornerstone works of detective fiction. In fact, the *Times* of London soon put it on its list of the one hundred best detective stories ever written. One of the many remarkable attributes of the novel that justify this verdict is the thoroughness with which it sets in place a framework sturdy and intricate enough to sustain an epic that ultimately would encompass more than ten thousand pages. This framework appears, of course, to depend on a system of comic order that Wolfe has ordained for himself and those living under his roof and which outsiders, whether clients or intruders—and that includes the constabulary (the FBI as well as New York's Finest)—are compelled to recognize and accommodate. Wolfe holds to an unvarying regimen. He will not leave his brownstone house, on West Thirty-fifth Street, on business. (Perhaps as many as a score of times he violates this rule, but, over a period of more than forty years, that amounts to no more than an infinitesimal breach of conduct). Women are given no role in his meticulously managed household, yet the housekeeping arrangements are flawless. For that reason, Clara Fox, in *The Rubber Band* (1936), is moved to say, " 'You know, Mr. Goodwin, this house represents the most insolent denial of female rights the mind of man has ever conceived. No woman in it from top to bottom, but the routine is faultless, the food is perfect, and the sweeping and dusting impeccable.' "

Wolfe eats breakfast in his bedroom at eight. Between nine and eleven he tends his ten thousand orchid plants in his rooftop greenhouse. From eleven till one-fifteen he is in his office, and then after lunch he is there until four. From four to six he again sojourns, virtually incommunicado, among his orchids. He returns then to his office, where he stays till his dinner hour, seven-thirty. Only in the most extraordinary circumstances does he tolerate any breach of this routine. Actually, however, Wolfe perceives that the order he decrees within his own household is a working model—a microcosm if you will—of that ideal order that civilization must move toward if it is to endure and prevail.

That Rex Stout should, from the outset, regulate with clocklike precision, the context of the world in which Nero Wolfe would function, comes as no surprise to those who knew him. A genius in his own right (he had an IQ of 185), it was usual with him, at the outset of a new enterprise, to visualize it right down to its most minute articulations, because he wanted to be certain it could stand up under every stress and strain before he set it in motion. This he had done, in 1916, with the school banking system—the Educational Thrift Service—that earned millions of dollars for the Stout family in the years before he turned to writing. For three days he locked himself in his room at the Schenley Hotel, in Pittsburgh, brainstorming every particular of it before it was launched.

The relentless logic that Nero Wolfe applies to the problems that beset him found its pattern in the flawlessly functioning mind of Rex Stout—a mind that enabled Stout to write his stories with such assurance that he got them right on first try. Sometimes he leaned his head against his typewriter until the frame grew hot, plotting the next step, but when he struck the keys he was certain of what he wanted to say. The first draft was always the final draft. When he pulled the last page from the typewriter, the manuscript was ready to put in the mail. Writing four to six pages a day, in a nine-hour stint, he usually finished a book in thirty-eight days. "If I had to rewrite a book to get it right," Rex said, "I would have done so. But I never had to." Lucetta Stout, Rex's mother, once said that she named him Rex "because when he came out, he came out like a king." Nero Wolfe also came out like a king.

Over many years various explanations have been advanced to account for the favor detective fiction finds with a multitude of readers. Somerset Maugham thought it found its public among those who like their stories well made. Ronald Knox surmised it is popular because man, by nature, is a puzzle-solving animal. Phoebe Atwood Taylor mischievously alleged that it gives men a chance to channel off their hostilities by allowing them to participate vicariously in the act of murder. Edgar Allan Poe suggested that it justified itself by exercising the mind in the pursuit of its proper end—the attainment of truth. Charles Brady proposed that it commends itself to serious notice because it upholds fixed moral values in an increasingly relativistic world. Rex Stout himself whimsically contended that it owes its acceptance to its success in perpetuating the illusion that man is a rational animal. The essence of these many claims is distilled in Mark Van Doren's declaration that "the detective story must remain civilized because that is what the literature of detection is all about; the protection of civilization by those courageous and competent enough to save it." Because Rex Stout realized this fact, Van Doren concluded, he "never subscribed to the theory that the detective must be a thug, a drunkard, and a lecher." Indeed, sex and violence have only a small role to play in the Wolfe corpus. Yet Rex Stout was no prude. "Sex and violence," he told me, "like all other items of human behavior, are acceptable and desirable in a detective story if they are essential to the story. In mine, apparently, they are not."

In a compelling assessment of the saga of Nero Wolfe, David Anderson sees the cycle of stories steadily broadening from a concern with personal order, as embodied in the individual family, e.g., *The League of Frightened Men* (1935), *The Red Box* (1936), *Too Many Cooks* (1938), *Some Buried Caesar* (1939), and *Where There's a Will* (1941), to a concern with political order, embodied in the state, e.g., *Over My Dead Body* (1939), *The Silent Speaker* (1946), and *The Second Confession* (1949), to a concern with ethical order, which upholds man's place in the scheme of creation, e.g., *The Final Deduction* (1961), *A Right to Die* (1964), and *Death of a Doxy* (1966).

While Nero Wolfe is preeminently a man of intellect—a veritable embodiment of reason—simultaneously, as he readily and frequently acknowledges, he is an ardent romantic, cherishing a vision of an ideal society. Within his brownstone house he can anticipate some success in securing and maintaining the ideal order that he envisages. Yet, as David Anderson observes, "His daily schedule is as much an insistence on order as a tribute to it." To the extent that it is possible for him to do so, he isolates himself to safeguard his romantic vision. He even accounts for his obesity (in peak form he weighs 285 pounds) as a condition fostered to insulate himself from emotions. His alleged misogyny is ascribed to the same cause. As he says in *Too Many Cooks*, " 'Not like women? They are astounding and successful animals. For reasons of convenience, I merely preserve an appearance of immunity.' " This does not keep him from instructing Archie, on occasion, to seat an attractive lady client where he can observe a well-turned calf.

But Wolfe has no more chance of limiting his struggle for order to his own carefully manipulated environment than Poe's potentate in "The Masque of the Red Death" had of isolating his household from the pestilence raging outside the confines of his subterranean palace. Even his right to isolate himself in this fashion may be questioned, just as Doctor Joseph Fletcher, the eminent situation ethics expert, questioned the propriety of isolating David, "the bubble boy," from the hazards of a world nature had not fitted him to cope with. The ideal human community Wolfe seeks to create, the chaotic world beyond his doors—the point of origin of many harsh intrusions—and, ironically, Wolfe's dependency on that chaos for the money he needs to underwrite his fantasy of an ideal world are irreconcilable, and the issues involved must, of course, ultimately be confronted.

As much as Wolfe reverences his ideal environment, he is not blind to reality. In "Door to Death" (1950), he tells Joseph G. Pitcairn, " 'It would be foolhardy to assume that you would welcome a thorn for the sake of such abstractions as justice or truth, since that would make you a rarity almost unknown.' " Yet Nero Wolfe himself is such a rarity. When he confronts the crime lord, Arnold Zeck, in *In the Best Families* (1950), he realizes that the safety and stability of the brownstone will exist as a mere sham if he does not meet the challenge Zeck has thrown to him. Accordingly, he abandons his snug, secure haven and goes forth into the world to suffer what, for him, are unspeakable indignities before he brings his quarry to ground. It was not with irreverence that Stout caused Wolfe to abandon his sanctuary, leaving the door ajar behind him, on East Sunday, for he too, in secular terms, was coming forth as a savior who had voluntarily assumed a martyr's role to redeem his fellow man—in this instance freeing mankind from the scourge of a corrupt individual who threatens the stability of the social order.

At this juncture the man of reason, compelled by reason to become a man of action, displaces the romantic idealist. In "Grim Fairy Tales" (1949), Rex Stout would say, "We enjoy reading about people who love and hate and covet—about gluttons and martyrs, misers and sadists, whores and saints, brave men and cowards. But also, demonstrably, we enjoy reading about a man who gloriously acts and decides, with no exception and no compunction, not as his emotions brutally command, but as his reason instructs." In *In the Best Families*, the very apogee of the orbit of the Wolfe epic, Wolfe emerges as the epitome of such a man. In Greek myth the Furies, with stern, dispassionate justice, exact retribution for disruptions of the moral order. Wolfe, fully cognizant of their role, proclaims himself to be of their company, "one of the Erinyes." In this role, of course, he exactly parallels the behavior of his creator, Rex Stout, who, at the start of World War II, forsook the idyllic life he had created at High Meadow—his beautiful country estate in Danbury, Connecticut—to live in an apartment in New York City, and, as chairman of the vital Writers War Board (overseeing the activities of more than two thousand writers), engage in a campaign to bring down Adolf Hitler and his Axis allies. That campaign has been called the most successful propaganda effort ever mounted by a major nation in wartime.

During this period of service to his country and to mankind—for which he accepted neither salary nor expense money—Rex Stout stopped writing Nero Wolfe stories. This sacrifice, nonetheless, did not go uncompensated, for when he resumed writing he came to his task with a vision more broadly based and with, as well, the realization, which he had before lacked, that he should bend all his narrative efforts to writing Nero Wolfe stories. It was in these stories that his vision and his artistry came together in perfect harmony to express those views that were his contribution to the preservation of the social order and the dignity of the human condition. It may here be noted that in the Wolfe corpus, even while he entertains us, Rex Stout attacks a broad spectrum of social evils: fascism, communism, McCarthyism, racism, censorship, mercantile greed, commercial radio; abuses in the law profession, in government agencies, in labor unions, in the National Association of Manufacturers, and in the publishing industry; exploitation of displaced persons; the Nixon government; and social pretense wherever encountered. This is not done with calculated didacticism but with an earnestness remote from preachment or overt chastisement that gives it a wholesome, organic relevance to the narrative at hand.

To Jacques Barzun, dean of American critics, Nero Wolfe stands as "a portrait of the Educated Man." Readers who feel intimidated by that formidable description will feel somewhat reassured, perhaps, by James M. Cain's assertion that "Nero Wolfe is one of the master creations." It was left to British novelist Kingsley Amis, however, to characterize Wolfe in terms that no true votary of detective fiction can ignore. "Wolfe," said Amis, "is the most interesting 'great detective' of them all." It cannot surprise the reader, then, to learn that newcomers to the corpus have been known to put the question to long-standing Neronians, Are we supposed to like Nero Wolfe? For many detective heroes the scrutiny such a question invites would be lethal. With Wolfe that is not a problem. What we know about Wolfe is what we are told by his indispensable dogsbody, Archie Goodwin, the first person narrator of all the Nero Wolfe stories.

We see Wolfe as Archie sees him. Like Archie we can be exasperated by Wolfe's arrogance, obstinacy, and aloofness. Sometimes relations between the two men seem at the breaking point. But Archie admits that Wolfe is his "favorite fatty," and as we come to deepen our acquaintance with both men, we see why. Wolfe has none of those qualities spoken of as endearing. But he is just, sincere, humane, honest, fair-minded, dignified, witty, learned, loyal, profound, and astute. Above all, he is relentlessly logical and, as a result, ultimately invincible. He grows on us with each encounter until we come to respect him and, at length, to cherish him quite as Archie does. We even become solicitous and distressed for his sake when his comforts are interfered with. Maybe his plant schedule is unreasonable and his fear of moving vehicles ludicrous. Maybe his beer drinking is excessive and his gourmet preferences (e.g., chicken fattened on blueberries), outrageous. But we come to believe that the world owes something to this unique and heroic man and that gratifying his indulgences is a small price to pay in exchange for the services he renders to humanity. A God-the-Father figure, he is awesome but deserving of our obeisance. If he looks upon his orchids as pampered concubines that merit the attention they get because of the beauty they bestow, then we must concede that he himself should be indulged without stint because he is a superior being who, by operating mentally and morally at the level he does, exalts the human race.

Archie, on the other hand, has no trouble enlisting our loyalty, sympathy, and devotion. We find ourselves, though we know better, strangely partial to the resolute lady who showed up at a Poughkeepsie bookstore and asked for "one of those Archie books." The bookseller ruminated for a minute, then said, "You mean the Nero Wolfe books!" "Nonsense," the customer rejoined. "We know who does all the work." Even Rex Stout was able to relate to this outlook. As the saga progressed he enlarged Archie's role and, occasionally, as in *Too Many Women* (1947), kept Archie center stage while Wolfe lurked in the background. Rex's mail so consistently told him how much Archie was esteemed, he was able at last to concede, "It's Archie who really carries the stories as narrator. Whether the readers know it or not, it's Archie they really enjoy." Rex did not resent Archie's eminence. After all, though Wolfe was his achieved self, the man of intellect he became over the years, Archie was his spontaneous self, the person he most naturally was.

Many people whose judgment has to be respected have admired Archie. Agatha Christie said, "Archie is a splendid character to have invented." Leslie Charteris, creator of the Saint, maintained, "It always seemed to me that Archie was a creation worth noticing. Goodwin has his own personality, can carry out an assignment with intelligence and efficiency, and is not incapable of occasional irreverence towards some of the affectations and grandiosities of the boss. Which I found a most refreshing change from the usual formula in this genre." Charteris is referring here to the Dr. Watson stereotype, dubbed by Stephen Leacock "the Poor Sap," and by Agatha Christie (notwithstanding Captain Hastings), "the Idiot Friend," because he seems to exist either solely to reenforce the ego of the great detective with constant exclamations of astonishment, reverence, and approval, or, forgive me, to pit the reader against an observer who is stupider than he is.

When, in 1965, Jacques Barzun turned away for a moment from his duties as dean of the Columbia University Graduate School to take a close look at Archie, he came to a warmhearted conclusion: "If he had done nothing more than to create Archie Goodwin, Rex Stout would deserve the gratitude of whatever assessors watch over the prosperity of American literature. For surely Archie is one of the folk heroes in which the modern American temper can see itself transfigured." P. G. Wodehouse was willing to go further and wasted no words in saying so. "Stout's supreme triumph," he said, "was the creation of Archie Goodwin. A Watson of some sort to tell the story is unavoidable, and the hundreds of Watsons who have appeared in print since Holmes's simply won't do. Archie is a Watson in the sense that he tells the story, but in no other way is there anything Watsonian about him. And he brings excellent comedy into the type of narrative where comedy seldom bats better than .100." Barzun is in wholehearted agreement: "Archie is the lineal descendant of Huck Finn. Above all, he commands a turn of humor that goes to the heart of character and situation: not since Mark Twain and Mr. Dooley has the native spirit of comedy found an interpreter of equal force. Our other professional humorists of the last half century have been solid and serviceable, but their creations are not in a class with Archie."

Discussion of the corpus is not ended with an acknowledgment of the merits of Wolfe and Archie. The brownstone house is itself a palpable presence in the stories, as is the intimate family group that Wolfe has gathered about him. With most detective stories our interest centers on the impact the detectives have on the crime. With the Wolfe corpus our locus of interest is the impact the crime has on the detectives because it is them that we really care about. "Like P. G. Wodehouse," says Donald Westlake, "Rex Stout created a world." David Anderson, concurring, amplifies on that claim: "A writer can create a world in one novel—as Rex Stout did in Fer-de-Lance—but a world developed and established over seventy-two tales and forty-two years becomes more than a fictive world—it becomes a fictive home."

In addition to those residing in the brownstone with Wolfe—

Archie; Fritz Brenner, Swiss chef and general factotum; and
Theodore Horstmann, who tends the orchids—Wolfe's intimate
world includes also his "professional family," as Fred Durkin
calls it, which, in addition to Fred, includes Saul Panzer,
Orrie Cather, Johnny Keems (slain in the line of duty), and
Bill Gore (dropped because he bored his creator). These are
the operatives, men of varying excellence, who along with
Theodolinda Bonner and Sally Colt, supplement Archie when
need arises. By extension we can add three more to this
number, newsman Lon Cohen, Lily Rowan, Archie's girl-
friend—"I would tackle a tiger bare-handed to save her from
harm," Rex told me when a reader had the consummate
nerve to propose that he should kill her off—and Inspector L.
T. Cramer who, occasionally at least, is cordially received at
West Thirty-fifth Street, though by no means always. In their
supportive roles, as the bulwark that helps to hold off the
menacing forces of the world beyond the brownstone, these
individuals make Wolfe's edenic haven seem more probable
and more possible.

Archie, who sometimes indiscreetly boasts that Wolfe needs
him to goad him into action—rather like a mahout prodding
an elephant—on occasion has been described as Wolfe's
tinderbox. But if this is so, then Inspector Cramer is the
bellows that quickens the flame. Quite commonly in detective
fiction, when the detective is a private investigator, his
efficiency is underscored by emphasizing the incompetence
and ineptitude of the police. Rex Stout avoids that snare.
Lieutenant Rowcliff is despised, of course, and his shortcomings
stressed over many years till finally he receives his comeup-
pance in the penultimate Nero Wolfe novel, *Please Pass the
Guilt* (1973). Since George Rowcliff was modeled on a naval
officer under whom Rex Stout served in 1905–1906 when he
was pay yeoman on Theodore Roosevelt's presidential yacht,
the officer must have left deep wounds. But Lieutenant Perley
Stebbins and Cramer are portrayed with consideration. In
fact, one of Rex Stout's favorite scenes in the corpus came in
The Doorbell Rang (1965), when Cramer, meeting secretly
with Archie to give him some background on the case they
were working on, brought with him a carton of milk for
Archie since he knew that that was Archie's preferred beverage.
"I think I wrote that very well," Rex told me, "I think that's
done just the way such an episode should be done." Rex
resented any suggestion that he came down hard on the

police in the Wolfe corpus. Indeed, he thought it a fine endorsement of the democratic system that, in his books, he showed that private investigators could disagree with the police now and again yet not be prevented from carrying on independently of them—a situation that would not have been conceivable in a totalitarian state. Indeed, Rex was delighted when he learned that readers in the Soviet Union were impressed that Rex Stout, in *The Doorbell Rang*, could take on J. Edgar Hoover himself and not be imprisoned or silenced.

Back in the 1950s when a college president and his wife were disembarking from a cab on West Thirty-seventh Street in New York City, the lady said to her husband, "Isn't this where Nero Wolfe lives?" Before he could answer, the shocked cabbie intervened. "Oh, no," he said. "Wolfe lives on West Thirty-fifth Street." The cabbie was justified in his indignation for, after all, he had a right to expect this fact to be common knowledge. In the fifty years that have elapsed since *Fer-de-Lance* was first published, the Nero Wolfe stories have been translated into twenty-seven languages and have sold, in all editions, more than one hundred million copies. The London *Times* has reported that of all the writers who ever wrote in English the two who sell best behind the Iron Curtain now are Agatha Christie and Rex Stout. What is even more remarkable, Stout is available there only in contraband editions. "Do not mail me any of Stout's books," a Prague editor wrote to me sadly, "because I would not be allowed to have them."

During World War II FDR sometimes read the Wolfe stories to relax from the burdens of office. Dwight D. Eisenhower read *Prisoner's Base* (1952) while recovering from a heart attack during his first term as president. In England, Anthony Eden, as prime minister of Great Britain, devoured the novels with enthusiasm. Former French president Giscard d'Estaing, more recently, confessed that Nero Wolfe was his favorite reading. John Cardinal Wright, a member of the Vatican Curia, liked the stories well enough to write Rex Stout a fan letter. William Faulkner quoted Nero Wolfe in his Nobel Prize acceptance speech. John Steinbeck wrote a poem about Wolfe and Archie. Moss Hart schemed to write a play about them. The Vermont Symphony Orchestra, in the dead of winter, premiered a "Wolfe and Archie Overture." Ian Fleming introduced Nero Wolfe into a James Bond thriller and asserted that Stout's was "one of the most civilized minds ever to concern itself with detective fiction." He asked Rex to collaborate with him on a Wolfe and Bond novel. "No," said Rex, "Bond would get the girl. Archie wouldn't like that."

Other admirers of the Wolfe corpus whom Stout sometimes heard from included Hubert Humphrey, Graham Greene, Georges Simenon, Marlene Dietrich, T. E. Lawrence (Lawrence of Arabia), Alfred Lunt and Lynn Fontanne, Aldous Huxley, J. B. Priestley, Henry Miller, Norman Cousins, Richard Rodgers, Oscar Hammerstein II, Bertrand Russell, Norbert Wiener, Robert Parker, John Wayne, Robert Penn Warren, Henry Morgan, Louis Untermeyer, Mary Stewart, Ellery Queen, Sir Hugh Greene, Joseph Wood Krutch, Marian Anderson, Havelock Ellis, Karl Menninger, Jerome Weidman, Clifton Fadiman, Herblock, and the Maharajah of Indore. No less appreciated were the letters he had from shopgirls, cowhands, college boys, soldiers, switchboard operators, housewives, lawyers, doctors, professors, scientists (including Lew Kowarski, senior physicist at the European Center for Nuclear Research), and men and women in prison.

Eric Ambler wrote: "Those who like the detective story have special reason to be grateful to Rex Stout because a considerable body of work such as his, with its consistent ingenuity and fine craftsmanship raises the whole standard of the genre a further notch above the mundane." Ross Macdonald carried praise a step further: "Rex Stout is one of the half-dozen major figures in the development of the American detective novel. With great wit and cunning, he devised a form which combined the traditional values of Sherlock Holmes and the English school with the fast-moving vernacular narrative of Dashiell Hammett." Mark Van Doren, with glorious abandon, added this accolade: "Rex is a perfect writer—economical, rapid, free of cliche, epigrammatic, intelligent, charming. What else? That's enough." Lawrence Block sums up, not without a note of anguish: "I've found Rex Stout's books about Nero Wolfe endlessly rereadable. There's nothing ordinary about Wolfe and it's not only his corpulence that makes him larger than life. Ordinary? Scarcely that. But so real that I sometimes have to remind myself that Wolfe and Goodwin are the creations of a writer's mind, that no matter how many doorbells I ring in the West Thirties, I'll never find the right house." As realists we should agree with him. But can we be sure?

The death of Rex Stout, on October 27, 1975, was front-page news in *The New York Times*. That autumn fifty-seven Nero Wolfe books were in print, more books than any other living American writer had available at the time. On the "Evening News," Harry Reasoner told an ABC-TV audience, "The odds are overwhelming that when historians look at the bright blue late October of 1975 the only thing they will keep about the twenty-seventh is that it was the day Rex Stout died. Rex Stout was a lot of things during his eighty-eight years, but the main thing he was was the writer of seventy-two mysteries about Nero Wolfe and Archie Goodwin. A lot of more pretentious writers have less claim on our culture and our allegiance." The Sunday London *Times* marked Rex's death with "Ave Atque Vale," a thirty-six line elegy by Edmund Crispin, author and composer.

To those who knew Rex, and Wolfe, and Archie, this recognition came as no surprise. They were merely getting their due.

Rex Stout said once that he was curious to know "what, of course, I'll never know," that is, how Nero Wolfe would be looked on a century hence, if remembered at all. He had no cause for anxiety. Nearly a decade after his death the Wolfe corpus still is selling briskly. The Wolfe Pack, called into existence by admiring fans, has members in every corner of the globe. There is a Wolfe Pack *Gazette* and a *Rex Stout Newsletter*, both quarterlies. More than a hundred articles have been written about the corpus, and seven books. Another three books are in progress. Mia Gerhardt, a professor at the University of Utrecht (in the Netherlands), has drawn a favorable comparison between Quixote and Wolfe and Panza and Archie. Wolfe's likeness has appeared on postage stamps in Nicaragua and the republic of San Marino. The Authors League has established a Rex Stout Award; the Wolfe Pack, a Nero Wolfe Award. Wolfe, who has appeared in two Hollywood movies and three radio serials in the past, has been the subject of a TV movie, based on *The Doorbell Rang*, and two TV series, one in the U.S., the other in Italy. He has had an orchid named after him. And a Yale man who, on a visit to London, shouted the name Nero Wolfe at Paddington Station, found himself besieged by eager admirers of the brainy sleuth. Never doubt it. At fifty Wolfe and Archie are alive and well.

The Wolfe corpus opens in June 1933 and carries through to November 1974. Rex Stout was forty-seven when he wrote *Fer-de-Lance* and eight-eight when he wrote *A Family Affair*.

When, at the behest of publisher John Farrar, he wrote
Fer-de-Lance he did not foresee that so many stories would
follow. What would he have said in 1934 had someone given
him a glimpse of the labors that lay ahead of him? "Nuts!" he
told me. Nonetheless, though the events in each story always
correspond to the year in which it was written, and often to
the very days, Rex Stout prudently kept Wolfe and Archie at
the same ages they were when he introduced them in *Fer-de-
Lance* (fifty-eight and thirty-four), almost as though he
anticipated the difficulty of having to deal with a Nero Wolfe
who would be ninety-nine in 1974 and an Archie who would
be (we shudder at the thought), seventy-five. He believed it
would be easier for him to adopt the persona of a man thirty-
four, through the medium of Archie, than to deal with aged
heroes. And this, though he admitted at the end that the
effort was taking an increasing lot out of him, he was able to
do. Incredibly, when he wrote *A Family Affair*, in his eighty-
ninth year, he still caught to perfection, in Archie's breezy
style, the spirit of a man of thirty-four. Not for him Agatha
Christie's dilemma of having a centenarian Hercule Poirot
doing his final bit of detecting from a wheelchair. When Rex
finished *A Family Affair*, he had a stroke from which he did
not recover. But he had done what he had set out to do,
without a hitch, and to him that was all that mattered.

While it is possible to pick up with the Wolfe corpus at any
point and to read the stories in any sequence, since, like a
cask, each narrative rests on its own bottom, something is to
be gained from reading them in chronological order on a
second if not a first reading. In addition to the mounting
sophistication that comes with the author's expanding social
and ethical vision, the characters themselves show change
and growth. At the outset Archie is somewhat rawboned and
rough edged, as befits a youth not so many years off the farm
at Chillicothe, Ohio. After prolonged association with Wolfe—a
true Renaissance man—Archie sheds the more disagreeable
qualities that link him to detective fiction's hard-boiled tradition.
Wolfe, for his part, enters into a more paternal relationship
with Archie, a relationship of the kind that emerges when a
grown son succeeds to a condition of friendship with a father
who respects him for his maturity and achievements. Most of
all, a chronological reading brings us to a full comprehension
of Wolfe's success in coming to terms, despite his romantic
ideals, with the reality of the world he lives in.

In *The Honorary Consul* Graham Greene speaks of the comfort to be had from a detective story: "The story of a dream world where justice is always done." At the end of *A Family Affair* the front door of the brownstone is shattered—not left merely ajar as it was in *In the Best Families* (which novel readily pairs with this one as the titles invite us to notice), but utterly demolished—reminding Wolfe that our responsibilities carry beyond our own threshold and there is no denying that fact. We may try to shut out the reality of evil in our own lives, to create a paradise from which evil is forever excluded. Yet in the end it will seek us out. Wolfe does not flinch from this truth. He does his duty and cleans his own house. But something is changed for good and always. He is compelled to realize that we cannot isolate ourselves from the rest of mankind—we are all members, one of another, mutually interdependent. He knows that the tide of chaos has reached his doors. Years before he had said, "For the sake of truth and justice we must be prepared to receive the thorn." When the thorn is offered now, he does not refuse it.

We need not suppose, however, that Wolfe, in confronting reality, abandoned his faith in an ordered universe. Rex Stout, planning a further Nero Wolfe story at the time of his death, last spoke of Wolfe contentedly rereading Jane Austen's *Emma*, one of Rex's own favorites. Emma Woodhouse's follies and her way of dealing with them remind us that decency and honor, no matter how severely besieged, may emerge strengthened and triumphant if we do not abandon faith in mankind's basic decency, for the human spirit is, after all, touched by the attar of divinity.

When, toward the close of his life, Rex Stout was asked if he had plans to send Wolfe to his grave, even as Agatha Christie had done unto Poirot, and Doyle sought to do with Holmes, Rex Stout cocked one eyebrow (a talent he shared in common with Archie), and said, "I hope he lives forever!" We have no cause to think that that hope will not be met. Indeed, new strength constantly is being added to the ranks of those who echo Phyllis McGinley's rallying refrain:

> Come, mark them down with a big black zero
> Who don't love Archie, Rex, and Nero.

John McAleer
Mount Independence
25 March 1984

Chapter 1

There was no reason why I shouldn't have been sent for the beer that day, for the last ends of the Fairmont National Bank case had been gathered in the week before and there was nothing for me to do but errands, and Wolfe never hesitated about running me down to Murray Street for a can of shoe-polish if he happened to need one. But it was Fritz who was sent for the beer. Right after lunch his bell called him up from the kitchen before he could have got the dishes washed, and after getting his orders he went out and took the roadster which we always left parked in front. An hour later he was back, with the rumble seat piled high with baskets filled with bottles. Wolfe was in the office—as he and I called it, Fritz called it the library—and I was in the front room reading a book on gunshot wounds which I couldn't make head or tail of, when I glanced through the window and saw Fritz pull up at the curb. It was a good excuse to stretch my legs, so I went out and helped him unload and carry the baskets into the kitchen, where we were starting to stow the bottles away in a cupboard when the bell rang. I followed Fritz into the office.

Wolfe lifted his head. I mention that, because his head was so big that lifting it struck you as being quite a job. It was probably really bigger than it looked, for the rest of him was so huge that any head on top of it but his own would have escaped your notice entirely.

"Where's the beer?"

"In the kitchen, sir. The lower cupboard on the right, I thought."

"I want it in here. Is it cold? And an opener and two glasses."

"Mostly cold, yes, sir. Very well."

1

I grinned and sat down on a chair to wonder what Wolfe was doing with some pieces of paper he had cut into little discs and was pushing around into different positions on the desk blotter. Fritz began bringing in the beer, six at a time on a tray. After the third trip I had another grin when I saw Wolfe glance up at the array on the table and then around at Fritz's back going through the door. Two more trays full; whereupon Wolfe halted the parade.

"Fritz. Would you inform me when this is likely to end?"

"Very soon, sir. There are nineteen more. Forty-nine in all."

"Nonsense. Excuse me, Fritz, but obviously it's non-sense."

"Yes, sir. You said one of every kind procurable. I went to a dozen shops, at least that."

"All right. Bring them in. And some plain salt crackers. None shall lack opportunity, Fritz, it wouldn't be fair."

It turned out that the idea was, as Wolfe explained to me after he had invited me to draw my chair up to the desk and begin opening the bottles, that he had decided to give up the bootleg beer, which for years he had bought in barrels and kept in a cooler in the basement, if he could find a brand of the legal 3.2 that was potable. He had also decided, he said, that six quarts a day was unnecessary and took too much time and thereafter he would limit himself to five. I grinned at that, for I didn't believe it, and I grinned again when I thought how the place would be cluttered up with empty bottles unless Fritz ran his legs off all day long. I said to him something I had said before more than once, that beer slowed up a man's head and with him running like a brook, six quarts a day, I never would understand how he could make his brain work so fast and deep that no other man in the country could touch him. He replied, also as he had before, that it wasn't his brain that worked, it was his lower nerve centers; and as I opened the fifth bottle for him to sample he went on to say—not the first time for that either—that he would not insult me by acknowledging my flattery, since if it was sincere I was a fool and if it was calculated I was a knave.

He smacked his lips, tasting the fifth brand, and holding up the glass looked through the amber at the light. "This is a pleasant surprise, Archie. I would not have believed it. That of course is the advantage of being a pessimist; a pessimist gets nothing but pleasant surprises, an optimist nothing but unpleasant. So far, none of this is sewage. As you see, Fritz has marked the prices on the labels, and I've started with the cheap ones. No, here, take this next."

It was at that moment that I heard the faint buzz from the kitchen that meant the front door, and it was that buzz that started the ball rolling. Though at the time it appeared to be nothing interesting, just Durkin asking a favor.

Durkin was all right up to the neck. When I consider how thick he was in most respects I am surprised how he could tail. I know bull terriers are dumb, but good tailing means a lot more than just hanging on, and Fred Durkin was good. I asked him once how he did it, and he said, "I just go up to the subject and ask him where he's headed for, and then if I lose him I know where to look." I suppose he knew how funny that was; I don't know, I suspect him. When things got so Wolfe had to cut down expenses like everybody else from bankers to bums, Saul Panzer and I got our weekly envelopes sliced, but Durkin's was stopped altogether. Wolfe called him in when he was needed and paid him by the day, so I still saw him off and on and knew he was having hard sledding. Things had been slow and I hadn't run across him for a month or more when the buzzer sounded that day and Fritz brought him to the door of the office.

Wolfe looked up and nodded. "Hello, Fred. Do I owe you something?"

Durkin, approaching the desk with his hat in his hand, shook his head. "How are you, Mr. Wolfe. I wish to God you did. If there was anybody owed me anything I'd be with him like a saddle on a horse."

"Sit down. Will you sample some beer?"

"No, thanks." Fred stayed on his feet. "I've come to ask a favor."

Wolfe looked up again, and his big thick lips pushed out a little, tight together, just a small movement, and back again, and then out and back again. How I loved to watch him doing that! That was about the only time I ever got excited, when Wolfe's lips were moving like that. It didn't matter whether it was some little thing like this with Durkin or when he was on the track of something big and dangerous. I knew what was going on, something was happening so fast inside of him and so much ground was being covered, the whole world in a flash, that no one else could ever really understand it even if he had tried his best to explain, which he never did. Sometimes, when he felt patient, he explained to me and it seemed to make sense, but I realized afterward that that was only because the proof had come and so I could accept it. I said to Saul Panzer once that it was like being with him in a dark room which neither of you has ever seen before, and he describes all of its contents to you, and then when the light is turned on his explanation of how he did it seems sensible because you see everything there before you just as he described it.

Wolfe said to Durkin, "You know my failing on the financial side. But since you haven't come to borrow money, your favor is likely granted. What is it?"

Durkin scowled. Wolfe always upset him. "Nobody needs to borrow money worse than I do. How do you know it's not that?"

"No matter. Archie will explain. You're not embarrassed enough, and you wouldn't have brought a woman with you. What is it?"

I leaned forward and broke in, "Damn it, he's alone! My ears are good anyhow!"

A little ripple, imperceptible except to eyes like mine that had caught it before, ran over Wolfe's enormous bulk. "Of course, Archie, splendid ears. But there was nothing to hear; the lady made no sound audible at this distance. And Fritz did not speak to her; but in greeting Fred there was a courtesy in his tone which he saves for softer flesh. If I should hear Fritz using that tone to a lone man I'd send him to a psychoanalyst at once."

Durkin said, "It's a friend of my wife's. Her best friend, you know my wife's Italian. Maybe you don't know, but she is. Anyway, this friend of hers is in trouble, or thinks she is. It sounds to me like a washout. Maria keeps after Fanny and Fanny keeps after me and they both keep after me together, all because I told Fanny once that you've got a devil in you that can find out anything in the world. A boob thing to say, Mr. Wolfe, but you know how a man's tongue will get started."

Wolfe only said, "Bring her in."

Durkin went out to the hall and came right back with a woman in front of him. She was little but not skinny, with black hair and eyes, and Italian all over though not the shawl kind. She was somewhere around middle age and looked neat and clean in a pink cotton dress and a black rayon jacket. I pulled over a chair and she sat down facing Wolfe and the light.

Durkin said, "Maria Maffei, Mr. Wolfe."

She tossed Fred a smile, showing little white teeth, and then said to Wolfe, "Maria Maffei," pronouncing it quite different.

Wolfe said, "Not Mrs. Maffei."

She shook her head. "No, sir. I'm not married."

"But in trouble anyhow."

"Yes, sir. Mr. Durkin thought you might be good enough—"

"Tell us about it."

"Yes, sir. It's my brother Carlo. He has gone."

"Gone where?"

"I don't know, sir. That's why I am afraid. He has been gone two days."

Where did he—no, no. These are not phenomena, merely facts." Wolfe turned to me. "Go on, Archie."

By the time he had finished his "no, no" I had my notebook out. I enjoyed this sort of business in front of Wolfe more than at any other time because I knew damn well I was good at it. But this wasn't much of a job; this woman knew what to get down as well as I did. She told her tale quick and straight. She was housekeeper at a swell apartment on Park Avenue and lived there. Her brother Carlo, two years older than her, lived in a rooming-house on Sullivan Street. He was a metal-worker, first class she said; for years he had made big money working on jewelry for Rathbun & Cross, but because he drank a little and occasionally didn't turn up at the shop he had been one of the first to go when the depression came. For a while after that he had got odd jobs here and there, then he had used up his small savings, and for the past winter and spring he had been kept going by his sister. Around the middle of April, completely discouraged, he had decided to return to Italy and Maria had agreed to furnish the necessary funds; she had, in fact, advanced the money for the steamship ticket. But a week later he had suddenly announced that the trip was postponed; he wouldn't say why, but he had declared that he would need no more money, he would soon be able to return all she had lent him, and he might stay in this country after all. He had never been very communicative, but regarding the change in plans he had been stubbornly mysterious. Now he was gone. He had telephoned her on Saturday that he would meet her Monday evening, her evening off, at the Italian restaurant on Prince Street where they often dined

together, and had added gaily that he would have enough
money with him to pay back everything and lend her some
into the bargain if she needed it. Monday evening she had
waited for him until ten o'clock, then had gone to his
rooming-house and been told that he had left a little after
seven and had not returned.

"Day before yesterday," I observed.

Durkin, I saw, had his notebook open too, and now he
nodded. "Monday, June fourth."

Wolfe shook his head. He had been sitting as still and
unobservant as a mountain with his chin lodged on his chest,
and now without moving otherwise his head shook faintly as he
murmured, "Durkin. Today is Wednesday, June seventh."

"Well?" Fred stared. "Okay with me, Mr. Wolfe."

Wolfe wiggled a finger at Maria. "Was it Monday?"

"Yes, sir. Of course. That's my evening off."

"You should know that evening. Durkin, annotate your
notebook, or, better perhaps, throw it away. You are a full
twelvemonth ahead of your times; next year Monday will be
June fourth." He turned to the woman. "Maria Maffei, I am
sorry to have to give you a counsel of desperation. Consult the
police."

"I have, sir." A gleam of resentment shot from her eyes.
"They say he has gone to Italy with my money."

"Perhaps he has."

"Oh no, Mr. Wolfe. You know better. You have looked at
me. You can see I would not know so little of a brother as
that."

"Do the police tell you what boat your brother sailed on?"

"How could they? There has been no boat. They do not
investigate or even consider. They merely say he has gone to
Italy."

"I see, they do it by inspiration. Well. I'm sorry I can't
help you. I can only guess. Robbery. Where is his body then?
Again consult the police. Sooner or later someone will find it
for them and your puzzle will be solved."

Maria Maffei shook her head. "I don't believe it, Mr.
Wolfe. I just don't believe it. And there was the phone call."

I broke in, "You mentioned no phone call."

She smiled at me with her teeth. "I would have. There
was a phone call for him at the rooming-house a little before
seven. The phone there is in the downstairs hall and the girl
heard him talking. He was excited and he agreed to meet

someone at half-past seven." She turned to Wolfe. "You can help me, sir. You can help me find Carlo. I have learned to look cool like the grass in the morning because I have been so long among these Americans, but I am Italian and I must find my brother and I must see anyone who has hurt him."

Wolfe only shook his head. She paid no attention.

"You must, sir. Mr. Durkin says you are very tight about money. I still have something left and I could pay all expenses and maybe a little more. And you are Mr. Durkin's friend and I am Mrs. Durkin's friend, my friend Fanny."

Wolfe said, "I am nobody's friend. How much can you pay?"

She hesitated.

"How much have you got?"

"I have—well—more than a thousand dollars."

"How much of it would you pay?"

"I would pay—all of it. If you find my brother alive, all of it. If you find him not alive and show him to me and show me the one who hurt him, I would still pay a good deal. I would pay first for the funeral."

Wolfe's eyelids lowered slowly and raised slowly. That, as I knew, meant his approval; I had often looked for that sign, and frequently in vain, when I was reporting to him. He said, "You're a practical woman, Maria Maffei. Moreover, possibly, a woman of honor. You are right, there is something in me that can help you; it is genius; but you have not furnished the stimulant to arouse it and whether it will be awakened in search of your brother is problematical. In any event, routine comes first, and the expense of that will be small."

He turned to me.

"Archie, go to Carlo Maffei's rooming-house; his sister will accompany you as authority. See the girl who heard the phone call; see others; examine his room; if any trail is indicated phone here for Saul Panzer any time after five; returning here bring with you any articles that seem to you unimportant."

I thought it was unnecessary for him to take that dig at me before a stranger, but I had long since learned that there was no point in resenting his pleasantries. Maria Maffei got up from her chair and thanked him.

Durkin took a step forward. "About that being tight with

money, Mr. Wolfe, you know how a man's tongue will get started—"

I rescued him. "Come on, Fred, we'll take the roadster and I might as well drop you on the way."

Chapter 2

When I parked the big shiny black roadster in front of the number on Sullivan Street Maria Maffei had given me I felt that I might never see it alive and happy again—the roadster I mean—for the street was littered with rubbish and full of wild Italian kids yelling and dashing around like black-eyed demons. But I had had the roadster in worse places than that, as for instance the night I chased young Graves, who was in a Pierce coupé with a satchel of emeralds between his knees, from New Milford all over Pike County, up and down a dozen mountains in a foot of mud and the worst rain I ever saw. It was Wolfe's orders that after every little rub the roadster should be fixed up as good as new, and of course that pleased me just as well.

It was just another rooming-house. For some reason or other they're all alike, whether it's a high-hat affair in the Fifties or a brownstone west of Central Park full of honest artist girls or an Italian hangout like this one on Sullivan Street. With, of course, a difference in details like garlic. Maria Maffei took me first to the landlady, a nice fat woman with wet hands and a pushed-in nose and rings on her fingers, and then upstairs to her brother's room. I looked around a little while Maria Maffei went to get the girl who had heard the phone call. It was a good-sized room on the third floor with two windows. The rug was worn and the furniture old and sort of broken, but it was clean and really not a bad room except for the noise from the hoodlums below when I opened the window to see if the roadster was still on its feet. Two large traveling bags were stacked in a corner, one flimsy and old and done for, the other one old too but sturdy and good. Neither was locked. The flimsy one was empty; the good one contained a lot of small tools of different shapes and sizes, some of which had pawnshop tags hanging on them, and some pieces of wood and metal and odds and ends like coil springs. The closet contained an old suit of clothes, two overalls, an overcoat, two pairs of shoes, and a felt hat. In the drawers of the bureau which stood between the windows was an assortment, not scanty for a man who had been living on his sister for a year, of shirts, ties, handkerchiefs, socks, and a lot of miscellaneous junk like shoestrings, lead pencils, snapshots, and empty pipe-tobacco cans. In an upper drawer was a bundle of seventeen letters in envelopes all with Italian postage stamps, fastened with a rubber band. Scattered around in the same drawer were receipts and paid bills, a tablet of writing-paper, a few clippings from newspapers and magazines, and a dog collar. On top of the bureau, along with comb and brush and similar impedimenta as Wolfe would say, were half a dozen books, all in Italian except one that was full of pictures and designs, and a big stack of magazines, different monthly issues for three years back all with the same name, *Metal Crafts*. In the corner by the right window was a plain rough wood table with its top scarred and cut all over, and on it was a small vise, a grinder and buffer with an electric cord long enough to reach the lamp socket, and some more tools like those in the traveling bag. I was looking over the grinder to see how recently it had been used when Maria Maffei came in with the girl.

"This is Anna Fiore," the woman said.

I went over and shook hands with her. She was a homely kid about twenty with skin like stale dough, and she looked like she'd been scared in the cradle and never got over it. I told her my name and said that I had learned from Miss Maffei that she had heard Mr. Maffei answering the phone call before he went out Monday evening. She nodded.

I turned to the woman. "I expect you'd like to get along back uptown, Miss Maffei. Anna and I will get along."

She shook her head. "If I'm back by dinner it will be all right."

I got a little gruff. The truth was that I agreed with Durkin that it was a washout and that there was nothing to be expected from it but fanning the air. So I told Maria Maffei that I could easily do without her and she'd better trot along and she'd hear from Wolfe if there was anything to hear. She shot a glance at the girl and showed her teeth to me, and left us.

I pulled a couple of chairs face to face and got the girl deposited on one in front of me, and pulled out my notebook.

"You've got nothing to be scared of," I told her. "The worst that can happen to you is that you'll do a favor to Miss Maffei and her brother and she might give you some money. Do you like Miss Maffei?"

She seemed startled, as if surprised that anyone should think it worth the trouble to learn her likes and dislikes, but the answer was ready behind the surprise. "Yes, I like her. She is nice."

"Do you like Mr. Maffei?"

"Yes, of course, everybody does. Except when he drinks, then a girl should stay away from him."

"How did you happen to hear the phone call Monday evening? Were you expecting it?"

"How could I be expecting it?"

"I don't know. Did you answer the phone?"

"No, sir. Mrs. Ricci answered it. She told me to call Mr. Maffei and I called upstairs. Then I was clearing the table in the dining-room and the door was open and I could hear him talking."

"Could you hear what he said?"

"Of course." She looked a little scornful. "We always hear everything anyone says on the telephone. Mrs. Ricci heard him too, she heard the same as I did."

"What did he say?"

"First he said *hello*. Then he said *well this is Carlo Maffei what do you want*. Then he said *that's my business I'll tell you when I see you*. Then he said *why not here in my room*. Then he said *no I'm not scared I'm not the one to be scared*. Mrs. Ricci says it was *it's not me that's scared,* but she don't remember right. Then he said *sure I want the money and a lot more*. Then he said *all right seven-thirty at the corner of*. Then he said *shut up yourself what do I care*. Then he said *all right seven-thirty I know that car*."

She stopped. I said, "Who was he talking to?"

I supposed of course that the answer would be that she didn't know, since Maria Maffei had not known, but she said at once, "The man that called him up before."

"Before? When?"

"Quite a few times. In May. One day twice. Mrs. Ricci says nine times before Monday altogether."

"Did you ever hear his voice?"

"No, sir. Mrs. Ricci always answers."

"Did you ever hear this man's name?"

"No, sir. After Mrs. Ricci got curious she asked it, but he always just said *never mind tell him he's wanted on the phone.*"

I began to think there might be some fun in this somewhere, possibly even some money. Not that the money interested me; that was for Wolfe; it was the fun I was after. Anyway it might not be just a stick-up and a stiff in the East River. I decided to see what I could get, and I went after that girl. I had heard Wolfe do it many a time, and while I knew most of his results came from a kind of feeling that wasn't in me, still a lot of it was just patience and hit-or-miss. So I went after her. I kept at it two hours, and collected a lot of facts, but not one that meant anything to me. Once I thought I might be getting warm when I learned that Carlo Maffei had two different women with whom he appeared publicly on different occasions, and one of them was married; but when I saw that wouldn't tie up with the phone call I threw it out. Maffei had mentioned going to Italy but had given no details. He had pretty well kept his business in his own bosom. He had never had callers except his sister and a friend from his old prosperous days with whom he had occasionally gone to dine. I pumped her for two hours and couldn't see a gleam anywhere, but something about that phone call kept me from calling it a dull day and putting on my hat. Finally I said to her:

"You stay here a minute, Anna, while I go down and see Mrs. Ricci."

The landlady confirmed the girl's version of the phone call and said she had no idea who the caller was though she had tried on several occasions to find out. I asked her a few questions here and there, and then requested permission to take Anna with me uptown. She said no, she couldn't be left alone with the dinner to get, so I produced a dollar bill, and she asked what time she might expect the girl back, saying that it must not be later than nine o'clock.

After taking my dollar! I told her, "I can make no promises, Mrs. Ricci, when my boss gets started asking questions nights and days are nothing. But she'll be back safe and sound as soon as possible."

I went upstairs and got Anna and some of the stuff from

the bureau drawer and when we got to the street was relieved to find that the roadster hadn't lost a fender or a spare tire.

I moseyed along uptown taking it easy, not wanting to reach Thirty-fifth Street too soon, since Wolfe was always upstairs with the plants from four to six and it wasn't a good idea to disturb him during those two hours unless you had to. Anna was overwhelmed by the roadster; she kept her feet pulled back against the seat and her hands folded tight in her lap. That tickled me and I felt kindly toward her, so I told her that I might give her a dollar if she told my boss anything that would help him out. It was a minute or two after six when I pulled up in front of the old brownstone less than a block from the Hudson River where Wolfe had lived for twenty years and where I had been with him a third of that.

Anna didn't get home that night by nine o'clock. It was after eleven when Wolfe sent me to the *Times* office for the papers, and it was well past midnight when we finally hit on the spot that Anna recognized. By that time Mrs. Ricci had telephoned three times, and when I got to Sullivan Street with the girl a little before one the landlady was waiting out in front, maybe with a knife in her sock. But she didn't say a word, only glared at me. I had given Anna her dollar, for something had happened.

I had reported to Wolfe up in the front plant-room, the sun-room, leaving Anna down in the office. He sat there in the big chair with a red and tan orchid eight inches wide tickling the back of his neck, looking not interested. He really wasn't interested. He barely glanced at the papers and things I had brought with me from Maffei's room. He admitted that the phone call had a dash of possibility in it, but couldn't see that there was anything to bother about. I tried to persuade him that since the girl was already downstairs he might as well take it up and see what he could get; and I added with malice:

"Anyway, she cost a dollar. I had to give the landlady a dollar."

"That was your dollar, Archie."

"No, sir, it was an expense dollar. It's down in the book."

I went with him to the elevator. If he had had to do his own lifting and lowering I don't think he would ever have gone upstairs, even for the plants.

He began on Anna at once. It was beautiful. Five years earlier I wouldn't have appreciated it. It was beautiful because it was absolutely comprehensive. If there was anything in that girl, any bit of knowledge, any apparently forgotten shred of feeling or reaction, that could show us a direction or give us a hint, it simply could not have kept away from him. He questioned her for five hours. He asked her about Carlo Maffei's voice, his habits, his clothing, his meals, his temper, his table manners, his relations with his sister, with Mrs. Ricci, with Anna herself, with everyone Anna had ever seen him with. He asked her about ,Mrs. Ricci, about all the residents of the rooming-house for two years, about the neighbors, and about the tradesmen who delivered things to the house. All this he did easily and leisurely, careful not to tire her—quite different from the time I watched him with Lon Graves; him he wore down and drove halfway crazy in an afternoon. It seemed to me he got only one thing out of the girl, and that wasn't much, only an admission that she had removed something from Maffei's room that very morning, Wednesday. Little pieces of paper from his bureau drawer with mucilage on the back, and printed on the front S.S. *LUCIA* and S.S. *FIORENZA*. Of course they were steamship luggage stickers. From the newspaper file I learned that the *Lucia* had sailed on the 18th of May and the *Fiorenza* on the 3rd of June. Evidently Maffei had decided on Italy not once, but twice, and had given it up both times. Anna had taken them, she said, because they were pretty colors and she wanted to paste them on the box she kept her clothes in. During dinner, which the three of us ate together in the dining-room, he let Anna alone entirely and talked to me, mostly about beer; but with the coffee he moved us back to the office and went at it again. He doubled back and recovered the ground, he darted around at random on things so irrelevant and inconsequential that anyone who had never seem him pull a rabbit out of that hat before would have been sure he was merely a nut. By eleven o'clock I was through, yawning and ready to give up, and I was exasperated that he showed not the slightest sign of impatience or discouragement.

Then all at once he hit it.

"So Mr. Maffei never gave you any presents?"

"No, sir. Except the box of chalk I told you about. And the newspapers, if you call that a present."

"Yes. You said he always gave you his morning paper. The *Times*."

"Yes, sir. He told me once he took the *Times* for the classified ads. You know, the job ads."

"Did he give you his paper Monday morning?"

"He always gave it to me in the afternoon. Monday afternoon, yes, sir."

"There was nothing peculiar about it that morning, I suppose."

"No, sir."

Apparently Wolfe caught some faint flicker in her eye, some faint movement that I missed. Anyway he insisted.

"Nothing peculiar about it?"

"No, sir. Except—of course, the cut-out."

"The cut-out?"

"A piece cut out. A big piece."

"Did he often cut out pieces?"

"Yes, sir. Mostly the ads. Maybe always the ads. I used the papers to take the dirt up in and I had to watch for the holes."

"But this was a big piece."

"Yes, sir."

"Not an advertisement then. You will pardon me, Miss Fiore, if I do not say *ad*. I prefer not to. Then it wasn't an advertisement he cut out of Monday's paper."

"Oh no, it was on the front page."

"Indeed. Had there ever been a piece cut out on the front page before?"

"No, sir. I'm sure not."

"Never anything but advertisements before?"

"Well, I'm not sure of that. Maybe only ads, I think it was."

Wolfe sat for a minute with his chin on his chest. Then he turned to me. "Archie, run up to Forty-second Street and get twenty copies of Monday's *Times*."

I was glad for something to wake me up. Not that it was anything to get excited about, for I could see that Wolfe was just taking a wink at the only crack that had shown any chance of light; I wasn't expecting anything and I didn't think he was. But it was a fine June night, cool but soft and pleasant, and I filled my lungs with good air snatched from the breeze I made as I rolled crosstown to Broadway and turned north. At Times Square I saw a cop I knew, Marve Doyle who used to pound the cement down on Fourteenth Street, and he let me leave the car against the Broadway curb while I ran across the street to the *Times* office. The theater and movie mob was slopping off the sidewalks into the street, deciding between two dollars at a speak and two nickles at a Nedick's.

When I got back to the office Wolfe was giving the girl a rest. He had had Fritz bring in some beer and she was sipping at a glass like it was hot tea, with a stripe of dried foam across her upper lip. He had finished three bottles, though I couldn't have been gone more than twenty minutes at the outside. As I came in he said:

"I should have told you city edition."

"Sure, that's what I got."

"Good." He turned to the girl. "If you don't mind, Miss Fiore, it would be better if you did not overlook our preparations. Turn her chair around, Archie; there, the little table for her beer. Now the papers. No, don't rip it off; better intact I think; that's the way she first saw it. Remove the second sections, they'll be a find for Miss Fiore, think of all the dirt they'll hold. Here."

I spread open a first section on the desk before him and he pulled himself up in his chair to hunch over it. It was like seeing a hippopotamus in the zoo get up for a feed. I took out all the second sections and stacked them on a chair and then took a front page for myself and went over it. At the first glance it certainly looked hopeless; miners were striking in Pennsylvania, the NRA was saving the country under three different headings, two boys had crossed the Atlantic in a thirty-foot boat, a university president had had heart failure on a golf course, a gangster had been tear-gassed out of a Brooklyn flat, a negro had been lynched in Alabama, and someone had found an old painting somewhere in Europe. I glanced at Wolfe; he was drinking the whole page. The only thing that looked to me worth trying at all was the painting which had been found in Switzerland and was supposed to have been stolen from Italy. But when Wolfe finally reached for the scissors out of the drawer it wasn't that one he clipped, it was the gangster piece. Then he laid the paper aside and called for another one. I handed it to him, and this time I grinned as I saw him go after the article about the painting; I came in second anyhow. When he called for a third paper I was curious, and as he ran the scissors around the edges of the story about the university president I stared at him. He saw me. He said without looking up, "Pray for this side, Archie. If it's this one we shall have an *Angræcum sesquipedale* for Christmas." I could spell that because I kept his accounts for

him on orchids as on everything else, but I could no more have
pronounced it than I could have imagined any connection
between the university president and Carlo Maffei.

Wolfe said, "Show her one."

The last one he had clipped was on top, but I reached
under it and got the next one; the painting piece had been in a
large box in the lower right quarter of the page. As I held it
out, spread open, to Anna, Wolfe said, "Look at that, Miss
Fiore. Is that the way the piece was cut out Monday morning?"

She gave it only a glance. "No, sir. It was a big piece out
of the top, here, let me show you—"

I snatched it out of the way before she could get hold of
it, tossed it back to the table, and picked up another. I spread
it in front of her. This time she took two glances, then she said,
"Yes, sir."

"You mean that's it?"

"It was cut out like that, yes, sir."

For a moment Wolfe was silent, then I heard him breathe
and he said, "Turn her around, Archie." I took the arm of her
chair and whirled it around with her in it. Wolfe looked at her
and said, "How sure are you, Miss Fiore, that the paper was
cut out like that?"

"I know it was, sir. I'm sure."

"Did you see the piece he had cut out? In his room, in the
wastebasket perhaps, or in his hand?"

"No, I never saw it. It couldn't have been in the wastebasket because there isn't any."

"Good. If only all reasons were as good as that. You may
go home now, Miss Fiore. You have been a good girl, good and
patient and forbearing, and unlike most of the persons I avoid
meeting by staying inside my house, you are willing to confine
your tongue to its proper functions. But will you answer just
one more question? I ask it as a favor."

The girl was completely tired out, but there was enough
life left in her to let the bewilderment show in her eyes. She
stared at him. Wolfe said, "Just one more question. Have you
ever at any time seen a golf club in Carlo Maffei's room?"

If he was looking for a climax he got it, because for the
first time in all these hours the girl shut up on him. It was
funny how plain you could see it happen. For an instant she
just looked, then when the question had clicked what little
color she had left her till she was dead white and her mouth

dropped half open; she looked absolutely like an idiot, and she began to tremble all over.

Wolfe bored at her, quiet. "When did you see it?"

All of a sudden she shut her lips tight, and her hands in her lap closed into fists. "No, sir." It was just a mumble. "No, sir, I never did."

Wolfe looked at her a second, then he said, "All right. It's quite all right, Miss Fiore." He turned to me. "Take her home."

She didn't try to stand up till I went over and touched her shoulder. Then she put her hands on the arms of the chair and got to her feet. He had certainly got her somehow, but she didn't seem exactly scared, just caved in. I got her jacket from the back of a chair and helped her put it on. As she started for the door I turned to say something to Wolfe, and couldn't believe my eyes. He was raising himself out of his chair to stand up! Actually. I had at one time seen him refuse to take that trouble for the departure from that room of a woman worth twenty million American dollars who had married an English duke. But anyway I said what I had started to say:

"I told her I'd give her a dollar."

"Then you'll have to do it, I'm afraid." He raised his voice a little to reach the door: "Good night, Miss Fiore."

She didn't reply. I followed her to the hall and took her out to the roadster. When we got to Sullivan Street Mrs. Ricci was waiting in front with a glare in her eye that made me decide not to stop for any amenities.

Chapter 3

By the time I had garaged the car and walked the two blocks back to Thirty-fifth Street the office was dark and when I went up a flight I saw a ribbon of light under the door of Wolfe's bedroom. I often wondered how he ever got his clothes off, but I know Fritz never helped him. Fritz slept up above, across the hall from the plant-rooms; my room was on the second floor, the same floor as Wolfe's, a fair-sized room in front with its own bath and a pair of windows. I had lived there seven years, and it certainly was home; and seemed likely to remain so for another seven, or even twenty-seven, for the only girl I had ever been really soft on had found another bargain she liked better. That was how I happened to meet Wolfe—but that story isn't for me to tell, at least not yet. There are one or two little points about it that will need clearing up some day. But that room was certainly home. The bed was big and good, there was a desk with plenty of drawer-space and three chairs all roomy and comfortable, and a real carpet all over, no damn little rugs to slide you around like a piece of butter on a hot cake. The pictures on the walls were my own, and I think they were a good selection; one of Mount Vernon, the home of George Washington, a colored one of a lion's head, another colored one of woods with grass and flowers, and a big framed photograph of my mother and father, who both died when I was just a kid. Also there was a colored one called September Morn, of a young woman apparently with no clothes on and her hair hanging down in front, but that was in the bathroom. There was nothing unusual about the room, it was just a good room to live in, except the big gong on the wall under the bed, and that was out of sight. It was connected up so that when Wolfe turned on a switch in his room, which he did every night, the gong would sound if anyone stepped in the hall within five feet of his door or if any of his windows was disturbed, and also it was connected with all entrances to the plant-rooms. Wolfe told me once, not as if it mattered much, that he really had no cowardice in him, he only had an intense distaste for being touched by anyone or for being compelled without warning to make any quick movements; and when I considered the quantity he had to move I was willing to believe him. For some reason questions like that of cowardice have never interested me as regards Wolfe, though ordinarily if I have cause to suspect that a man is yellow as far as I'm concerned he can eat at another table.

I took one of the newspapers from the office upstairs with me, and after I had undressed and got into pajamas and slippers, I made myself comfortable in a chair with cigarettes and ash tray handy and read that university president article three times. It was headed like this:

PETER OLIVER BARSTOW
DEAD DROM STROKE

PRESIDENT OF HOLLAND
SUCCUMBS ON LINKS

Friends Reach His Side
With His Last Breath

It was quite a piece, with a full column on the front page, another column and a half on the inside, and in another article a long obituary with comments from a lot of prominent people. The story itself didn't amount to much and there was really nothing to it except another man gone. I read the paper every day and this one was only two days old, but I couldn't remember noticing this. Barstow, 58-year-old president of Holland University, had been playing golf Sunday afternoon on the links of the Green Meadow Club near Pleasantville, thirty miles north of New York, a foursome, with his son Lawrence and two friends named E. D. Kimball and Manuel Kimball. On the fairway of the fourth hole he had suddenly pitched forward and landed on his face, flopped around on the ground a few seconds, and then lay still. His caddy had jumped to him and grabbed his arm, but by the time the others got to him he was dead. Among the crowd that collected from the clubhouse and other players was a doctor who was an old friend of Barstow's, and he and the son had taken the body in Barstow's own car to the Barstow home six miles away. The doctor had pronounced it heart disease.

The rest was trimmings, all about Barstow's career and achievements and a picture of him and this and that, and how his wife had collapsed when they brought him home and his son and daughter bore up well. After the third reading I just yawned and threw up the sponge. The only connection that I could see between Barstow's death and Carlo Maffei was the fact that Wolfe had asked Anna Fiore if she had seen a golf club, so I tossed the paper away and got up saying to myself aloud, "Mr. Goodwin, I guess you haven't got this case ready for the closed business file." Then I took a drink of water and went to bed.

It was nearly ten o'clock when I got downstairs the next morning, for I need eight hours' sleep when I can get it, and of course Wolfe wouldn't be down till eleven. He arose always at eight, no matter what time he went to bed, had breakfast in his room with a couple of newspapers, and spent the two hours from nine to eleven in the plant-rooms. Sometimes I could hear old Horstmann, who tended the plants, yelling at him, while I was dressing or taking a bath. Wolfe seemed to have the same effect on Horstmann that an umpire had on John J. McGraw. Not that the old man really disliked Wolfe, I'm sure he didn't; I wouldn't wonder if he was worried for fear Wolfe's poundage, having at least reached the limit of equilibrium, would topple over and make hash of the orchids. Horstmann didn't think any more of those plants than I do of my right eye. He slept in a little room partitioned off of a corner, and I wouldn't have been surprised if he had walked the floor with them at night.

After I got through in the kitchen with a dish of kidneys and waffles and a couple of glasses of milk—for I absolutely refused to let Fritz dress up the dining-table for my breakfast, which I always had alone—I went out for ten minutes' worth of air, hoofing it down around the piers and back again, and then settled down at my corner desk in the office with the books, after dusting around a little and opening the safe and filling Wolfe's fountain pen. His mail I left on his desk unopened, that was the custom; there wasn't any for me. I made out two or three checks and balanced my expense book, not much to that, things had been so quiet, and then began going over the plant records to be sure Horstmann had his reports up to date. I was in the middle of that when I heard the buzzer in the kitchen, and a minute later Fritz came to the door and said a man named O'Grady wanted to see Mr. Wolfe. I took the card and looked at it and saw it was a new one on me; I knew a lot of the dicks on the Homicide Squad, but I had never seen this O'Grady. I told Fritz to usher him in.

O'Grady was young, and very athletic judging from his make-up and the way he walked. He had a bad eye, conscientious and truculent; from the way he looked at me you might have thought I had the Lindbergh baby in my pocket.

He said, "Mr. Nero Wolfe?"

I waved at a chair. "Have a seat." I glanced at my wrist. "Mr. Wolfe will be down in nineteen minutes."

He scowled. "This is important. Couldn't you call him? I sent in my card, I'm from the Homicide Squad."

"Sure, I know, that's all right. Just have a seat. If I called him he'd throw something at me."

He took the chair and I went back to the plant records. Once or twice during the wait I thought I might try pumping him just for the fun of it, but a glance at his face was enough; he was too young and trustworthy to bother with. For nineteen minutes he sat as if he was in church, not saying a word.

He got up from the chair as Wolfe entered the office. Wolfe, as he made steady progress from the door to the desk, bade me good morning, asked me to open another window, and shot a glance at the visitor. Seated at the desk he saw the card I had laid there, then he took a look at the mail, flipping the corners of the envelopes with his quick fingers the way a bank teller does the checks when he is going over a deposit. He shoved the mail aside and turned to the dick.

"Mr. O'Grady?"

O'Grady stepped forward. "Mr. Nero Wolfe?"

Wolfe nodded.

"Well, Mr. Wolfe, I want the papers and other articles you took yesterday from Carlo Maffei's room."

"No!" Wolfe lifted his head to see him better. "Really? That's interesting, Mr. O'Grady. Have a chair. Pull him up a chair, Archie."

"No, thanks, I've got a job on. I'll just take those papers and—things."

"What things?"

"The things you took."

"Enumerate them."

The dick stuck his chin out. "Don't try to get funny. Come on, I'm in a hurry."

Wolfe wiggled a finger at him. "Easy, Mr. O'Grady." Wolfe's voice was clear and low, with a tone he didn't use very often; he had used it on me only once, the first time I had ever seen him, and I had never forgotten how it sounded; it had made me feel that if he had wanted to he could have cut my head off without lifting a hand. He went on with it, "Easy now. Sit down. I mean it, really, sit down."

I had a chair shoved behind the dick's knees, and he came down onto it slowly.

"What you are getting is a free but valuable lesson," Wolfe said. "You are young and can use it. Since I entered this room you have made nothing but mistakes. You were without courtesy, which was offensive. You made a statement contrary to fact, which was stupid. You confused conjecture with knowledge, which was disingenuous. Would you like me to explain what you should have done? My motives are entirely friendly."

O'Grady was blinking. "I don't charge you with motives—"

"Good. Of course you had no way of knowing how ill-advised it was to imply that I made a journey to Carlo Maffei's room; unfamiliar with my habits, you were not aware that I would not undertake that enterprise though a *Cattleya Dowiana aurea* were to be the reward. Certainly not for some papers and—as you say—things. Archie Goodwin," a finger circled in my direction, "doesn't mind that sort of thing, so he went. What you should have done was this. First, answered me when I wished you good morning. Second, made your request courteous, complete, and correct as to fact. Third —though this was less essential—you might as a matter of professional civility have briefly informed me that the body of the murdered Carlo Maffei has been found and identified and that the assistance of these papers is required in the attempt to discover the assassin. Don't you agree with me that that would have been better, Mr. O'Grady?"

The dick stared at him. "How the hell—" he started, and stopped, and then went on, "So it's already in the papers. I didn't see it, and his name couldn't have been for it's only two hours since I learned it myself. You're quite a guesser, Mr. Wolfe."

"Thank you. Neither did I see it in the papers. But since Maria Maffei's report of her brother's disappearance did not arouse the police beyond a generous effort at conjecture, it seemed to me probable that nothing less than murder would stir them to the frenzy of discovering that Archie had visited his room and removed papers. So. Would you mind telling me where the body was found?"

O'Grady stood up. "You can read it tonight. You're a lulu, Mr. Wolfe. Now those papers."

"Of course." Wolfe didn't move. "But I offer a point for your consideration. All I ask of you is three minutes of your time and information which will be available from public sources within a few hours. Whereas—who knows?—today, or tomorrow, or next year, in connection with this case or another, I might happen upon some curious little fact which conveyed to you would mean promotion, glory, a raise in pay; and, I repeat, you make a mistake if you ignore the demands of professional civility. Was the body by any chance found in Westchester County?"

"What the hell," O'Grady said. "If I hadn't already looked you up, and if it wasn't so plain you'd need a boxcar to get around in, I'd guess you did it yourself. All right. Yes, Westchester County. In a thicket a hundred feet from a dirt road three miles out of Scarsdale, yesterday at eight p.m. by two boys hunting birds' nests."

"Shot perhaps?"

"Stabbed. The doctor says that the knife must have been left in him for a while, an hour or more, but it wasn't there and wasn't found. His pockets were empty. The label on his clothes showed a Grand Street store, and that and his laundry mark were turned over to me at seven o'clock this morning. By nine I had his name, and since then I've searched his room and seen the landlady and the girl."

"Excellent," Wolfe said. "Really exceptional."

The dick frowned. "That girl," he said. "Either she knows something, or the inside of her head is so unfurnished that she can't remember what she ate for breakfast. You had her up here. What did you think when she couldn't remember a thing about the phone call that the landlady said she heard every word of?"

I shot a glance at Wolfe, but he didn't blink an eyelash. He just said, "Miss Anna Fiore is not perfectly equipped, Mr. O'Grady. You found her memory faulty then?"

"Faulty? She had forgot Maffei's first name!"

"Yes. A pity." Wolfe pushed his chair back by putting his hands on the edge of the desk and shoving; I saw he meant to get up. "And now those papers. The only other articles are an empty tobacco can and four snapshots. I must ask a favor of you. Will you let Mr. Goodwin escort you from the room? A personal idiosyncrasy; I have a strong disinclination for opening my safe in the presence of any other person. No offense of course. It would be the same, even perhaps a little accentuated, if you were my banker."

I had been with Wolfe so long that I could usually almost keep up with him, but that time I barely caught myself. I had my mouth open to say that the stuff was in a drawer of his desk, where I had put it the evening before in his presence, and his look was all that stopped me. The dick hesitated, and Wolfe assured him, "Come, Mr. O'Grady. Or go rather. There is no point in surmising that I am creating an opportunity to withhold something, because even if I were there would be nothing you could do to prevent it. Suspicions of that sort between professional men are futile."

I led the dick into the front room, closing the door behind us. I supposed Wolfe would monkey with the safe door so we could hear the noise, but just in case he didn't take the trouble I made some sort of conversation so O'Grady's ears wouldn't be disappointed. Pretty soon we were called back in, and Wolfe was standing on the near side of the desk with the tobacco can and the envelope I had filed the papers and snapshots in. He held them out to the dick.

"Good luck, Mr. O'Grady. I give you this assurance, and you may take my words for what they are worth: if at any time we should discover anything that we believe would be of significance or help to you, we shall communicate with you at once."

"Much obliged. Maybe you mean that."

"Yes, I do. Just as I say it."

The dick went. When I heard the outer door close I went to the front room and through a window saw him walking away. Then I returned to the office and approached Wolfe's desk, where he was seated again, and grinned at him and said:

"You're a damn scoundrel."

The folds of his cheeks pulled away a little from the corners of his mouth; when he did that he thought he was smiling. I said, "What did you keep?"

Out of his vest pocket he pulled a piece of paper about two inches long and half an inch wide and handed it to me. It was one of the clippings from Maffei's top bureau drawer, and it was hard to believe that Wolfe could have known of its existence, for he had barely glanced through that stuff the evening before. But he had taken the trouble to get O'Grady out of the room in order to keep it.

> METAL-WORKER, *must be expert both design and mechanism, who intends returning to Europe for permanent residence, can get lucrative commission. Times L467 Downtown.*

I ran through it twice, but saw no more in it than when I had first read it the afternoon before in Maffei's room. "Well," I said, "if you're trying to clinch it that he meant to go for a sail I can run down to Sullivan Street and pry those luggage stickers off of Anna's wardrobe. And anyway, granting even that it means something, when did you ever see it before? Don't tell me you can read things without looking at them. I'll swear you didn't—" I stopped. Sure, of course he had. I grinned at him. "You went through that stuff while I was taking Anna home last night."

He waited till he was back around the desk and in his chair again before he murmured sarcastically, "Bravo, Archie."

"All right," I said. I sat down across from him. "Do I get to ask questions? There's three things I want to know. Or am I supposed to go up front and do my homework?" I was a little sore, of course; I always was when I knew that he had tied up a nice neat bundle right in front of me without my even being able to see what was going in it.

"No homework," he said. "You are about to go for the car and drive with reasonable speed to White Plains. If the questions are brief—"

"They're brief enough, but if I've got work to do they can wait. Since it's White Plains, I suppose I'm to take a look at the hole in Carlo Maffei and any other details that seem to me unimportant."

"No. Confound it, Archie, stop supposing aloud in my presence; if it is inevitable that in the end you are to be classed with—for instance—Mr. O'Grady, let us at least postpone it as long as possible."

"O'Grady did a good job this morning, two hours from a coat label and a laundry mark to that phone call."

Wolfe shook his head. "Cerebrally an oaf. But your questions?"

"They can wait. What is it at White Plains if it's not Maffei?"

Wolfe gave me his substitute for a smile, an unusually prolonged one for him. Finally he said, "A chance to make some money. Does the name Fletcher M. Anderson mean anything to you without referring to your files?"

"I hope so." I snorted. "No thanks for a bravo either. Nineteen-twenty-eight. Assistant District Attorney on the Goldsmith case. A year later moved to the country and is now District Attorney for Westchester County. He would admit that he owes you something only if the door were closed and he whispered in your ear. Married money."

Wolfe nodded. "Correct. The bravo is yours, Archie, and I shall manage without the thanks. At White Plains you will see Mr. Anderson and deliver a provocative and possibly lucrative message. At least that is contemplated; I am awaiting information from a caller who is expected at any moment." He reached across his rotundity to remove the large platinum watch from his vest pocket and glance at it. "I note that a dealer in sporting goods is not more punctual than a skeptic would expect. I telephoned at nine; the delivery would be made at eleven without fail; it is now eleven-forty. It really would be well at this point to eliminate all avoidable delay. It would have been better to send you— Ah!"

It was the buzzer. Fritz passed the door down the hall; there was the sound of the front door opening and another voice and Fritz's in question and answer. Then heavy footsteps drowning out Fritz's, and there appeared on the threshold a young man who looked like a football player bearing on his shoulder an enormous bundle about three feet long and as big around as Wolfe himself. Breathing, he said, "From Corliss Holmes."

At Wolfe's nod I went to help. We got the bundle onto the floor and the young man knelt and began untying the cord, but he fumbled so long that I got impatient and reached in my pocket for my knife. Wolfe's murmur sounded from his chair, "No, Archie, few knots deserve that," and I put my knife back. Finally he got it loose and the cord pulled off, and I helped him unroll the paper and burlap, and then stood up and stared. I looked at Wolfe and back again at the pile on the floor. It was nothing but golf clubs, there must have been a hundred of them, enough I thought to kill a million snakes, for it had never seemed to me that they were much good for anything else.

I said to Wolfe, "The exercise will do you good."

Still in his chair, Wolfe told us to put them on the desk, and the young man and I each grabbed an armload. I began spreading them in an even row on the desk; there were long and short, heavy and light, iron, wood, steel, chromium, anything you might think of. Wolfe was looking at them, each one as I put it down, and after about a dozen he said, "Not these with iron ends. Remove them. Only those with wooden ends." To the young man, "You do not call this the end?"

The young man looked amazed and superior. "That's the head."

"Accept my apologies—your name?"

"My name? Townsend."

"Accept my apologies, Mr. Townsend. I once saw golf clubs through a shop window while my car was having a flat tire, but the ends were not labeled. And these are in fact all varieties of a single species?"

"Huh? They're all different."

"Indeed. Indeed, indeed. Plain wooden faces, inset faces, bone, composition, ivory—since this is the head I presume that is the face?"

"Sure, that's the face."

"Of course. And the purpose of the inset? Since everything in life must have a purpose except the culture of Orchidaceæ."

"Purpose?"

"Exactly. Purpose."

"Well—" The young man hesitated. "Of course it's for the impact. That means hitting the ball, it's the inset that hits the ball, and that's the impact."

"I see. Go no further. That will do r ely. And the handles, some wood, really fine and sensitive, and steel— I presume the steel handles are hollow."

"Hollow steel shaft, yes, sir. It's a matter of taste. That one's a driver. This is a brassie. See the brass on the bottom? Brassie."

"Faultless sequitur," Wolfe murmured. "That, I think, will be all, the lesson is complete. You know, Mr. Townsend, it is our good fortune that the exigencies of birth and training furnish all of us with opportunities for snobbery. My ignorance of this special nomenclature provided yours; your innocence of the elementary mental processes provides mine. As to the object of your visit, you can sell me nothing; these things will forever remain completely useless to me. You can reassemble your bundle and take it with you, but let us assume that I should purchase three of these clubs and that the profit on each should be one dollar. Three dollars? If I give you that amount will it be satisfactory?"

The young man had, if not his own dignity, at least that of Corliss Holmes. "There is no obligation to purchase, sir."

"No, but I haven't finished. I have to ask a favor of you. Will you take one of these clubs—here, this one—and stand there, beyond that chair, and whirl it about you in the orthodox manner?"

"Whirl it?"

"Yes; club, strike, hit, whatever you call it. Pretend that you are impacting a ball."

Beyond snobbery, the young man was now having difficulty to conceal his contempt. He took the driver from Wolfe, backed away from the desk, shoved a chair aside, glanced around, behind, and up, then brought the driver up over his shoulder and down and through with a terrific swish.

Wolfe shuddered. "Ungovernable fury," he murmured. "Again, more slowly?"

The young man complied.

"If possible, Mr. Townsend, more slowly yet?"

This time he made it slow motion, a cartoon, derisive, but Wolfe watched it keenly and soberly. Then he said:

"Excellent. A thousand thanks, Mr. Townsend. Archie, since we have no account at Corliss Holmes, will you please give Mr. Townsend three dollars? A little speed now, if you don't mind. The trip I mentioned is imminent and even urgent."

After the quiet weeks that had passed it made my heart jump to hear Wolfe ask for speed. The young man and I had the package together again in no time; I went to let him out the front door, and then back to the office. Wolfe was sitting there with his lips fixed to whistle, but with no sound that could be heard six feet away; you only knew the air was going in and out by his chest rising and falling. Sometimes, when close enough to him, I had tried to hear if he really thought he was doing a tune, but without success. He stopped as I came in and said:

"This will only take a minute, Archie. Sit down. You won't need your notebook."

Chapter 4

When I'm driving I don't see much of anything except the road, for I have the type of mind that gets on a job and stays there until it's time for another one. That day I hit a good clip, too; on account of the traffic it took a long while to get to Woodlawn, but from there to White Plains my clock covered just twenty-one minutes. But in spite of my type of mind and the hurry I was in I enjoyed the Parkway out of the corner of my eye. Lots of the bushes were covered with flowers, the new crop of leaves on the trees was waving easy in the breeze like a slow dance, and the grass was thick and green. I thought to myself that they couldn't make a carpet if it cost ten thousand dollars that would be as nice to walk on as that grass.

The hurry didn't help any. When I got to the courthouse there was nothing but bad luck. Anderson was away and wouldn't be back until Monday, four days. In the Adirondacks, they said, but wouldn't give me his address; it wouldn't have been a bit unpleasant to head the roadster for Lake Placid and step on it. His chief assistant, whose name, Derwin, I had never heard before, was still out to lunch and wouldn't be back for half an hour. No one around seemed to care about being helpful.

I went down the street to a phone and got Wolfe in New York. He said to wait for Derwin and try it on him; and I didn't mind having time for a couple of sandwiches and a glass of milk before he was expected back. When I returned Derwin was in his office, but I had to wait for him twenty minutes, I suppose for him to finish picking his teeth. The place was certainly dead.

When I consider the different kinds I've seen it seems silly to say it, but somehow to me all lawyers look alike. It's a sort of mixture of a scared look and a satisfied look, as if they were crossing a traffic-filled street where they expect to get run over any minute but they know exactly the kind of paper to hand the driver if they get killed and they've got one right in their pocket. This Derwin looked like that; otherwise he seemed very respectable, well-dressed and well-fed, somewhere around forty, under rather than over, with his dark hair brushed back slick and his face happy and pleased-looking. I laid my panama on a corner of his desk and took a chair before I said:

"I'm sorry to have missed Mr. Anderson. I don't know if you'll be interested in my message, but I'm pretty sure he would."

Derwin was leaning back in his chair with a politician's smile. "If it is connected with the duties of my office, I certainly will, Mr. Goodwin."

"It's connected all right. But I'm at a disadvantage since

you don't know my employer, Nero Wolfe. Mr. Anderson knows him."

"Nero Wolfe?" Derwin wrinkled his forehead. "I've heard of him. The private detective, you mean of course. This is only White Plains, you see, the provinces begin a little farther north."

"Yes, sir. Not that I would call Nero Wolfe a private detective. As a description—well, for one thing it's a little too active. But that's the man I work for."

"You have a message from him?"

"Yes, sir. As I say, the message was for Mr. Anderson, but I telephoned him half an hour ago and he said to give it to you. It may not work out the same, for I happen to know that Mr. Anderson is a rich man, and I don't know that much about you. Maybe you're like me, maybe your salary is the only rope that holds Saturday and Sunday together for you."

Derwin laughed, just a trick laugh, for in a second his face was solemn and businesslike. "Maybe I am. But although I am not particularly rushed this afternoon, I am still waiting for the message."

"Yes, sir. It's like this. Last Sunday afternoon, four days ago, Peter Oliver Barstow, president of Holland University, died suddenly while playing golf on the links of the Green Meadow Club over toward Pleasantville. You know about that?"

"Of course. It was a loss to the community, to the whole country in fact. Of course."

I nodded. "His funeral was Tuesday and he was buried at Agawalk Cemetery. Mr. Nero Wolfe wants to bet you—he would rather bet Mr. Anderson but he says you'll do—that if you'll have the body lifted and an autopsy made you'll find proof of poison. He will bet ten thousand dollars and will deposit a certified check for that amount with any responsible person you name."

I just grinned as Derwin stared at me. He stared a long time, then he said, "Mr. Nero Wolfe is crazy."

"Oh no," I said. "Whatever you bet on, don't bet on *that*. I haven't finished yet with Nero Wolfe's bet. The rest of it is that somewhere in Barstow's belly, probably just below the stomach, somewhere between one and three inches in from the skin, will be found a short, sharp, thin needle, probably of steel but possibly of very hard wood. It will be pointing upward, approximately at an angle of forty-five degrees if not deflected by a bone."

Derwin kept staring at me. When I stopped he tried his trick laugh again, but it didn't work so well. "This is about as big a bunch of nonsense as I've ever heard," he said. "I suppose there is a point to it somewhere, if you're not crazy too."

"There's a point all right." I reached in my pocket for the check Wolfe had given me. "There are very few people in the world who would risk ten thousand on a bunch of nonsense, and you can take it from me that Nero Wolfe isn't one of them. Peter Oliver Barstow was murdered, and he's got that needle in him. I say it, Nero Wolfe says it, and this ten grand says it. That's a lot of testimony, Mr. Derwin."

The lawyer was beginning to look not nearly as happy and pleased as he had when I went in. He got up from his chair and then sat down again. I waited. He said, "It's preposterous. Absolutely preposterous."

"Wolfe isn't betting on that." I grinned. "He's just betting that it's true."

"But it can't be. It's merely preposterous and—and monstrous. Whatever the stunt may be you're trying to pull, you've hit the wrong man; I happen to be acquainted with the Barstow family and therefore know the facts. I won't recite them to you; such idiotic nonsense. Do you know who signed the death certificate? I don't suppose—"

"Sure," I put in, "Dr. Nathaniel Bradford. Coronary thrombosis. But if all the doctors in the world were as good as him, and if they all said coronary thrombosis, Nero Wolfe's money is still right here ready to talk."

I had seen the change come over Derwin's face; he had got over his shock and was now ready to be clever. His voice was sharp. "See here, what's your game?"

"No game at all. None. Except to win ten grand."

"Let me see that check."

I handed it to him. He looked it over thoroughly and then pulled his desk telephone over, took off the receiver and in a moment spoke to someone: "Miss Ritter, please get me the Thirty-fourth Street branch of the Metropolitan Trust Company." He sat and looked at the check and I folded my arms and got patient. When the bell rang he took the phone again and began asking questions, plenty of them; he certainly made sure there could be no mistake. When he hung up I said pleasantly:

"Anyway we're getting started, now that you know it's real dollars."

He paid no attention, but just sat frowning at the check. Finally he said in a shrewd voice, "Do you mean that you are actually empowered to wager this money on that proposition as you stated it?"

"Yes, sir. That check is made out to me, and certified. I can endorse it just like that. If you want to phone Wolfe, the number is Bryant nine, two-eight-two-eight. In order to avoid any misunderstanding, I would suggest that you have your stenographer type a memorandum of the details for us to sign. I should tell you that Wolfe undertakes to furnish no reasons or suggestions or clues and will not discuss the matter. It's a bet, that's all."

"Bet, hell. You're not expecting any bet. Who do you expect to bet with you, Westchester County?"

I grinned. "We hoped for Mr. Anderson, but lacking him we're not particular. Anyone with ten thousand dollars; Wolfe wouldn't care; a chief of police or a newspaper editor or maybe some prominent Democrat with a strong sense of civic duty."

"Indeed!"

"Yes, sir, indeed. My instructions are to do my best to get the money covered before dark."

Derwin got up, kicking his chair back. "Hah! Bet? Bluff."

"You think so, sir? Try me. Try covering it."

Evidently he had decided something, for with my words he was crossing the room. At the door he turned to say, "Will you wait here for me ten minutes? I imagine you will, since I have your check in my pocket."

It wasn't endorsed. He was gone before I could toss a nod at him. I settled down to wait. How was it going, I wondered. Had I passed up any advantages? Would it have been better to postpone my last threat for more stubbornness if he had it in him? How could I force him to act quick? And after all, did this third-rater have the authority or the guts to undertake a thing like this with his boss gone? What Wolfe wanted was quick action; of course I knew he no more expected a bet than I expected him to give me the ten grand for my birthday; he was after an autopsy and that needle. I could see now how he had guessed the needle, but how he had ever connected it with Carlo Maffei in the first place—I stopped myself to switch back to the immediate job. If this Derwin laid down and played dead on me, where would I go next? Between four and six I would have to use my own judgment; I wouldn't dare to interrupt Wolfe with a phone call while he was upstairs with the damn plants. It was now two-fifty. Derwin had been gone ten minutes. I began to feel silly. What if he left me sitting there holding my fingers all afternoon, and him with the check? If I let a third-rate brief-shark do that to me I'd never be able to look Wolfe in his big fat face again. I should never have let him out of my sight, certainly not without getting the check back. I jumped out of my chair and crossed the room, but at the door I calmed down and took it easy; softly I turned the knob and pulled and stuck my head out. There was a dinky hall leading to the outer office, and I could hear the girl on the telephone.

"No, operator, person-to-person. No one but Mr. Anderson will do."

I waited till she had hung up, then I went on out and over to her desk. "Would it be much bother to tell me where Mr. Derwin has gone to?"

She seemed interested in me; she took a good look. But she answered straight enough. "He's in Mr. Anderson's room telephoning."

"You wouldn't lie to me just for practice?"

"I don't need any practice, thanks."

"All right. If you don't mind, I'll try one of these chairs. It was awful in there all alone."

I sat down within three feet of the entrance door, and I had no sooner got disposed than the door opened and a man came in, a husky, busy-looking man in a blue suit and black shoes, with a stiff straw hat. From where I sat, as he went toward the girl with his back to me, it was easy to see that he had a gun on his hip. The girl said, "Howdedo, Mr. Cook, Mr. Derwin's in Mr. Anderson's room." When the man had gone on through another door I said to the girl, "Ben Cook maybe?" She nodded without looking at me, and I grinned, and sat and waited.

It was all of fifteen minutes more before the door of Anderson's room opened again and Derwin appeared and called to me, "Come in here, Goodwin."

I went. When I got inside and saw that they had actually staged me it was too funny not to laugh. Ben Cook was in a chair that had been drawn alongside the one by the desk—that one of course for Derwin—and one had been placed just right for me, quite close and facing them and the light.

"Amused, huh," the husky man grunted. Derwin waited till he was back in his chair to inform me. "This is the chief of police."

I was pretending to blink at the light. "Don't tell me," I said. "Do you think Ben Cook's reputation stops at Bronx Park?"

Derwin went stern on me. Lord, it was funny. He even went so far as to shake a finger at me. "Goodwin, I've been pretty busy for half an hour, and now I'm ready to tell you what comes next. You'll tell us what you know, if anything, while we're waiting for Wolfe. What reason have you—"

I hated to interrupt the show, but I couldn't help it. It was involuntary. "Waiting for Wolfe? Here?"

"Certainly, here. If he knows what's good for him, and I think I made that plain on the telephone."

I didn't laugh. I just said, "Listen, Mr. Derwin. This is one of your bad days. You never had a chance at so many rotten bets in your life. Nero Wolfe is about as apt to come here as I am to tell you who killed Barstow."

"Yeah?" It was Ben Cook. "You'll tell us plenty. Plenty."

"Maybe. But I won't tell you who killed Barstow, because I don't know. Now if you want to ask about roads, for instance—"

"Cut it out." Derwin got sterner. "Goodwin, you have made a most startling accusation in a most sensational manner. I won't pretend that I have a lot of questions ready for you, because I obviously have nothing to base them on. I have just one question, and I want a prompt and complete answer. For what reason and for what purpose did your employer send you here today?"

I sighed and looked solemn. "I've told you, Mr. Derwin, to get a bet down."

"Come on, act as if you had some sense. You can't get away with that, you know damn well you can't. Come on. Let's hear it."

Ben Cook said, "Don't try to be bright. You'd be surprised how we treat bright boys up here sometimes."

I could have kept it going all night, I suppose, if I had wanted to, but time was passing and they gave me a pain. I said, "Listen a minute, gentlemen. Of course you're peeved and that's too bad, but I can't help it. Let's say I tell you to go to hell and get up and walk out, what are you going to do—? Yes, Chief, I know it's only a short distance to the station, but I'm not going that way. Honest, you're acting like a pair of dumb flatfeet. I'm surprised at you, Mr. Derwin. Nero Wolfe offers to let you in right at the beginning of a big thing, and the first thing you do is spill it to Ben Cook and the next is to drive me to take it away from both of you and toss it to the wolves. You can't touch me, don't be silly. Nero Wolfe would love a suit for false arrest, and I never go to police stations except to visit friends unless you can show me a warrant, and think how funny it would be after the reporters got my story and then the proof followed of Barstow's murder. As a matter of fact, I'm beginning to get a little bit sore and I've got half a mind to demand that check back and walk out on you. Get this: I'll tell you exactly nothing. You understand that maybe? Now you can give me that check or talk sense yourself."

Derwin sat with his arms folded and looked at me without making any effort to open his mouth. Ben Cook said, "So you've come out to the country to show the hayseeds how it's done. Sonny, I'm plenty big enough to take you to the station with nothing at all but the inclination. That's all I need."

"You can afford to be breezy," I told him. "Derwin has handed you a firecracker that he might have to set off himself, and you know it." I turned to Derwin. "Who did you telephone to in New York? Headquarters?"

"No. The District Attorney."

"Did you get him?"

Derwin unfolded his arms, pulled himself back in his chair and looked at me helplessly. "I got Morley."

I nodded. "Dick Morley. What did he tell you?"

"He told me that if Nero Wolfe was offering to bet ten thousand dollars on anything whatever he would appreciate it if I'd take him on for another thousand, only he would give me ten to one."

I was too sore to grin. I said, "And still you invite me in here to tea instead of getting a spade and beating it to Agawalk Cemetery. I repeat that I'll tell you nothing and Wolfe will tell you nothing, but if ever you had a sure thing to go on it's right now. The next thing to do is to give me back that check, and then what?"

Derwin let out a sigh and cleared his throat, but he had to clear it again. "Goodwin," he said, "I'll be frank with you. I'm out of my depth. That's not for publication, Ben, but it's a fact

anyhow. I'm clear out of my depth. Good Lord, don't you
know what it would mean—an exhumation and autopsy on
Peter Oliver Barstow?"

I put in, "Rot. Any of a dozen excuses is enough."

"Well, maybe I'm not good at excuses. Anyway, I know
that family. I can't do it. I've telephoned Anderson at Lake
Placid and couldn't get him. I'll have him before six o'clock,
before seven sure. He can take a sleeper and be here
tomorrow morning. He can decide it then."

"That lets today out," I said.

"Yes. Not a chance. I won't do it."

"All right." I got up. "I'll go down to the corner and phone
Wolfe and see if he'll wait that long, and if he says okay I'll
head south away from the hayseeds. I might as well have that
check."

Derwin took it from his pocket and handed it to me.

I grinned at Ben Cook. "Shall I give you a lift as far as the
station, Chief?"

"Run along, sonny, run along."

Chapter 5

Wolfe was as nice as pie that evening. I got home in time to eat
dinner with him. He wouldn't let me say anything about
White Plains until the meal was over; in fact, there wasn't any
conversation to speak of about anything, for he had the radio
going. He was accustomed to say that this was the perfect era
for the sedentary man; formerly such a man could satisfy any
amount of curiosity regarding bygone times by sitting down
with Gibbon or Ranke or Tacitus or Greene but if he wanted to
meet his contemporaries he had to take to the highways,
whereas the man of today, tiring for the moment of Galba or
Vitellius, had only to turn on the radio and resume his chair.
One program Wolfe rarely missed was the Joy Boys. I never
knew why. He would sit with his fingers interlaced on his
belly, his eyes half closed, and his mouth screwed up as if
there was something in it he would spit out any minute.

Frequently I went for a walk at that time, but of course when dinner was a little early so that it came then I was caught. I have my radio favorites all right, but the Joy Boys seem to me pretty damn vulgar.

In the office after dinner it didn't take me long to report. I hated apologizing to Wolfe because he was so invariably nice about it; he always took it for granted that I had done everything possible and that there was nothing to criticize but the contrariety of the environment, as he put it. He made no comments and didn't seem much interested in the report or the apology either. I tried to get him started, tried for instance to find out if he had really had some sort of wild idea that I might kid a District Attorney into covering a bet of ten thousand dollars just like that, but he only stayed nice and quiet. I asked him if he thought it likely that I could have taken any line at all that would have persuaded Derwin to start the digging that afternoon. He said probably not.

"Frogs don't fly." He was sitting at his desk examining with a magnifying glass the rostellum from a *Cymbidium Alexanderi* that Horstmann had brought down wilty on the stem. "He would have needed a touch of imagination, just a touch, but I would judge from your description that he lacks it. I beg you not to reproach yourself. This affair may prove unprofitable in the end. With Fletcher M. Anderson it might have been different. He is a rich man with professional ambitions, and no fool. He might easily have reflected that if a quiet and unadvertised autopsy proved me wrong he would win ten thousand dollars; if it proved me right he would have to pay me, but he would get a remarkable and sensational case in return, and he might also infer that having pocketed his money I would have further information to be placed at his disposal. Your errand at White Plains was in essence a primitive business enterprise: an offer to exchange something for something else. If Mr. Anderson had only been there he would probably have seen it so. It may yet materialize; it is still worth some small effort. I believe though it is getting ready to rain."

"What are you doing now, changing the subject?" I stuck to the chair near his desk, though I saw that I was being regarded as a mild nuisance, for I had some questions to ask. "It was clouding up as I came in. Is it going to rain all over your clues?"

He was placid, still bent over the magnifying glass. "Some

day, Archie, when I decide you are no longer worth tolerating, you will have to marry a woman of very modest mental capacity to get an appropriate audience for your wretched sarcasms. When I mentioned the rain I had your own convenience and comfort in mind. This afternoon it struck me as desirable that you should visit Sullivan Street, but tomorrow will do as well."

It was hard to believe unless you were as well acquainted with him as I was; I knew that he was really serious, he thought that leaving the house at any time was an unpleasant venture, but to go out in the rain was next to foolhardy. I said, "What do you think I am, the Chinese army? Of course I'll go. That was one of my questions. Why do you suppose Anna Fiore closed up so hard on O'Grady? Because he wasn't all grace and charm like you and me?"

"Likely. Excellent conjecture, Archie. The more so because when I sent Panzer for her today she confessed only reluctantly to her name and she would not budge. So your grace and charm will be needed. If it would be convenient have her here in the morning at eleven. It's not of great importance but can do no harm for passing the time, and such stubbornness deserves a siege."

"I'll go get her now."

"No. Really. Tomorrow. Sit down. I would prefer to have you here, idle and useless, while I purposelessly inspect this futile flower. Futile and sterile apparently. As I have remarked before, to have you with me like this is always refreshing because it constantly reminds me how distressing it would be to have someone present—a wife, for instance—whom I could not dismiss at will."

"Yes, sir." I grinned. "Go on with the rest of it."

"Not just now. Not with the rain falling. I dislike it."

"All right, then tell me a few things. How did you know Carlo Maffei had been murdered? How do you know Barstow was poisoned? How do you know he's got a needle in him? Of course I see how it got there since you had the boy from Corliss Holmes show us, but how did you get that far?"

Wolfe laid down his magnifying glass and sighed. I knew I was making him uncomfortable, but aside from curiosity it was a matter of business. He never seemed to realize that while it was all very well for me to feel in my bones that he would never get us committed to a mistake, I could do my part with a little more intelligence if I knew what was making the wheels go round. I don't believe he ever would have opened up once, on any case big or little, if I hadn't kept nudging him.

He sighed. "Must I again remind you, Archie, of the reaction you would have got if you had asked Velasquez to explain why Aesop's hand was resting inside his robe instead of hanging by his side? Must I again demonstrate that while it is permissible to request the scientist to lead you back over his footprints, a similar request of the artist is nonsense, since he, like the lark or the eagle, has made none? Do you need to be told again that I am an artist?"

"No, sir. All I need to be told is how you knew Barstow was poisoned."

He took up the magnifying glass. I sat and waited, lighting another cigarette. I had finished it, and had about decided to go to the front room for a book or magazine, when he spoke.

"Carlo Maffei is gone. Common enough, beaten and robbed probably, until the telephone call and the advertisement. The telephone call as a whole does not lack interest, but it is the threat, *I'm not the one to be scared,* that has significance. The advertisement adds a specification; to that point Maffei has been this and that, he now becomes also a man who may have made something intricate and difficult that would *work*. The word *mechanism* made that a good advertisement, but it also offered magnificent suggestions to an inquiring mind. Then, quite by accident just as the creation of life was an accident, Maffei becomes something else: a man who clipped the Barstow news from the paper on the morning of his disappearance. So, read the Barstow news again and find the aspect of it that closely concerned Carlo Maffei. An obscure Italian metal-worker immigrant; a famous learned wealthy university president. Still there must be a connection, and the incongruity of the elements would make it only the more plain if it was visible at all. There is the article; find the link if it is there; stop every word and give it passage only if its innocence is sure. But little effort is required; the link is so obvious that it is at once apparent. At the moment of, and for some time immediately preceding, his collapse, Barstow had in his hands and was using not one, but an entire assortment, of instruments which if they were not intricate and difficult mechanisms were admirably adapted to such a use. It was a perfectly composed picture. But while it needed no justification, nothing indeed but contemplation, as a work of art, if it were to be put to practical uses a little fixative would help. So I merely asked Miss Fiore if she had ever seen a golf club in Maffei's room. The result was gratifying."

"All right," I said "But what if the girl had just looked and said no, she never saw one anywhere?"

"I have told you before, Archie, that even for your amusement I shall not advise replies to hypothetical questions."

"Sure, that's an easy out."

Wolfe shook his head regretfully. "To reply is to admit the validity of your jargon, but I have learned not to expect better of you. How the devil do I know what I would have done *if* anything? Probably bade her good night. Would I have found varnish for my picture elsewhere? Maybe; maybe not. Shall I ask you how you would have seen to eat if your head had been put on backwards?"

I grinned. "I wouldn't have starved. Neither will you; if I know anything I know that. But how did you know that Maffei had been murdered?"

"I didn't, until O'Grady came. You heard what I said to him. The police had searched his room. That could only be if he had been taken in a criminal act, or been murdered. The first was unlikely in the light of other facts."

"All right. But I've saved the best till the last. Who killed Barstow?"

"Ah." Wolfe murmured it softly. "That would be another picture, Archie, and I hope an expensive one. Expensive for the purchaser and profitable for the artist. Also, one of its characters would be a worthy subject. To continue my threadbare metaphor, we shan't set up our easel until we are sure of the commission.—Yet in point of fact that isn't strictly true. We shall get in a spot of the background tomorrow morning if you can bring Miss Fiore here."

"Let me get her now. It's only a little after nine."

"No—hear the rain? Tomorrow will do."

I knew there was no use insisting, so after a try at a couple of magazines had got me good and bored I got a raincoat from upstairs and went out for an hour at a movie. I wouldn't have admitted to anyone else, but I did to myself, that I wasn't any too easy in my mind. I had had the same kind of experience often before, but that didn't make me like it any better. I did absolutely feel in my bones that Wolfe would never let us tumble into a hole without having a ladder we could climb out with, but in spite of that I had awful doubts sometimes. As long as I live I'll never forget the time he had a bank president pinched, or rather I did, on no evidence whatever except that the fountain pen on his desk was dry. I was never so relieved in my life as I was when the guy shot himself an hour later. But there was no use trying to get Wolfe to pull up a little; I hardly ever wasted time on that any more. If I undertook to explain how easy he might be wrong he would just say, "You know a fact when you see it, Archie, but you have no feeling for phenomena." After I had looked up the word phenomena in the dictionary I couldn't see that he had anything, but there was no use arguing with him.

So here I was uneasy again. I wanted to think it over, so I got my raincoat and went to a movie where I could sit in the dark with something to keep my eyes on and let my mind work. It wasn't hard to see how Wolfe had doped it out. Someone wanted to kill Barstow, call him X. He put an ad in the paper for an expert to make him something, fixing it to get someone intending to leave the country for good so if he had any curiosity later on it wouldn't hurt him any. Maffei answered the ad and got the job, namely to make an arrangement inside a golf club so that when the inset on the face hit a ball it would release a trigger and shoot a needle out of the handle at the other end. Probably X presented it as a trial of skill for the European commission to follow; but he gave the Italian so much money for doing it that Maffei decided not to go back home after all. That started an argument inside a golf club so that when the inset on the face anyhow, X proceeded to use the club for its calculated purpose, putting it in Barstow's bag (it had of course been made identical in appearance with Barstow's own driver). Then Maffei happened to read Monday's *Times* and put two and two together, which wasn't strange considering the odd affair he had been paid to construct. X had telephoned; Maffei had met him, made him a present of his suspicions, and tried blackmail. X didn't wait this time for an expert design and mechanism, he just used a knife, leaving it in Maffei's back to keep from soiling the upholstery of the car. He then drove around the Westchester hills until he found a secluded spot, put the body in a thicket and pulled out the knife and later tossed it into a handy stream or reservoir. Arriving home at a decent hour, he had a drink or two before going to bed, and when he got up in the morning put on a cutaway instead of a business suit because he was going to his friend Barstow's funeral.

Of course that was Wolfe's picture, and it was a lulu, but what I figured as I sat in the movie was this, that though it used all the facts without any stretching, anyone could have said that much a thousand years ago when they thought the sun went around the earth. That didn't stretch any of the facts they knew, but what about the ones they didn't know? And here was Wolfe risking ten grand and his reputation to get Barstow dug up. Once one of Wolfe's clients had told him he was insufferably blithe. I liked that; Wolfe had liked it too. But that didn't keep me from reflecting that if they cut Barstow open and found only coronary thrombosis in his veins and no oddments at all in his belly, within a week everybody from the D.A. down to a Bath Beach flatfoot would be saving twenty cents by staying home and laughing at us instead of going to a movie to see Mickey Mouse. I wasn't so dumb, I knew anyone may make a mistake, but I also knew that when a man sets himself up as cocksure as Wolfe did, he had *always* got to be right.

I was dumb in a way though. All the time I was stewing I knew damn well Wolfe *was* right. It was that note I went to sleep on when I got home from the movie and found that Wolfe had already gone up to his room.

The next morning I was awake a little after seven, but I dawdled in bed, knowing that if I got up and dressed I would have to dawdle anyway, since there was no use bringing Anna Fiore until time for Wolfe to be down from the plant-rooms. I lay, yawning, looking at the picture of the woods with grass and flowers, and at the photograph of my father and mother, and then closed my eyes, not to nap for I was all slept out, but to see how many different noises from the street I could recognize. I was doing that when there was a knock on the door and in answer to my call Fritz came in.

"Good morning," I said. "I'll have grapefruit juice and just a tiny cup of chocolate."

Fritz smiled. He had a sweet sort of faraway smile. He could catch a joke but never tried to return it. "Good morning. There's a gentleman downstairs to see Mr. Wolfe."

I sat up. "What's his name?"

"He said Anderson. He had no card."

"What!" I swung myself to the edge of the bed. "Well well well well. He's not a gentleman, Fritz, he's a noovoh reesh. Mr. Wolfe is hoping that soon he'll be less reesh. Tell him—no, don't bother. I'll be right down."

I doused some cold water over my face, got on enough clothes for an emergency, and gave my hair a few swipes with a brush. Then I went down.

Anderson didn't get up from his chair when I entered the office. He was so sunburned that on the street it would have taken me a second glance to recognize him. He looked sleepy and sore and his hair hadn't been brushed any better than mine.

I said, "My name's Archie Goodwin. I don't suppose you remember me."

He kept his chair. "I suppose not, I'm sorry. I came to see Wolfe."

"Yes, sir. I'm afraid you'll have to wait a little. Mr. Wolfe isn't up yet."

"Not long I hope."

"I couldn't say. I'll see. If you'll excuse me."

I beat it to the hall and stood there at the foot of the stairs. I had to decide whether this was a case when Wolfe would want to break a rule. It was a quarter to eight. Finally I went on upstairs and down the hall to a point about ten feet from his door where there was a push-button in the wall. I pushed it, and right away heard his voice faintly:

"Well?"

"Turn off the switch. I'm coming in."

I heard the little click and then: "Come."

You would never believe there was such a thing in the world as Wolfe in bed if you didn't see it. I had seen it often, but it was still a treat. On top was a black silk puffy cover which he always used, winter and summer. From the mound in the middle it sloped precipitously on all sides, so that if you wanted to see his face you had to stand well up front, and then you had to stoop to look under the canopy arrangement that he had sticking out from the head of the bed. It was also of black silk, and extended a foot beyond his chin and hung quite low on all three sides. Inside it on the white pillow his big fat face reposed like an image in a temple.

His hand came from beneath the cover to pull a cord that hung at his right, and the canopy folded back against the headboard. He blinked. I told him that Fletcher M. Anderson was downstairs and wanted to see him.

He cursed. I hated to hear him curse. It got on my nerves. The reason for that, he told me once, was that whereas in most cases cursing was merely a vocal explosion, with him it was a considered expression of a profound desire. He did it seldom. That morning he cursed completely. At the end he said, "Leave, get out, go."

I hated to stammer, too. "But—but—Anderson—"

"If Mr. Anderson wishes to see me he may do so at eleven o'clock. But that is unnecessary. What do I pay you for?"

"Very well, sir. Of course you're right. I break a rule and I get bawled out. But now that that's done with may I suggest that it would be a good idea to see Anderson—"

"You may not."

"Ten thousand dollars?"

"No."

"In the name of heaven, sir, why not?"

"Confound it, you badger me!" Wolfe's head turned on the pillow, and he got a hand around to wiggle a finger. "Yes, you badger me. But it is a valuable quality at times and I won't cavil at it. Instead I'll answer your question. I shall not see Mr. Anderson for three reasons: first, being still in bed I am undressed and in an ugly temper. Second, you can do our business with him just as well. Third, I understand the technique of eccentricity; it would be futile for a man to labor at establishing a reputation for oddity if he were ready at the slightest provocation to revert to normal action. Go. At once."

I left the room and went downstairs to the office and told Anderson that if he wanted to wait he could see Mr. Wolfe at eleven o'clock.

Of course he couldn't believe his ears. As soon as he became able to credit the fact that the message was like that and that it was meant for him, he blew up. He seemed especially indignant that he had come straight to Wolfe's place from a sleeper at Grand Central Station, though I couldn't see why. I explained to him several times how it was, I told him it was eccentricity and there was no help for it. I also told him that I had been to White Plains the day before and was acquainted with the situation. That seemed to calm him a little and he began asking me questions. I fed it to him in little pieces, and had the fun of seeing the look on his face when I told him about Derwin calling Ben Cook in. When he had the whole story he sat back and rubbed his nose and looked over my head.

Finally he brought his look down to me. "This is a startling conclusion Wolfe has made. Isn't it?"

"Yes, sir. It is indeed."

"Then he must have some startling information."

I grinned. "Mr. Anderson, it is a pleasure to talk with you, but there's no use wasting time. As far as startling information is concerned, Wolfe and I are the same as two mummies in a museum until that grave is opened and Barstow is cut up. Not a chance."

"Well. That's too bad. I might offer Wolfe a fee as a special investigator—a sort of inquiry and report."

"A fee? That's like saying as long as a piece of string."

"Say, five hundred dollars."

I shook my head. "I'm afraid he's too busy. I'm busy too, I may have to run up to White Plains this morning."

"Oh." Anderson bit his lip and looked at me. "You know, Goodwin, I rarely go out of my way to be offensive, but doesn't it occur to you that this whole thing is fairly nasty? It might be better to say unethical."

I got sore at that. I looked back at him and said, "Look here, Mr. Anderson. You said you didn't remember me. I remember you. You haven't forgotten the Goldsmith case five years ago. It wouldn't have hurt you a bit to let people know what Wolfe handed you on that. But let them go, let's say you needed to keep it for yourself. We wouldn't have minded that so much. But how ethical was it for you to turn it around so that Wolfe got a nice black eye instead of what was really coming to him? You tend to your own ethics maybe."

"I don't know what you're talking about."

"All right. But if I go to White Plains today somebody will know what I'm talking about. And whatever you get this time you'll pay for."

Anderson smiled and got up. "Don't bother, Goodwin. You won't be needed at White Plains today. On information that I have received I have decided definitely on the exhumation of Barstow's body. You will be here throughout the day, or Wolfe? I may wish to get in touch with him later."

"Wolfe is always here, but you can't get him between nine and eleven or four and six."

"Well. Such an eccentric!"

"Yes, sir. Your hat's in the hall."

I went to the front room window and watched his taxi roll off. Then I turned to the office, to the telephone. I hesitated; but I knew Wolfe was right, and if he wasn't, a little publicity wouldn't make it any harder for us. So I called the *Gazette* office for Harry Foster, and by luck he was in.

"Harry? Archie Goodwin. Here's something for you, but keep it so quiet you can hear a pin drop. This morning at White Plains, Anderson, the District Attorney, is going to get a court order for an exhumation and autopsy on Peter Oliver Barstow. He'll probably try to keep it mum, but I thought you might like to help him out. And listen. Some day, when the time comes, I'd be glad to tell you what it was that made Anderson so curious. Don't mention it."

I went upstairs and shaved and did my dressing over. By the time I had finished with that, and with breakfast and a little chat in the kitchen with Fritz about fish, it was nine-thirty. I went to the garage for the roadster and filled up with gas and oil, and headed south for Sullivan Street.

Since it was school hours it wasn't as noisy and dirty around there as it had been before, and it was different otherwise. I might have expected the decorations, but it hadn't occurred to me. There was a big black rosette with long black ribbons hanging on the door and above it was a large wreath of leaves and flowers. A few people were standing around, mostly across the street. A little distance off a cop stood on the sidewalk looking uninterested; but when my roadster pulled up some yards short of the door with the wreath on it I saw him cock an eye at me. I got out and went over to him to say hello.

I handed him a card. "I'm Archie Goodwin of Nero Wolfe's office. We were engaged by Maffei's sister to look for him the day before his body was found. I've come to see the landlady and check up a little."

"Yeah?" The cop stuck my card in a pocket. "I don't know a thing except that I'm standing here. Archie Goodwin? Pleased to meet you."

We shook hands and as I moved off I asked him to keep an eye on my car.

Mrs. Ricci didn't seem very glad to see me, but I could understand that easy enough. That dick O'Grady had probably raked her over for letting me take stuff from Maffei's room, of course without any right or reason, but that wouldn't deter O'Grady. I grinned when I saw the landlady's lips go shut, getting ready for the questions she thought I had come to ask. It's never any fun having a murdered man lying upstairs, even when he was only a roomer. So I sympathized with her a little before I mentioned that I'd like to see Anna Fiore.

"She's busy."

"Sure. But this is important; my boss would like to see her. It would only take an hour or so, here, a couple of dollars—"

"No! For the love of God can't you let us alone in our house? Can't you let the poor woman bury her brother without cackling in her ears to drive her crazy? Who are you that—"

Of course she would have to pick me to blow up on. I saw it was hopeless to get any co-operation out of her, she wouldn't even listen to me, so I removed myself and went back to the front hall. The door to the dining-room was open, but the room was empty. After I had slipped in there I heard footsteps in the hall, and looking through the crack between the door and the jamb I saw Mrs. Ricci start upstairs. She went on up, and I could hear her continue the second flight. I stuck behind the door and waited, and luck came my way. Not more than ten minutes had passed before there were steps on the stairs, and using the crack again I saw Anna. I called her name, softly. She stopped and looked around. I called still softly, "In the dining-room." She came to the threshold and I moved around where she could see me.

"Hello, Anna. Mrs. Ricci told me to wait here till you came down."

"Oh. Mr. Archie."

"Sure. I came to take you for a ride. Mrs. Ricci was angry that I came for you, but you remember on Wednesday I gave her a dollar? Today I gave her two dollars, so she said all right. But hurry up; I told her we'd be back before noon."

I grabbed Anna's hand, but she held back. "In that car like the other day?"

"Sure. Come on."

"My jacket is upstairs and look at my dress."

"It's too warm for a jacket. Hurry; what if Mrs. Ricci changed her mind? We can buy you one—come on."

With my hand on her arm I worked her out of the dining-room and down the short hall to the entrance door, but I didn't want to look anxious outside; there was no telling how important that cop might think he was and any interruption might queer it. So I threw the door open and said, "Go on and get in, I'll tell Mrs. Ricci good-bye." I waited only a few seconds before I followed her; she was at the roadster opening the door. I went around to my side and climbed in, stepped on the starter, waved to the flatfoot and shot off down Sullivan

Street in second with the engine roaring so that no yelling from an upstairs window could hurt Anna's ears.

She certainly was a scarecrow. Her dress was a sight. But I wasn't ashamed to have her beside me as, headed uptown again, I circled through Washington Square and rolled into Fifth Avenue. Not a bit. The clock on the dash said twenty after ten.

Anna said, "Where are we going, Mr. Archie?"

I said, "You see how it is about your dress in this low seat? Nobody can see you anyway except your face and there's nothing wrong with that. What do you say we drive around Central Park? It's a beautiful morning."

"Oh yes."

I didn't say anything and she didn't either for about ten blocks and then she said again, "Oh yes."

She was certainly having a swell time. I went on up the Avenue and into the Park at Sixtieth. Up the west side to a Hundred and Tenth, across to Riverside Drive, up to Grant's Tomb where I circled around and turned downtown. I don't think she glanced at the trees or the grass or the river once; she kept looking at people in other cars. It was five minutes to eleven when I drew up in front of Wolfe's house.

Mrs. Ricci had already telephoned twice. Fritz had a funny look when he told me about it. I settled that at once by calling her up and giving her a piece about obstructing justice. I didn't know how much of it she heard with her yelling, but it seemed to work; we didn't hear another peep out of her before noon, when I left to take Anna home.

Wolfe came in while I was phoning Mrs. Ricci. I watched him stopping to tell the girl good morning on his way to the desk. He was elegant with women. He had some sort of a perverted idea about them that I've never caught the hang of but every time I had ever seen him with one he was elegant. I couldn't describe how he did it because I couldn't make it out myself; it was hard to see how that enormous lump of flesh and folds could ever be called elegant, but he certainly was. Even when he was bullying one of them, like the time he sweated the Diplomacy Club business out of Nyura Pronn. That was the best exhibition of squeezing a sponge dry I've ever seen.

He started softly with Anna Fiore. After he had flipped through the mail, he turned and looked at her a minute before he said, "We no longer need to indulge in any conjectures as to

the whereabouts of your friend Carlo Maffei. Accept my
condolences. You have viewed the body?"

"Yes, sir."

"It is a pity, a real pity, for he did not seek violence; he got
in its path by misadventure. It is curious on how slender a
thread the destiny of a man may hang; for example, that of the
murderer of Carlo Maffei may hang on this, Miss Fiore: when
and under what circumstances did you see a golf club in
Maffei's room?"

"Yes, sir."

"Yes. It will be easy to tell us now. Probably my question
the other day recalled the occasion to your mind."

"Yes, sir."

"It did?"

She opened her mouth but said nothing. I was watching
her, and she looked odd to me. Wolfe asked her again, "It
did?"

She was silent. I couldn't see that she was a bit nervous or
frightened, she was just silent.

"When I asked you about this the other day, Miss Fiore,
you seemed a little upset. I was sorry for that. Would you tell
me why you were upset?"

"Yes, sir."

"Was it perhaps your memory of something unpleasant
that happened the day you saw the golf club?"

Silence again. I saw that something was wrong. Wolfe
hadn't asked the last question as if it meant anything. I knew
the shades of the tones of his voice, and I knew he wasn't
interested; at least, not in that question. Something had him
off on another trail. All at once he shot another question at her
in another tone:

"When did you decide to say *Yes, sir*, to anything I might
ask you?"

No answer; but without waiting Wolfe went on: "Miss
Fiore, I would like to make you understand this. My last
question had nothing whatever to do with a golf club or with
Carlo Maffei. Don't you see that? So if you have decided to
reply nothing but *Yes, sir*, to anything I may ask about Carlo
Maffei that will be all right. You have an absolute right to do
that because that is what you decided to do. But if I ask you
about other things you have no right to say *Yes, sir*, then,
because that is not what you decided to do. About other things
you should talk just as anyone would. So, when you decided to

say nothing but *Yes, sir*, to me, was it on account of anything that Carlo Maffei had done?"

Anna was looking hard at him, right at his eye. It was clear that she wasn't suspecting him or fighting against him, she was merely trying to understand him. She looked and he looked back. After a minute of that she said:

"No, sir."

"Ah! Good. It was not on account of anything he had done. Then it had nothing to do with him, so it is all right for you to tell me anything about it that I may ask. You see that of course. If you have decided to tell me nothing of Carlo Maffei I won't ask you. But this other business. Did you decide to say *Yes, sir*, to Mr. O'Grady, the man that came and asked you questions yesterday morning?"

"Yes, sir."

"Why did you do that?"

She frowned, but said, "Because something happened."

"Good. What happened?"

She shook her head.

"Come, Miss Fiore." Wolfe was quiet. "There is no reason on earth why you shouldn't tell me."

She turned her head to look at me, and then back at him again. After a moment she said, "I'll tell Mr. Archie."

"Good. Tell Mr. Archie."

She spoke to me. "I got a letter."

Wolfe shot a glance at me and I took it up. "You got a letter yesterday?"

She nodded. "Yesterday morning."

"Who was it from?"

"I don't know. There was no name, it was on a typewriter, and on the envelope it said only Anna and the address, not the rest of my name. Mrs. Ricci gets the mail from the box and she brought it to me but I didn't want to open it where she was because I never get a letter. I went downstairs where I sleep and opened it."

"What did it say?"

She looked at me a moment without replying, and then suddenly she smiled, a funny smile that made me feel queer so that it wasn't easy to look at her. But I kept my eyes on hers. Then she said, "I'll show you what was in it, Mr. Archie," and reached down and pulled her skirt up above her knee, shoved her hand down inside of her stocking, and brought it out again with something in it. I stared as she unrolled five twenty-dollar bills and spread them out for me to see.

"You mean that was in the letter?"

She nodded. "One hundred dollars."

"So I see. But there was something typewritten."

"Yes. It said that if I would never tell anyone anything about Mr. Maffei or anything he ever did I could keep the money. But if I would not do that, if I told about him, I would have to burn it. I burned the letter, but I will not burn the money. I will keep it."

"You burned the letter?"

"Yes."

"And the envelope?"

"Yes."

"And you think you won't tell anyone about Mr. Maffei or about that golf club?"

"I never will."

I looked at her. Wolfe's chin was on his chest, but he was looking at her too. I got up from my chair. "Well, of all the damn fairy stories—"

"Archie! Apologize."

"But good heavens—"

"Apologize."

I turned to the girl. "I apologize, but when I think of all the gas I burned up riding you around the park—" I sat down.

Wolfe said, "Miss Fiore, did you happen to notice the postmark? The little round thing on the envelope that tells where it was mailed?"

"No, sir."

"Of course not. By the way, that money did not belong to the man who sent it to you. He took it from Carlo Maffei's pocket."

"I will keep it, sir."

"No doubt you will. You may not be aware that if the police knew of this they would take it from you ruthlessly. But do not be alarmed; your confidence in Mr. Archie is not misplaced." He turned to me. "Grace and charm are always admirable qualities and sometimes useful. Take Miss Fiore home."

I protested. "But why not—"

"No. Get her to burn those bills by replacing them from your expense book? No. She would not do it; but even if she would, I would not see money burned to save beauty herself from any grave that might be dug for her. The destruction of money is the only authentic sacrilege left us to abhor. Possibly you don't realize what that hundred dollars means to Miss Fiore; to her it represents the unimaginable reward for a desperate and heroic act. Now that she has it safely back in its crypt, take her home." He started to get himself out of his chair. "Good day, Miss Fiore. I have paid you a rare compliment; I have assumed that you mean what you say. Good morning."

I was at the door telling her to come on.

Going back downtown I let her alone. I was pretty sore, after kidnaping her and driving her around in style for nearly an hour to have her go moron on us, but there was no use wasting breath on her. At Sullivan Street I just dumped her out on the sidewalk with a good deal of satisfaction, thinking that Wolfe had been elegant enough for both of us.

She stood there. As I pulled the gear shift lever to go on she said, "Thank you, Mr. Archie."

She was being elegant! She had caught it from Wolfe. I said, "You're not welcome, Anna, but good-bye and no hard feelings," and rolled off.

Chapter 6 ·

It was during the half-hour that I was gone taking Anna Fiore home that Wolfe had a relapse. It was a bad one, and it lasted three days. When I got back to Thirty-fifth Street he was sitting in the kitchen, by the little table where I always ate breakfast, drinking beer with three bottles already gone, arguing with Fritz whether chives should be used in tomato tarts. I stood and listened a few minutes without saying anything, then I went upstairs to my room and got a bottle of rye from the closet and took a drink.

I had never really understood Wolfe's relapses. Sometimes it seemed plain that it was just ordinary discouragement and funk, like the time the taxi driver ran out on us in the Pine Street case, but other times there was no accounting for it at all. Everything would be sailing along and it would look to me as if we were about ready to wrap up the package and deliver it C.O.D., when for no reason at all he would lose interest. He was out and that was all there was to it. Nothing that I could say made the slightest dent on him. It might last anywhere from one afternoon up to a couple of weeks, or it was even possible that he was out for good and wouldn't come back until something new turned up. While it lasted he acted one of two different ways: either he went to bed and stayed there, living on bread and onion soup, refusing to see anyone but me and forbidding me to mention anything I had on my mind; or he sat in the kitchen telling Fritz how to cook things and then eating them on my little table. He ate a whole half a sheep that way in two days once, different parts of it cooked in twenty different ways. At such times I usually had my tongue out from running all over town from the Battery to Bronx Park, trying to find some herb or root or maybe cordial that they needed in the dish they were going to do next. The only time I ever quit Wolfe was when he sent me to a Brooklyn dock where a tramp steamer from China was tied up, to try to buy some badden-root from the captain. The captain must have had a cargo of opium or something to make him suspicious; anyway he took it for granted that I was looking for trouble and filled my order by having half a dozen skinny savages wrap things around my skull. I quit the next afternoon, phoning from the hospital, but a day later Wolfe came and took me home, and I was so astonished that he actually came himself that I forgot I had quit. That finished that relapse, too.

This day I knew it was a relapse as soon as I saw him sitting in the kitchen arguing with Fritz, and I was so disgusted that after I had gone upstairs and had a couple of drinks I came down again and went out. I started walking, but after a few blocks the appetite from the drinks was quite active and I stopped at a restaurant for a meal. No restaurant meal was much after seven years of Fritz's everyday cooking, but I wouldn't go home to eat; in the first place I was disgusted and in the second place those relapse menus couldn't be depended on—sometimes it was a feast for an epicure, sometimes it was a dainty little taste good for eighty cents in Schrafft's and sometimes it was just a mess.

But after the meal I felt better, and I walked back to Thirty-fifth Street and told Wolfe what Anderson had said that morning and added that it looked to me as if there would be something doing before the full moon came.

Wolfe was still sitting at the little table, watching Fritz stir something in a pan. He looked at me as if he was trying to remember where he had seen me before. He said, "Don't ever mention that shyster's name to me again."

I said, hoping to get him sore, "This morning I phoned Harry Foster at the *Gazette* and told him what was up. I knew you'd want plenty of publicity."

He didn't hear me. He said to Fritz, "Have boiling water ready in case it should disunite."

I went upstairs to tell Horstmann he'd have to nurse his babies alone that afternoon and maybe for a week. He would be miserable. It was always funny how he pretended to be annoyed when Wolfe was around but if anything happened to keep Wolfe from showing up on the dot at nine or four he was so worried and anxious you might have thought mealy bugs were after him. So I went upstairs to make him miserable.

That was two o'clock Friday afternoon, and the first sane look I got from Wolfe was eleven Monday morning, sixty-nine hours later.

In between things happened a little. First was the telephone call from Harry Foster Friday around four. I'd been expecting it. He said they had dug Barstow up and done the autopsy but wouldn't make any announcement. It wasn't his story any more; others had got wind of it and were hanging around the coroner's office.

A little after six the second phone call came. This time it was Anderson. I grinned when I heard his voice and glanced at my wrist; I could see him fuming around waiting for six o'clock. He said he wanted to talk to Wolfe.

"I'm sorry, Mr. Wolfe is busy. This is Goodwin."

He said he wanted Wolfe to come to White Plains. I laughed at him. He rang off. I didn't like it, he struck me as a bad guy. After thinking it over a little I called up Henry H. Barber at his apartment and got all the dope on things like accessories and arrests of material witnesses. Then I went to the kitchen and told Wolfe about the two phone calls. He wiggled a spoon at me.

"Archie. This Anderson is a disease. Cleanse the telephone. Did I forbid mention of his name?"

I said, "I'm sorry, I should have known better. You know

what I think, sir. A nut is always a nut even when it's you. I want to talk to Fritz."

Wolfe wasn't listening. I told Fritz that for dinner I would come and get sandwiches and take them to the office, and then I told him that when the buzzer rang, until further notice, he was not to go to the door, I would attend to it. Under no circumstances was he to open the door.

I knew it was probably uncalled-for precaution, but I was taking no chances on anyone busting in there with Wolfe in one of his Bloomingdale moods. I was glad he hadn't tried to send me for anything and I hoped he wouldn't, for I wouldn't have gone. If it was a washout, all right, but I wasn't going to let them make ninnies of us if I could help it. Nothing happened that night. The next morning I stayed out of Wolfe's way, mostly in the front room, opening the door to a gas man and an expressman, and once to a slick youth that wanted to get helped through college. I helped him as far as the bottom of the stoop. It was around eleven when I obeyed the buzzer by opening the door again and found a big husky standing against it, coming in with it, his foot sliding along. I gave him a good solid stiff-arm and pushed him back, and went on out, shutting the door behind me.

I said, "Good morning. Who invited you?"

He said, "It wasn't you anyhow. I want to see Nero Wolfe."

"You can't. He's sick. What do you want?"

He smiled, being smooth, and handed me a card. I looked at it.

"Sure. From Anderson's office. His right-hand man? What do you want?"

"You know what I want," he smiled. "Let's go in and talk it over."

I didn't see any sense in trying to be coy. Anyway I had no idea when Wolfe might kick out of it, and that made me sick. So I covered it all in as few words as possible. I told him that Wolfe didn't know one thing that they didn't know, at least nothing that applied to Barstow, and that what he did know came to him in a dream. I told him that if they wanted Wolfe on the case at a price to say so and name the price and he would take it or leave it. I told him that if they wanted to try any funny warrants they would be surprised how funny they'd turn out to be before Wolfe get through with them. Then I told him that I could see that he weighed twenty pounds more than

I did and that therefore I wouldn't attempt to go back in the house until he had departed, and that I would appreciate it if he would get a move on because I was reading an interesting book. He inserted a few remarks as I went along, but when I finished all he said was:

"Tell Wolfe he can't get away with it."

"Sure. Any other message?"

"Just go to hell for you."

I grinned, and stood on the stoop watching him as he walked off, headed east. I had never heard of him before, but I didn't know Westchester very well. The name on the card was H. R. Corbett. I went back to the front room and sat and smoked cigarettes.

After lunch, some time around four, I heard a newsy out in the street calling an extra. I went out and called him and bought one. There it was taking up half of the front page: BARSTOW POISONED—DART FOUND IN BODY. I read it through. If ever I had a pain in the neck it was then. Of course Wolfe and I weren't mentioned; I hadn't expected that; but to think of what that piece might have meant to us! I kicked myself for bungling with Derwin, and again with Anderson, for I was sure it could have been handled somehow to let us in, though it was hard to see how. And I kicked Wolfe for his damn relapse. At least I wanted to. I read it again. It wasn't a dart at all, it was a short steel needle, just as Wolfe had said, and it had been found below the stomach. Sore as I was at Wolfe, I handed it to him. There was his picture.

I went to the kitchen and laid the paper on the table in front of Wolfe without a word, and went out again. He called after me, "Archie! Get the car, here's a list for you."

I pretended I didn't hear. Later Fritz went.

Next day the Sunday papers were full of it. They had sent their packs running around sniffing all over Westchester County, but they hadn't found a thing. I read all the articles through, and I learned a lot of details about the Green Meadow Club, the Barstow family, the Kimballs who had been in the foursome, the doctor who had pulled a boner, and a lot besides, but nobody really knew any more than Wolfe had known Wednesday evening when he had asked Anna Fiore if she had ever seen a golf club in Carlo Maffei's room. Not as much, for there was no accepted theory as to how the needle got in Barstow's belly. All the papers had pieces by experts on poisons and what they do to you.

Sunday evening I went to a movie, telling Fritz to open the door to no one. Not that I expected anything; it looked as if Anderson was playing his own hand. Possibly, through motive or discoveries he had made, he was really lining it up. I would have got drunk that evening if it hadn't been Sunday. When I got back from the movie Wolfe had gone up to his room, but Fritz was still in the kitchen washing up. I fried a piece of ham to make myself a sandwich and poured a glass of milk, for I hadn't had much dinner. I noticed that the *Times* I had put there in the morning for Wolfe was still on top of the refrigerator just as I had left it. It was ten to one he hadn't looked at it.

I read in my room until after midnight and then had trouble going to sleep on account of my mind working. But apparently there was no trouble about it after I once got started, for when I pried my eyes open in the morning enough to glance at the clock on the stand it was after nine. I was sitting on the edge of the bed yawning when I heard a noise overhead that woke me up good. Either that was two pairs of footsteps and I knew both of them or I was still dreaming. I went out in the hall and listened a minute and then ran downstairs. Fritz was in the kitchen drinking coffee. "Is that Mr. Wolfe up with Horstmann?"

"And how." That was the only slang Fritz ever used and he always welcomed a chance to get it in. He smiled at me, glad to see me excited and happy. "Now I will just get a leg of lamb and rub garlic on it."

"Rub poison ivy on it if you want to." I went back up to dress.

The relapse was over! I was excited all right. I shaved extra clean and whistled in the bathtub. With Wolfe normal again anything might happen. When I got back down to the kitchen a dish of figs and a fat omelet were ready for me, and the newspaper was propped up against the coffeepot. I started on the headlines and the figs at the same time, but halfway through a fig I stopped chewing. I raced down the paragraphs, swallowing the mouthful whole to get it out of the way. It was plain, the paper stated it as a fact. Although no confirmation was needed, I turned the pages over, running my eyes up and down and across. It was on page eight toward the bottom, a neat little ad in a neat little box:

I WILL PAY FIFTY THOUSAND DOLLARS RE-
WARD TO ANY PERSON OR PERSONS WHO
WILL FURNISH INFORMATION RESULTING
IN THE DISCOVERY AND RIGHTEOUS PUN-
ISHMENT OF THE MURDERER OF MY HUS-
BAND PETER OLIVER BARSTOW.

ELLEN BARSTOW

I read it through three times and then tossed the paper away and got calm. I finished the fruit and omelet, with three pieces of toast and three cups of coffee. Fifty grand, with the Wolfe bank balance sagging like a clothesline under a wet horse blanket; and not only that, but a chance of keeping our places on the platform in the biggest show of the season. I was calm and cool, but it was only twenty minutes after ten. I went to the office and opened the safe and dusted around and waited.

When Wolfe came down at eleven he looked fresh but not noticeably good-humored. He only nodded for good morning and didn't seem to care much whether I was there or not as he got himself into his chair and started looking through the mail. I just waited, thinking I would show him that other people could be as hard-boiled as he was, but when he began checking off the monthly bill from Harvey's I popped at him:

"I hope you had a nice weekend, sir."

He didn't look at me, but I saw his cheeks folding. "Thank you, Archie. It was delightful; but on awakening this morning I felt so completely water-logged that with only myself to consider I would have remained in bed to await disintegration. Names battered at me: Archie Goodwin, Fritz Brenner, Theodore Horstmann; responsibilities; and I arose to resume my burden. Not that I complain; the responsibilities are mutual; but my share can be done only by me."

"Excuse me, sir, but you're a damn liar, what you did was look at the paper."

He checked off items on the bill. "You can't rile me, Archie, not today. Paper? I have looked at nothing this morning except life, and that not through a newspaper."

"Then you don't know that Mrs. Barstow has offered fifty thousand dollars for her husband's murderer?"

The pencil stopped checking; he didn't look at me, but the pencil was motionless in his fingers for seconds. Then he placed the bill under a paperweight, laid the pencil beside it, and lifted his head.

"Show it to me."

I exhibited first the ad and then the first page article. Of the ad he read each word; the article he glanced through.

"Indeed," he said. "Indeed. Mr. Anderson does not need the money, even granting the possibility of his earning it, and only a moment ago I was speaking of responsibilities. Archie, do you know what I thought in bed this morning? I thought how horrible and how amusing it would be to send Theodore away and let all those living and breathing plants, all that arrogant and pampered loveliness, thirst and gasp and wither away."

"Good God!"

"Yes. Just an early morning fantasy; I haven't the will for such a gesture. I would be more likely to offer them at auction —should I decide to withdraw from responsibilities—and take passage for Egypt. You know of course that I own a house in Egypt which I have never seen. The man who gave it to me, a little more than ten years ago—yes, Fritz, what is it?"

Fritz was a little awry, having put on his jacket hurriedly to go to the door.

"A lady to see you, sir."

"Her name?"

"She had no card, sir."

Wolfe nodded, and Fritz went out. In a moment he was back on the threshold, bowing in a young woman. I was on my feet. She started toward me, and I inclined my head in Wolfe's direction. She looked at him, stopped, and said:

"Mr. Nero Wolfe? My name is Sarah Barstow."

"Be seated," Wolfe said. "You must pardon me; for engineering reasons I arise only for emergencies."

"This is an emergency," she said.

Chapter 7

From the newspapers I was pretty well up on Sarah Barstow. She was twenty-five, popular, a graduate of Smith, and prominent both in university society at Holland and in various groups in summer Westchester. Of course beautiful, according to the papers. I thought to myself that this time that detail was accurate, as she arranged herself in a chair in front of Wolfe and sat with her eyes on him. She wore a tan linen dress with a coat to match and a little black hat on sideways. Her gloves showed that she was driving. Her face was a little small but everything on it was in place and well arranged; her eyes were too bright in the pupils and too heavy around the edges from tiredness, and from crying perhaps, and her skin was pale, but health and pleasantness showed through that. Her voice was low and had sense in it. I liked her.

She started to explain herself, but Wolfe wiggled a finger at her. "It is unnecessary, and possibly painful to you, Miss Barstow, I know. You are the only daughter of Peter Oliver Barstow. All you need tell is why you have come to me."

"Yes." She hesitated. "Of course you would know, Mr. Wolfe. It is a little difficult—perhaps I wanted a preamble." She had a try at a smile. "I am going to ask you a favor, I don't know how much of a favor it will be."

"I can tell you that."

"Of course. First I must ask you, do you know that my mother had an advertisement in the paper this morning?"

Wolfe nodded. "I have read it."

"Well, Mr. Wolfe, I—that is, we, the family—must ask you to disregard that advertisement."

Wolfe breathed and let his chin down. "An extraordinary request, Miss Barstow. Am I supposed to be as extraordinary in granting it, or do I get reasons?"

"There are reasons of course." She hesitated. "It is not a family secret, it is known that my mother is—in some degree and on various occasions—irresponsible." Her eyes were earnest on him. "You must not think there is anything ugly about this or that it has anything to do with money. There is plenty of money and my brother and I are not niggardly. Nor must you think that my mother is not a competent person —certainly not in the legal sense. But for years there have been times when she needed our attention and love, and this —this terrible thing has come in the middle of one of them. She is not normally vengeful, but that advertisement—my brother calls it a demand for blood. Our close friends will of course understand, but there is the world, and my father—my father's world was a wide one—we are glad if they help us mourn for him but we would not want them—Father would not want them—to watch us urging on the bloodhounds—"

She gave a little gasp and stopped, and glanced at me and back at Wolfe. He said, "Yes, Miss Barstow, you are calling me a bloodhound. I am not offended. Go on."

"I'm sorry. I'm a tactless fool. It would have been better if Dr. Bradford had come."

"Was Dr. Bradford considering the enterprise?"

"Yes. That is, he thought it should be done."

"And your brother?"

"Well—yes. My brother greatly regrets it, the advertisement I mean. He did not fully approve of my coming to see you. He thought it would be—fruitless."

"On the theory that it is difficult to call off a bloodhound. Probably he understands dogs. Have you finished, Miss Barstow? I mean, have you any further reasons to advance?"

She shook her head. "Surely, Mr. Wolfe, those are sufficient."

"Then as I understand it, your desire is that no effort be made to discover and punish the persons who murdered your father?"

She stared at him. "Why—no. I didn't say that."

"The favor you ask of me is that I refrain from such an effort?"

Her lips closed. She opened them enough to say, "I see. You are putting it as badly as possible."

"Not at all. Clearly, not badly. Understandably, your mind is confused; mine is lucid. Your position as you have so far expressed it is simply not intelligent. You may make any one of several requests of me, but you may not ask them all at once, for they are mutually exclusive. You may, for instance, tell me that while you are willing that I should discover the

murderer, you request me not to expect to be paid for it as
your mother has offered. Is that your request?"

"It is not. You know it is not."

"Or you may tell me that I may find the murderer if I can,
and collect the reward if I choose to take advantage of the legal
obligation, but that the family disapproves of the offer of
reward on moral grounds. Is that it?"

"Yes." Her lip trembled a little, but in a moment she
pulled it up firm. Then suddenly she stood up and shot at him:
"No! I'm sorry I came here. Professor Gottlieb was wrong; you
may be clever—good day, Mr. Wolfe."

"Good day, Miss Barstow." Wolfe was motionless. "The
engineering considerations keep me in my chair."

She was going. But halfway to the door she faltered, stood
a moment, and turned. "You *are* a bloodhound. You are. You
are heartless."

"Quite likely." Wolfe crooked a finger. "Come back to
your chair. Come, do; your errand is too important to let a
momentary resentment ruin it. That's better; self-control is an
admirable quality. Now, Miss Barstow, we can do one of two
things: either I can flatly but gracefully refuse your original
request as you made it and we can part on fairly bad terms; or
you can answer a few questions I would like to ask and we can
then decide what's to be done. Which shall it be?"

She was groggy, but game. She was back in her chair and
had a wary eye on him. She said, "I have answered many
questions in the past two days."

"I don't doubt it. I can imagine their tenor and their
stupidity. I shall not waste your time or insult your intelligence. How did you learn that I knew anything of this
business?"

She seemed surprised. "How did I learn it? Why, you are
responsible for it. That is, you discovered it. Everyone knows
it. It was in the paper—not New York, the White Plains
paper."

I had a grin at that. Derwin would phone Ben Cook to
come and assist me to the station, would he?

Wolfe nodded. "Have you asked the favor of Mr. Anderson that you have asked of me?"

"No."

"Why not?"

She hesitated. "Well—it didn't seem necessary. It didn't
seem— I don't know how to express it."

"Use your wits, Miss Barstow. Was it because it appeared unlikely that he would do any discovering worthy the name?"

She was holding herself tight. Her hands—damn good hands with strong fingers and honest knuckles—were little fists in her lap. "No!" she said.

"Very well. But what made you think it likely, at least possible, that my discovering might be more to the point?"

She began, "I didn't think—" But he stopped her:

"Come, control yourself. It is an honest plain question. You did think me more competent at discovery than Mr. Anderson, did you not? Was it because I had made the original discovery?"

"Yes."

"That is, because I had somehow known that your father was killed by a poisoned needle propelled from the handle of a golf club?"

"I—don't—know. I don't know, Mr. Wolfe."

"Courage. This will soon be over. Curiosity alone prompts the next question. What gave you the strange idea that I was so rare a person as to respond favorably to the idiotic request you meant to make of me?"

"I didn't know. I didn't have that idea really. But I was ready to try, and I had heard a professor at the university, Gottlieb, the psychologist, mention your name—he had written a book called *Modern Crime Detection*—"

"Yes. A book that an intelligent criminal should send as a gift to every detective he knows."

"Perhaps. His opinion of you is more complimentary. When I telephoned Professor Gottlieb he said that you were not susceptible of analysis because you had intuition from the devil, and that you were a sensitive artist as well as a man of probity. That sounded—well, I decided to come to see you. Mr. Wolfe, I beg you—I beg of you—"

I was sure she was going to cry and I didn't want her to. But Wolfe brusquely brought her up:

"That's all, Miss Barstow. That is all I need to know. Now I shall ask a favor of you: will you permit Mr. Goodwin to take you upstairs and show you my plants?"

She stared; he went on, "No subterfuge is intended. I merely wish to be alone with the devil. Half an hour perhaps; and to make a telephone call. When you return I shall have a proposal for you." He turned to me. "Fritz will call you."

She got up and came with me without a word. I thought

that was pretty good, for she was shaky and suspicious all over.
Instead of asking her to walk up two flights of stairs I took her
down the hall and used Wolfe's elevator. As we got out on the
top floor she stopped me by catching my arm.

"Mr. Goodwin. Why did Mr. Wolfe send me up here?"

I shook my head. "No good, Miss Barstow. Even if I knew
I wouldn't tell you, and since I don't know we might as well
look at the flowers." As I opened the door to the passage
Horstmann appeared from the potting room. "All right, Horstmann. May we look around a little?" He nodded and trotted
back.

As many times as I had been there, I never went in the
plant-rooms without catching my breath. It was like other
things I've noticed, for instance no matter how often you may
have seen Snyder leap in the air and one-handed spear a hot
liner like one streak of lightning stopping another one, when
you see it again your heart stops. It was that way in the
plant-rooms.

Wolfe used concrete benches and angle-iron staging, with
a spraying system Horstmann had invented for humidity.
There were three main rooms, one for Cattleyas Laelias and
hybrids, one for Odontoglossums, Oncidiums and Miltonia
hybrids, and the tropical room. Then there was the potting
room, Horstmann's den, and a little corner room for propaga-
tion. Supplies-pots, sand, sphagnum, leafmold, loam, osmun-
dine, charcoal, and crocks were kept in an unheated and
unglazed room in the rear alongside the shaft where the
outside elevator came up.

Since it was June the lath screens were on, and the slices
of shade and sunshine made patterns everywhere—on the
broad leaves, the blossoms, the narrow walks, the ten thousand pots. I liked it that way, it seemed gay.

It was a lesson to watch the flowers get Miss Barstow. Of
course when she went in she felt about as much like looking at
flowers as I did like disregarding her mother's ad, and down
the first rows of Cattleyas she tried to be polite enough to
pretend there was something there to see. The first one that
really brought her up was a small side-bunch, only twenty or
so, of Laeliocattleya Lustre. I was pleased because it was one
of my favorites. I stopped behind her.

"Astonishing," she said. "I've never seen one like that.
The colors—amazing."

"Yes. It's a bigeneric hybrid, they don't come in nature like that."

She got interested. In the next walk were some Brassocattlaelias Truffautianas and I cut off a couple and handed them to her. I told her a little about hybridization and seedlings and so on, but maybe she didn't hear me. Then, in the next room, I had a disappointment. She liked the Odontoglossums better than the Cattleyas and hybrids! I suspected it was because they were more expensive and difficult, but it turned out that she hadn't known that. No accounting for tastes, I thought. And best of all, even after we had been through the tropical room, she liked a little thing I had never looked at twice, a Miltonia blueanaeximina. She talked about its delicacy and form. I nodded and began to lose interest, and anyway I was wondering what Wolfe was up to. Then at last Fritz appeared. He came down the walk clear up to us and bent himself at the middle and said that Mr. Wolfe expected us. I grinned and would have liked to dig him in the ribs as I went by, but I knew he'd never forgive me.

Wolfe was still in his chair, and there was no indication that he had been out of it. He nodded at Miss Barstow's chair and at mine, and waited till we were arranged to say:

"You liked the flowers?"

"They are wonderful." She had a new eye on him, I could see that. "They are too much beauty."

Wolfe nodded. "At first, yes. But a long intimacy frees you of that illusion, and it also acquaints you with their scantiness of character. The effect they have produced on you is only their bluff. There is not such a thing as too much beauty."

"Perhaps." She had lost interest in the orchids. "Yes, perhaps."

"Anyway they passed your time. And of course you would like to know how I passed mine. First I telephoned my bank and asked them to procure immediately a report on the financial standing of Ellen Barstow, your mother, and the details of the will of Peter Oliver Barstow, your father. I then telephoned Dr. Bradford and endeavored to persuade him to call on me this afternoon or evening, but he will be otherwise engaged. I then sat and waited. Five minutes ago my bank telephoned me the report I had requested. I sent Fritz for you. Those were my activities."

She was getting worked up again. Her lips were getting tight. Apparently she didn't intend to open them.

He went on. "I said I would have a proposal for you. Here it is. Your notebook, Archie. Verbatim, please. I shall use my best efforts to find the murderer of Peter Oliver Barstow. I shall disclose the result of my efforts to you, Sarah Barstow, and if you interpose no objection I shall also disclose them to the proper public authorities, and at the proper time shall expect a check for the sum your mother has offered as a reward. But if my inquiries lead to the conclusion that the murderer is actually the person you fear it is, whom you are now endeavoring to shield from justice, there will be no further disclosure. Mr. Goodwin and I will know; no one else ever will. Just a moment! This is a speech, Miss Barstow; please hear all of it. Two more points. You must understand that I can make this proposal with propriety. I am not a public servant, I am not even a member of the bar, and I have sworn to uphold no law. The dangerous position of an accessory after the fact does not impress me. Then: if your fears prove to be justified, and I withhold disclosure, what of the reward? I find I am too sentimental and romantic to make it part of this proposal that under those circumstances the reward shall be paid. The word blackmail actually strikes me as unpleasant. But though I am handicapped by romance and sentiment, at least I have not pride further to hamper me, and if you should choose to present a gift it would be accepted.—Read it aloud, Archie, to make sure it is understood."

Miss Barstow's voice was first: "But this—it's absurd! It—"

Wolfe wiggled a finger at her. "Don't. Please. You would deny that you came here with that nonsense to shield someone? Miss Barstow! Really now. Let us keep this on a decent level of intelligence. Read it, Archie."

I read it through from my notes. When I had finished Wolfe said, "I advise you to take it, Miss Barstow. I shall proceed with my inquiry in any event, and if the result is what you fear it would be convenient for you to have the protection I offer. The offer, by the way, is purely selfish. With this agreement I shall expect your interest and co-operation, since it would be well for you, no matter what the outcome, to get it over with as speedily as possible; without it I shall expect considerable obstruction. I am no altruist or *bon enfant*, I am merely a man who would like to make some money. You said there was too much beauty upstairs; no, but there is too much expense. Have you any idea what it costs to grow orchids like that?"

Sarah Barstow only stared at him.

"Come," Wolfe said. "There will of course be no signing. This is what is humorously called a gentlemen's agreement. The first step in fulfilling it will be for Mr. Goodwin to call at your home tomorrow morning—it can wait till then—to talk, with your permission, with yourself and your brother and mother and whosoever—"

"No!" she exploded. Then she shut up.

"But yes. I'm sorry, but it is essential. Mr. Goodwin is a man of discretion, common decency, and immeasurable valor. It really is essential.—I'll tell you what, Miss Barstow." He put his hands on the edge of the desk and shoved his chair back, moved his hands to the arms of the chair and got himself to his feet, and stood in front of her. "You go on home, or about your errands, whatever they may be. People often find it difficult to think in my presence, I do not leave enough space. I know you are suffering, your emotions are tormenting you with their unbearable clamor, but you must free your mind to do its work. Go. Buy hats, or keep a rendezvous, or attend to your mother, whatever you may have in mind. Telephone me this evening between six and seven and tell me what time Mr. Goodwin may arrive in the morning, or tell me that he is not to come and we are enemies. Go."

She stood up. "Well—I don't know—my God, I don't know—"

"Please! That is not your mind speaking, it's the foam of churned feelings and has no meaning. I do not wish to be your enemy."

She was right in front of him, facing him, with her chin tilted up so that her eyes could be on his. "I believe you," she said. "I really believe you don't."

"Indeed, I do not. Good day, Miss Barstow."

"Good day, Mr. Wolfe."

I took her to the front door and let her out. I thought she might have handed me a good day too, but she didn't. She didn't say anything. As she went out I saw her car at the curb, a dark blue coupé.

Back in the office, Wolfe was in his chair again. I stood on the other side of the desk looking at him.

"Well," I said, "what do you know about that?"

His cheeks folded. "I know I'm hungry, Archie. It is pleasant to have an appetite again. I've had none for weeks."

Naturally I was indignant; I stared at him. "You can say that, after Friday and Saturday and Sunday—"

"But no appetite. A desperate search for one. Now I'm hungry. Lunch will be in twenty minutes. Meantime: I have learned that there is a person attached to a golf club called a professional. Find out who fills that post at the Green Meadow Club; see if we have any grateful client who might introduce us on the telephone; invite the professional, urgently, to dine with us this evening. There is a goose left from Saturday. After lunch you will pay a visit to the office of Dr. Nathaniel Bradford, and stop at the library for some books I need."

"Yes, sir. Who do you think Miss Barstow—"

"Not now, Archie. I would prefer just to sit here quietly and be hungry. After lunch."

Chapter 8

At ten o'clock Tuesday morning, June 13, I drove the roadster through the entrance gate of the Barstow place, after it had been opened for me by a state trooper who was there on guard. Another husky was with him, a private watchman of the Barstows', and I had to furnish plenty of proof that I was the Archie Goodwin Sarah Barstow was expecting. It looked likely that many a newspaper man had been sent to climb a tree around there in the past three days.

The house was at the low point of a saddle between two hills about seven miles northeast of Pleasantville. It was built of stone, quite large, well over twenty rooms I should say, and there were a lot of outbuildings. After going through about three hundred yards of trees and shrubbery the drive circled around the edge of an immense sloping lawn and entered under the shelter of a roof with two steps up to a flagged terrace. This was really the side of the house; the front was around the corner looking over the lawn down the hill. There were gardens ahead as you entered, and more gardens at the other edge of the lawn, with boulders and a pool. As I eased the roadster along taking it in I thought to myself that fifty grand was nothing. I had on a dark blue suit, with a blue shirt and a tan tie, and of course my panama which I had had cleaned right after Decoration Day. I've found it's a good idea to consider what kind of a place you're going to, and dress accordingly.

Sarah Barstow was expecting me at ten, and I was right on the dot. I parked the roadster in a graveled space the other side of the entrance, and pushed the button at the door on the terrace. It was standing open, but double screen doors kept me from seeing much inside. Soon there were footsteps and one of the screens came out at me and with it a tall skinny guy in a black suit.

He was polite. "If you will excuse me, sir. Mr. Goodwin?"

I nodded. "Miss Barstow expects me."

"I know. If you will come this way. Miss Barstow would like you to join her in the garden."

I followed him across the terrace and along a walk to the other side of the house, then down an arbor and among a lot of shrubbery till we came to an acre of flowers. Miss Barstow was on a shady bench over in a corner.

"All right," I said. "I see her."

He stopped, inclined his head, and turned and went back.

She looked bad, worse than she had the day before. She probably hadn't slept much. Forgetting or disregarding Wolfe's instructions on that detail, she had telephoned before six o'clock. I had taken the call, and her voice had sounded as if she was having a hard time of it. She had been short and businesslike, just said she would expect me at ten in the morning and hung up.

She invited me to sit beside her on the bench.

At bedtime the evening before Wolfe had given me no instructions whatever. Saying that he preferred to leave me fancy free, he had merely repeated his favorite saying, any spoke will lead an ant to the hub, and had reminded me that our great advantage lay in the fact that no one was aware how much or how little we knew and that on account of our original coup we were suspected of omniscience. He had finished, after a yawn that would have held a tennis ball: "Return here with that advantage unimpaired."

I said to Miss Barstow, "You may not have any orchids here, but you certainly have a flower or two."

She said, "Yes, I suppose so.—I asked Small to bring you out here because I thought we should not be interrupted. You will not mind."

"No, indeed. It's nice out here. I'm sorry to have to pester you, but there's no other way to get the facts. Wolfe says that he feels phenomena and I collect facts. I don't think that means anything, having looked up the word phenomena in the dictionary, but I repeat it for what it's worth." I took out my notebook. "First just tell me things. You know, the family, how old are you, who you're going to marry and so on."

She sat with her hands together in her lap and told me. Some of it I had read in the papers or got out of Who's Who, but I didn't interrupt. There was only her mother, her brother and herself. Lawrence, her brother, was twenty-seven, two years older than her; he had graduated from Holland at twenty-one and had then proceeded to waste five years (and, I gathered between the lines, a good portion of his father's time and patience also). A year ago he had suddenly discovered a talent for mechanical design and was now devoted to that, especially as applied to airplanes. Her mother and father had been mutually devoted for thirty years. She could not remember the beginning of her mother's difficulty, for that had been years before when Sarah was a child; the family had never considered it a thing to be ashamed of or to attempt to conceal, merely a misfortune of a loved one to sympathize with and as far as possible to ameliorate. Dr. Bradford and two specialists described it in neurological terms, but they had never meant anything to Sarah, to her the terms had been dead and cold and her mother was alive and warm.

The place in Westchester was the old Barstow family estate, but the family was able to be there less than three months of the year since it was necessary to live at the university from September to June. They came each summer for ten or eleven weeks with the servants, and closed the place up each fall on leaving. They knew many people in the surrounding countryside; her father's circle of acquaintance had of course been wide not only in Westchester, and some of his best and oldest friends lived within easy driving distance from the estate. She gave the names of these and I took them down. I also listed the names of the servants and details regarding them. I was doing that when Miss Barstow suddenly got up from the bench and moved away to the path in the sunshine, from under the shelter of the trees that shaded us.

There was the sound of an airplane overhead, so close that it had forced us to raise our voices. I went on writing, "—Finnish, 6 yrs, N Y agcy, sgl," and then looked at her. Her head was way back showing all her throat, with her gaze straight above, and one arm was up waving a handkerchief back and forth. I jumped out from under the trees and cocked an eye at the airplane. It was right over us, down low, and two arms could be seen extended, one from one side and one from the other, waving back at her. The plane dipped a little, then swung around and headed back, and soon was out of sight behind the trees. She went back to the bench and I joined her; she was saying:

"That was my brother. This is the first time he has been up since my father—"

"He must be pretty reckless, and he certainly has long arms."

"He doesn't fly; at least, not solo. That was Manuel Kimball with him, it's Mr. Kimball's plane."

"Oh. One of the foursome."

"Yes."

I nodded and went back to facts. I was ready for golf. Peter Oliver Barstow had not been a zealot, she said. He had rarely played at the university, and not oftener than once a week, occasionally twice, during the summer. He had nearly always gone to Green Meadow, where he was a member; he of course had had a locker and kept his paraphernalia there. He had been quite good, considering the infrequency of his play, averaging from ninety-five to a hundred. He had played usually with friends his own age, but sometimes with his son and daughter. His wife had never tried it. The foursome of that fatal Sunday, E. D. Kimball and his son Manuel and Barstow and his son Lawrence, had never before played together, she thought. Probably it had been an accident of propinquity; her brother had not mentioned whether it had been prearranged, but she knew that he did sometimes have a game with Manuel. She especially doubted that the foursome had been arranged beforehand because it had been her father's first appearance at Green Meadow that summer; the Barstows had come to Westchester three weeks earlier than their custom on account of Mrs. Barstow's condition, and Barstow had expected to return to the university that Sunday night.

When she had said that Sarah Barstow stopped. I glanced up from my notebook. Her fingers were twisted together and she was staring off at the path, at nothing. She said, not to me, "Now he will not return there at all. All the things he wanted to do—all he would have done—not at all—"

I waited a little and then shook her out of it by asking, "Did your father leave his gold bag at Green Meadow all year?"

She turned back to me. "No. Why—of course not, because he sometimes used them at the university."

"He had only the one bag of clubs?"

"Yes!" She seemed emphatic.

"Then he brought them with him? You only got here Saturday noon. You drove down from the university and the luggage followed in a truck. Was the bag in the car or in the truck?"

It was easy to see that I was touching something raw. Her throat showed muscles and her arms pressed ever so little against her sides; she was tightening up. I pretended I didn't notice it, just waited with my pencil. She said, "I don't know. Really I don't remember."

"Probably in the truck," I said. "Since he wasn't much of a fan he probably wouldn't bother with it in the car. Where is it now?"

I expected that would tighten her up some more, but it didn't. She was calm but a little determined. "I don't know that either. I supposed you knew it can't be found."

"Oh," I said. "The golf bag can't be found?"

"No. The men from White Plains and Pleasantville have searched everywhere, this whole house, the club, even all over the links; they can't find it."

Yes, I thought to myself, and you, young lady, you're damn well pleased they can't! I said, "Do you mean to say that no one remembers anything about it?"

"No. That is, yes." She hesitated. "I understand that the boy who was caddying for Father says that he put the bag in the car, by the driver's seat, when they—when Larry and Dr. Bradford brought Father home. Larry and Dr. Bradford do not remember seeing it."

"Strange. I know I am not here to collect opinions, only facts, Miss Barstow, but if you will permit me, doesn't that strike you as strange?"

"Not at all. They were not likely to notice a golf bag at such a time."

"But after they got here—it must have been removed sometime—some servant, the chauffeur—"

"No one remembers it."

"I may speak with them?"

"Certainly." She was scornful. I didn't know what kind of a career she had mapped out, but I could have warned her not to try the stage.

That was that. It looked to me as if the kernel was gone, leaving practically no nut at all. I switched on her.

"What kind of a driver did your father use? Steel shaft or wooden?"

"Wood. He didn't like steel."

"Face plain or inset?"

"Plain, I think. I think so. I'm not sure I remember. Larry's has an inset, so has mine."

"You seem to remember your brother's all right."

"Yes." Her eyes were level at me. "This is not an inquisition, I believe, Mr. Goodwin."

"Pardon." I grinned at her. "Excuse it please, I'm upset. Maybe I'm even sore. There's nothing in Westchester County I'd rather look at than that golf bag, especially the driver."

"I'm sorry."

"Oh no, you're not. It raises a lot of questions. Who took the bag out of the car? If it was a servant, which one, and how loyal and incorruptible is he? Five days later, when it became known that one of the clubs had performed the murder it had been designed for, who got the bag and hid it or destroyed it? You or your brother or Dr. Bradford? You see the questions I'm up against. And where is it hid or how was it destroyed? It isn't easy to get rid of a thing as big as that."

She had got up while I was talking and stood very composed and dignified. Her voice was composed too. "That will do. It wasn't in the agreement that I was to listen to idiotic insinuations."

"Bravo, Miss Barstow." I stood up too. "You're absolutely right, but I meant no offense, I'm just upset. Now, if I could see your mother for a moment. I'll not get upset any more."

"No. You can't see her."

"That *was* in the agreement."

"You have broken it."

"Rubbish." I grinned. "It's the agreement that makes it safe for you to let me take liberties with it. I'll take no liberties with your mother. While I may be a roughneck, I know when to keep my gloves on."

She looked at me. "Will five minutes be enough?"

"I don't know. I'll make it as short as possible."

She turned and started for the path that led toward the house, and I followed her. On the way I saw a lot of pebbles I wanted to kick. The missing golf bag was a hot one. Of course I hadn't expected to have the satisfaction of taking that driver back to Wolfe that evening, since Anderson would certainly have copped it. I gave him credit for being able to put two and two together after they have been set down for him ready to add; and I had counted on a request from Sarah Barstow to persuade him to let me give it the once over. But now—the whole damn bag was gone! Whoever had done it, it not only gave me a pain, it struck me as pretty dumb. If it had been just the driver it would have made sense, but why the whole bag?

The house inside was swell. I mean, it was the kind of a house most people never see except in the movies. While there were plenty of windows, the light didn't glare anywhere, it came in soft, and the rugs and furniture looked very clean and careful and expensive. There were flowers around and it smelled good and seemed cool and pleasant, for outdoors the sun was getting hot. Sarah Barstow took me through a big hall and a big room through to another hall, and on the other side of that through a door. Then we were in a sort of sun-room, with one side all glazed, though most of the blinds were pulled down nearly to the floor so there wasn't much sunshine coming in. There were some plants, and a lot of wicker chairs and lounges. In one chair a woman sat by a table sorting out the pieces of a jig-saw puzzle. Miss Barstow went over to her.

"Mother. This is Mr. Goodwin. I told you he was coming." She turned to me and indicated a chair. I took it. Mrs. Barstow let the jig-saw pieces drop from her fingers and turned to look at me.

She was very handsome. She was fifty-six, her daughter had told me, but she looked over sixty. Her eyes were gray, deep-set and far apart, her hair was nearly white, and while her face with its fine features was quite composed, I got the impression that there was nothing easy or natural about that, it came from the force of a strong personal will. She kept looking at me without saying anything until I was guessing that I didn't look very composed myself. Sarah Barstow had taken a chair

some distance away. I was about ready to open up from my
end when Mrs. Barstow suddenly spoke:

"I know your business, Mr. Goodwin."

I nodded. "It really isn't my business, it is that of my
employer, Mr. Nero Wolfe. He asked me to thank you for
permitting me to come."

"He is welcome." The deep-set gray eyes never left me.
"Indeed, I am grateful that someone—even a stranger whom I
shall never see—should acknowledge my authority over the
doors of my house."

"Mother!"

"Yes, Sarah. Don't be offended, dear; I know—and it is of
no importance whether this Mr. Goodwin does or not—that
the authority has not been usurped. It was not you who forced
me to resign, it was not even your father. According to Than, it
was God; probably His hands were idle and Satan furnished
the mischief."

"Mother, please." Sarah Barstow had got up and approached us. "If you have anything to ask, Mr. Goodwin—"

I said, "I have two questions. May I ask you two questions, Mrs. Barstow?"

"Certainly. That is your business."

"Good. The first one is easy to ask, but may be hard to
answer. That is, it may require thought and a long memory. Of
all people, you are the one probably in the best position to
answer. Who wanted, or might have wanted, to kill Peter
Oliver Barstow? Who had a grievance against him, a new one
or maybe a very old one? What enemies did he have? Who
hated him?"

"That isn't a question. It is four questions."

"Well—maybe I can hitch them together."

"It isn't necessary." The composure did not escape from
the will. "They can all be answered at once. Myself."

I stared at her. Her daughter was beside her with a hand
on her shoulder.

"Mother! You promised me—"

"There, Sarah." Mrs. Barstow reached up and patted her
daughter's hand. "You have not permitted those other men to
see me, for which I have been thankful. But if Mr. Goodwin is
to ask me questions he must have the answers. You remember
what your father used to say? *Never lay an ambush for truth.*"

Miss Barstow was at me. "Mr. Goodwin! Please!"

"Nonsense." The gray eyes were flashing. "I have my own

security, daughter, as good as any you might provide for me.
Mr. Goodwin, I have answered your first question. The
second?"

"Don't rush me, Mrs. Barstow." I saw that if I just
pretended Sarah Barstow wasn't there, Old Gray Eyes would
be right with me. "I'm not done with the first one. There may
have been others, maybe you weren't the only one."

"Others who might have wanted to kill my husband?" For
the first time the will relaxed enough to let the twitch of a
smile show on the lips. "No. That is impossible. My husband
was a good, just, merciful and well-loved man. I see what you
would have me do, Mr. Goodwin: look back over all the years,
the happy ones and the miserable ones, and pick out of
memory for you a remorseless wrong or a sinister threat. I
assure you it isn't there. There is no man living my husband
wronged, and none his enemy. Nor woman either. He did not
wrong me. My answer to your question was direct and honest
and was a relief to me, but since you are so young, not much
more than a boy, it probably shocked you as it did my
daughter. I would explain the answer if I could. I do not wish
to mislead you. I do not wish to give pain to my daughter.
When God compelled me to resign my authority He did not
stop there. If by any chance you understand Him, you
understand my answer too."

"All right, Mrs. Barstow. Then the second question: why
did you offer a reward?"

"No!" Sarah Barstow stood between us. "No! No more of
this—"

"Sarah!" The voice was sharp; then it softened a little:
"Sarah dear. I *will* answer. This is my share. Will you stand
between us? Sarah!"

Sarah Barstow went to her mother's side, placed her arm
across her mother's shoulders, and lowered her forehead onto
the gray hair.

The will re-created the composure. "Yes, Mr. Goodwin,
the reward. I am not insane, I am only fantastic. I now greatly
regret that the reward was offered, for I see its sordidness. It
was in a fantastic moment that I conceived the idea of a unique
vengeance. No one could have murdered my husband since no
one could have wanted to. I am certain that his death has
never seemed desirable to any person except myself, and to
me only during torments which God should never impose
even on the guiltiest. It came to me that there might be

somewhere a man clever enough to bring God Himself to justice. I doubt if it is you, Mr. Goodwin; I do not know your employer. I now regret that I offered the reward, but if it is earned it will be paid."

"Thank you, Mrs. Barstow. Who is Than?"

"Sir?"

"Than. You said that Than told you God forced you to resign your authority."

"Oh. Of course. Dr. Nathaniel Bradford."

"Thank you." I closed my notebook and got up. "Mr. Wolfe asked me to thank you for your forbearance; I guess he knew there would be some if I got started filling up my notebook."

"Tell Mr. Wolfe he is welcome."

I turned and went on out, figuring that Miss Barstow could use my room for a while.

Chapter 9

Miss Barstow invited me to lunch.

I liked her better than ever. For ten minutes or more I waited for her in the hall which connected the sun-room with other apartments. When she joined me there she wasn't sore, and I could see why: I hadn't pulled Mrs. Barstow's leg for any of that stuff, she had just handed it to me on a platter, and that wasn't my fault. But how many people in Sarah Barstow's place would have stopped to consider that? Not one in a thousand. They would have been sore anyhow, even if they had realized I didn't deserve it and tried not to show it; but she just wasn't sore. She had made a bargain and she was going through with it, no matter how many sleepless nights it brought her and no matter how many kinds of bad luck she had. She certainly had just had some. I could see that ten minutes earlier or ten minutes later Mrs. Barstow might have had different ideas in her head and all I would have got out of it would have been to exchange the time of day with a polite clam. I had no idea what it was that had happened to make her feel like opening up, but if it was my blue shirt and tan tie I hadn't wasted the money I had spent on them.

As Saul Panzer would have said, lovin' babe!

She invited me to lunch. She said her brother would be present, and since I would want to see him anyway that would be convenient. I thanked her. I said, "You're a good sport, Miss Barstow. A real one. Thank the Lord Nero Wolfe is the cleverest man on earth and thought up that agreement with you, because if you're in for trouble that's the only thing that will help you out of it."

"If I'm in for trouble," she said.

I nodded. "Sure, I know you've got plenty, but the one that bothers you most is your fear that there's worse ahead. I just wanted to say that you're a good sport."

As it turned out, I not only met her brother at lunch, I met Manuel Kimball too. I was glad of that, for it seemed to me that what I had learned that morning made the members of that foursome more important than they had been before. The preceding afternoon after about two hours of telephoning, I had finally found a hook-up with the professional of the Green Meadow Club and he had accepted Wolfe's invitation to dinner. He had never had any dealings with Barstow, had only known him by sight, but Wolfe had got out of him twenty bushels of facts regarding the general set-up at the club and around the links. By the time the professional left to go home around midnight he had a bottle of Wolfe's best port inside of him, and Wolfe knew as much about a golf club as if he had been a professional himself. Among other things he learned that the members kept their bags in their lockers, that some of them left their lockers unlocked, and that even with the locked ones an ingenious and determined man could have got a duplicate key without any great difficulty. With such a key, of course, it would have been simple to await a propitious moment to open the locker, take the driver from the bag and substitute another one. So Barstow's companions in the foursome that Sunday were of no more importance than any of the members or attendants or visitors who had access to the locker-rooms.

But now that was out, since Barstow's bag had not been in his locker since the September before. He had brought it down with him from the university. That changed the picture and made the members of the foursome a little more interesting than lots of other people.

Where we ate surely wasn't the dining room because it wasn't big enough, but it had a table and chairs and windows that you couldn't see much through on account of a lot of shrubbery just outside. The tall skinny guy in the black suit —otherwise Small, the butler, as an established guest like myself was aware—waited on us, and while the meal seemed to me a little light it was nothing that Fritz would have been ashamed of. There was some stuff in tambour shells that was first class. The table was small. I sat across from Miss Barstow, with her brother on my right and Manuel Kimball on my left.

Lawrence Barstow didn't resemble his sister any, but I could see traces of his mother. He was well put together and had the assurance that goes with his kind of life; his features were good and regular without anything noticeable about them. I've seen hundreds of him in the lunch restaurants in the Wall Street section and in the Forties. He had a trick of squinting when he decided to look at you, but I thought that was perhaps due to the blowing his eyes had got in the airplane breeze. The eyes were gray, like his mother's, but they didn't have the discipline behind them that hers had.

Manuel Kimball was quite different. He was dark and very neat and compact, with black hair brushed straight back and black restless eyes that kept darting around at us and seemed to find any degree of satisfaction or repose only when they were looking at Sarah Barstow. He made me nervous, and it seemed to me that he set Sarah Barstow a little on edge too, though that may have been only because he didn't know where I came in on the family crisis and wasn't supposed to know. That morning she had informed me that there had been no intimacy between the Kimballs and Barstows; the only points of contact had been propinquity in their summer residences and the fact that Manuel was a skilled amateur pilot and his offers to take Larry Barstow up and teach him to fly had been most convenient since Larry had developed an interest in airplane design. She herself had been up with Manuel Kimball two or three times the summer before, but aside from those occasions she had scarcely ever seen him except as the companion of her brother. The Kimballs were newcomers, having bought their place, two miles south, only three years previously. E. D. Kimball, Manuel's father, was known to the Barstows only slightly, through chance and infrequent meetings at large social or public gatherings. Manuel's mother was dead, long since, she had vaguely gathered. She could not

remember that there had ever been more than a few casual
words exchanged between her father and Manuel Kimball
except one afternoon the preceding summer when Larry had
brought Manuel to the Barstow place to settle a wager at
tennis, and she and her father had acted as umpire and
linesman.

In spite of which, I was interested in Manuel Kimball. He
had at any rate been one of the foursome; and he looked like a
foreigner and had a funny combination for a name, and he
made me nervous.

At lunch the conversation was mostly about airplanes.
Sarah Barstow kept it on that, when there was any sign of
lagging, and once or twice when her brother started questions
on affairs closer to her bosom she abruptly headed him off. I
just ate. When Miss Barstow finally pushed her chair back,
punching Small in the belly with it, we all stood up. Larry
Barstow addressed me directly almost for the first time; I had
seen indications of his idea that I might as well have been
eating out back somewhere.

"You want to see me?"

I nodded. "If you can spare a quarter of an hour."

He turned to Manuel Kimball. "If you don't mind waiting, Manny. I promised Sis I'd have a talk with this man."

"Of course." The other's eyes darted to rest on Sarah
Barstow. "Perhaps Miss Barstow would be kind enough to help
me wait."

She said yes, without enthusiasm. But I got a word in:
"I'm sorry." To Miss Barstow, "May I remind you that you
agreed to be present with your brother?" It hadn't been
mentioned, but I had taken it for granted, and I wanted her
there.

"Oh." I thought she looked relieved. "Yes. I'm sorry, Mr.
Kimball; shall we leave you here with the coffee?"

"No, thanks." He bowed to her and turned to Larry. "I'll
trot along and have a book at that gas line. If one of your cars
can run me over? Thanks. I'll be expecting you at the hangar
any time— Thank you for a pleasant luncheon, Miss Barstow."

One thing that had surprised me about him was his voice.
I had expected him, on sight, to sound like a tenor, but the
effect he produced was more like that of a murmuring bull.
The voice was deep and had a rumble in it, but he kept it low
and quite pleasant. Larry Barstow went out with him to tell
someone to take him home. His sister and I waited for Larry to

come back, and then all three of us went out to the garden, to the bench where I had been taken on my arrival. Larry sat at one side on the grass, and Miss Barstow and I on the bench.

I explained that I wanted Miss Barstow present because she had made the agreement with Nero Wolfe and I wanted her to be satisfied that nothing was said or done that went beyond the agreement. I had certain things I wanted to ask Lawrence Barstow and if there was any question about my being entitled to answers she was the one to question it.

She said, "Very well, I'm here." She looked about played out. In the morning she had sat with her shoulders straight, but now she let them sag down.

Her brother said, "As far as I'm concerned—your name's Goodwin, isn't it?"

"That's it."

"Well, as far as I'm concerned, your agreement, as you call it, is nothing more than a piece of cheap insolence."

"Anything else, Mr. Barstow?"

"Yes. If you want it. Blackmail."

His sister had a flash left. "Larry! What did I tell you?"

"Wait a minute, Miss Barstow." I was flipping back the pages of my notebook. "Maybe your brother ought to hear it. I'll find it in a minute." I found the page. "Here it is." I read it just as Wolfe had said it, not too fast. Then I closed the notebook. "That's the agreement, Mr. Barstow. I might as well say that my employer, Mr. Nero Wolfe, keeps his temper pretty well under control, but every once in a while I blow up. If you call him a blackmailer once more the result will probably be bad all around. If you don't know a favor when you see it handed to you I suppose you'd think a sock on the jaw was a compliment."

He said, "Sis, you'd better go in the house."

"She can go in a minute," I said. "If the agreement is to go overboard she ought to see it sink. If you don't like it, why did you let her come to Wolfe's office alone to make it? He would have been glad to see you. He said to your sister, we shall proceed with the inquiry in any event. That's our business, not such a rotten one either, a few people think who have dealt with us. I say the same to you: agreement or no agreement, we're going to find out who murdered Peter Oliver Barstow. If you ask me, I think your sister made a swell bargain. If you don't think so there must be some reason, and that's one of the things we'll find out on the way."

"Larry," Miss Barstow said. Her voice was full of things. She repeated it. "Larry." She was telling him and asking him and reminding him all at the same time.

"Come on," I said. "You're all worked up and looking at me all through lunch didn't help you any, but if something goes wrong with your airplane you don't just kick and scream, do you? You pull your coat off and help fix it."

He sat looking not at me but his sister, with his lower lip stuck up and pushed out so that he looked half like a baby about ready to cry and half like a man set to tell the world to go to hell.

"All right, Sis," he said finally. He showed no signs of apologizing to me, but I thought that could wait for a rainy day.

When I began feeding him questions he snapped out of it. He answered prompt and straight and, as far as I could see, without any figuring or hesitation anywhere. Even about the golf bag, where his sister had flopped around like a fish on a bank, it was all clear and ready with him. The bag had been brought down from the university on the truck; there had been no luggage with them in the car except one suitcase, his mother's. When the truck had arrived at the house about three o'clock in the afternoon its load had been removed and distributed at once; presumably the golf bag had been taken straight to his father's room, though he had no knowledge of that. At Sunday breakfast he and his father had arranged to play golf that afternoon . . .

"Who suggested it? You or your father?"

He couldn't remember. When his father had come downstairs after lunch he had had the bag under his arm. They had driven to the Green Meadow Club in the sedan, parked, and his father had gone straight to the first tee, carrying his bag, while Larry had gone around by the hut for caddies. Larry wasn't particular about his caddy, but there had been one the preceding summer that his father had taken a fancy to, and by chance that boy was there and Larry had taken him with another. On his way to the first tee Larry had fallen in with the Kimballs, also ready to tee off, and since he hadn't seen Manuel for some months and was eager to discuss plans for the summer he had asked them to make it a foursome, feeling sure his father wouldn't mind. When they had reached the tee his father had been off to one side, practicing with a mashie. Peter

Oliver Barstow had been cordial with the Kimballs and had greeted his caddy with delight and sent him off to chase balls.

They had waited for two or three other matches to get started and had then teed off. Manuel Kimball had driven first, then Larry, then Barstow, and last the elder Kimball. Larry couldn't remember seeing his father take the driver from the bag or from his caddy; while they were waiting he had been busy talking with Manuel, and during the moments immediately preceding his father's drive Larry had been driving himself. But he remembered well his father's actual swing at the ball, on account of an unusual circumstance. At the end of the swing there had been a peculiar jerk of the club, and as the ball sailed away with a bad slice Barstow had made an exclamation, with a startled look on his face, and begun rubbing his belly. Larry had never seen his father so suddenly and completely abandon his accustomed dignity in public. They had asked him what was wrong, and he had said something about a wasp or a hornet and started to open his shirt. Larry had been impressed by his father's agitation and had looked inside his shirt at the skin. There had been a tiny puncture, almost invisible, and his father had regained his composure and insisted that it would be nothing. The elder Kimball had made his drive and they had proceeded down the fairway.

The rest had been detailed in the newspapers many times. Thirty minutes later, on the fairway of the fourth hole, Barstow had suddenly collapsed on the ground, kicking and clutching the grass. He had been still alive when his caddy seized his arm, but by the time the others reached him he was dead. A crowd had collected, among them Dr. Nathaniel Bradford, an old Barstow family friend. Manuel Kimball had gone for the sedan and driven it along the edge of the fairway to the scene. The body had been lifted into the back of the sedan, Dr. Bradford had sat on the seat holding the head of his old friend on his lap, and Larry had taken the wheel.

Larry could remember nothing of the golf bag. Absolutely nothing. He knew the caddy's story, that the bag had been placed in front leaning against the seat, but he could not remember seeing it there while driving or at any other time. He said that he had driven the six miles slowly and carefully, and that later, after getting home, he had found blood all along his lower lip where he had bit it. He was a better liar than his sister. If it had not been for her give-away I might have been fooled by his tale as he told it. I went after him from every angle I could think of, but he didn't leak once.

I passed that up and asked him about the Kimballs. His story was the same as his sister's. There had been no contact to speak of between the families; the only connection had been himself and Manuel, and the basis of that was Manuel's convenience as owner and pilot of an airplane; Larry had intended to get one for himself as soon as he secured a license.

Then I asked the question that had started the fireworks with Mrs. Barstow before lunch. I asked both Larry and his sister, but not only was there no fireworks, there was nothing at all. They declared that they knew of no one who had a serious grievance against their father, or hatred or enmity for him, and that it was unthinkable that there ever should have been such a person. In his remarkable career—he had achieved the presidency of Holland University at forty-eight, ten years before—he had many times faced opposition, but he had always known the trick of melting it instead of crushing it. His private life had been confined to his own home. His son, I gathered, had had deep respect for him and a certain affection; his daughter had loved him. They agreed that no one could have hated him; and as his daughter told me that, knowing what I had heard from her mother's lips only three hours previously, her eyes challenged me and appealed to me at once.

Next Dr. Bradford, I turned to Miss Barstow on that instead of her brother. The way the thing seemed to be shaping up I expected some hesitation and covering, but there certainly was no sign of it. She told me, simply, that Bradford had been a schoolmate at college with her father, that they had always been close friends, and that Bradford, who was a widower, had been almost like one of the family, especially during the summer since he was then also a neighbor. He had been the family physician, and it was on him they had chiefly relied to remove Mrs. Barstow's difficulty, though he had called in specialists to assist.

I asked Sarah Barstow, "Do you like him?"

"Like him?"

"Yes. Do you like Dr. Bradford?"

"Certainly. He is one of the best and finest men I know."

I turned to her brother. "Do you like him, Mr. Barstow?"

Larry frowned. He was tired; he had been pretty patient; I had been after him for two hours. "I like him well enough.

He's what my sister says all right, but he likes to preach. Not that he ever bothers me now, but when I was a kid I used to hide from him."

"You arrived here from the university Saturday noon. Was Dr. Bradford here between that hour and Sunday at two?"

"I don't know.—Oh yes, sure. He was here Saturday for dinner."

"Do you think there is any chance that he killed your father?"

Larry stared. "Oh, for God's sake. Is that supposed to shock me into something?"

"Do you, Miss Barstow?"

"Nonsense."

"All right, nonsense. Anyhow, who suggested first that Bradford should certify it as a heart stroke? Which one of you? Him?"

Larry glared at me. His sister said quietly, "You said you wanted me here to see the agreement was observed. Well, Mr. Goodwin. I've been—patient enough."

"Okay. I'll lay off of that." I turned to her brother. "You're sore again, Mr. Barstow. Forget it. People like you aren't used to impertinence, but you'd be surprised how easy it is to let it slide and no harm done. There's only a couple of things left. Where were you between seven o'clock and midnight on Monday evening, June fifth?"

He still glared. "I don't know. How do I know?"

"You can remember. This isn't another impertinence; I seriously request you to tell me. Monday, June fifth. Your father's funeral was on Tuesday. I'm asking about the evening before the funeral."

Miss Barstow said, "I can tell you."

"I'd rather he would, as a favor."

He did. "There's no reason I shouldn't. Or should either. I was here, at home."

"All evening?"

"Yes."

"Who else was here?"

"My mother and sister, the servants, and the Robertsons."

"The Robertsons?"

"I said so."

His sister spoke. "The Robertsons are old friends. Mr. and Mrs. Blair Robertson and two daughters."

"What time did they come?"

"Right after dinner. We hadn't finished. Around seven-thirty."

"Was Dr. Bradford here?"

"No."

"Wasn't that peculiar?"

"Peculiar? Why?—But yes, of course it was. He had to address a meeting in New York, some professional meeting."

"I see. Thank you, Miss Barstow." I turned back to her brother. "I have one more question. A request rather. Does Manuel Kimball have a telephone at his hangar?"

"Yes."

"Will you telephone him that I am coming to see him and that you would like him to give me an interview?"

"No. Why should I?"

Miss Barstow told me, "You have no right to ask it. If you wish to see Mr. Kimball that is your business."

"Correct." I closed my notebook and got up. "Positively correct. But I have no official standing in this affair. If I call on Manuel Kimball on my own he'll just kick me out on my own. He's a friend of the family, anyway he thinks so. I need an introduction."

"Sure you need it." Larry had got up too and was brushing grass from the seat of his trousers. "But you won't get it. Where's your hat, in the house?"

I nodded. "We can get it when you go in to telephone. Look here, it's like this. I've got to ask you to phone Manuel Kimball, and the Robertsons, and the Green Meadow Club. That's all I have on my mind at present but there may be more later. I've got to go around and see people and find out things, and the easier you make it for me the easier it will be for you. Nero Wolfe knew enough, and told the police enough, to make them dig up your father's body. That was a good deal, but he didn't tell them everything. Do you want to force me to go to the District Attorney and spill enough more beans so that he will give me a ticket that will let me in wherever I want to go? He's sore at us now because he knows we're holding out on him. I'd just as soon go and make a friend of him, I don't mind, I like to make friends. You folks certainly don't. If this strikes you as some more blackmail, Mr. Barstow, I'll just get my hat and call it a day as far as you're concerned."

It was a crime, but I had to do it. The trouble with those two, especially the brother, was that they were so used to being safe and independent and dignified all their lives that they kept forgetting how scared they were and had to be reminded. But they were plenty scared when it came to the point, and if I had cared to make them a present of all my ideas that afternoon I would have had to admit that it looked to me as if they had reason to be scared.

They gave in, of course. We went into the house together, and Sarah Barstow telephoned the Robertsons and her brother phoned the club and Manuel Kimball. I had decided that there wasn't a chance in a million that I would get anything out of any of the servants, particularly if they had been trained by that tall skinny butler, so as soon as the telephoning was over I got my panama from the hall and beat it. Larry Barstow went with me out to the side terrace, I suppose to make sure that I didn't sneak back in and listen at keyholes, and just as we came to the steps a car rolled along the drive and stopped in front of us. A man got out, and I had the pleasure of a good grin as I saw it was H. R. Corbett, the dick from Anderson's office who had tried to crash the gate at Wolfe's house the morning I was acting as doorman. I passed him a cheerful salute and was going on, but he called to me:

"Hey, you!"

I stopped and turned. Larry Barstow stood on the terrace watching us. I said, "Did you address me, sir?"

Corbett was moving into my neighborhood. He paid no attention to my fast one. "What the hell are you doing here?"

I stood and grinned at him a second and then turned to Larry Barstow on the terrace. "Since this is your home, Mr. Barstow, maybe it would be better if you would tell him what the hell I'm doing here."

It was plain from the look on Larry's face that although he might never send me a Christmas card, I would get one long before Corbett would. He said to the dick, "Mr. Goodwin has been here at my sister's invitation, to consult with us. He will probably be here again. Would you like to investigate that?"

Corbett grunted and glared at me. "Maybe you'd like a trip to White Plains."

"Not at all." I shook my head. "I don't like the town, it's so slow you can't get a bet down." I started to move off. "So long,

Corbett. I don't wish you any bad luck, because even with
good luck you won't have much of a tombstone."

Without bothering to think up an answer to the threats
and warnings he tossed at my back, I went over to the roadster
where it was parked, got in and turned around, and rolled off.

Chapter 10

I went to the Robertsons' first, because I knew it wouldn't take
long and I might as well get it done. Mrs. Robertson and both
of the daughters were at home, and expecting me after Sarah
Barstow's phone call. They said they had been at the Barstows'
the evening of June fifth, the day before the funeral, arriving
well before eight o'clock and leaving after midnight. They
were certain that Larry and Sarah and Mrs. Barstow had been
present the entire evening. I made sure there was no possibility of a mistake about the date, and then tried a few casual
questions about the Barstow family but soon gave it up. The
Robertsons weren't discussing their old friends that afternoon
with a stranger; they wouldn't even let on that Mrs. Barstow
was otherwise than completely all right, not aware how much I
knew.

I got to the Kimball place a little after five o'clock. It
wasn't as dressed up as the Barstow estate, but was much
larger; I drove over half a mile after I entered their private
road. It was mostly on low ground, with some of the old stone
fences still running through the meadows and a couple of
brooks wandering around. Some woods were at the left. The
house was on a knoll in a park of evergreens, with a well-kept
lawn not very large and no sign of flowers that I could see as I
drove up. Not as big as the Barstows', the house was brand-
new, wood with panels and a high steep slate roof, one of the
styles that I lumped all together and called Queen William.

Back of the house, over the knoll, was an immense flat
meadow. I was sent in that direction, along a narrow graveled
drive, by a fat man in a butler's uniform who came out of the
house as I drove up. In the large meadow were no stone

fences; it was level and clean and recently mowed and was certainly perfect for a private landing field. On the edge about halfway down its length was a low concrete building with a flat roof, and the graveled drive took me there. There was a wide and long concrete runway in front, and two cars were parked on it.

I found Manuel Kimball inside, washing his hands at a sink. The place was mostly full of airplane, a big one with black wings and a red body, sitting on its tail. In it tinkering with something was a man in overalls. Everything was neat and clean, with tools and oil cans and a lot of junk arranged on steel shelves that ran along one side. Besides the sink there was even a rack with three or four clean towels on it.

"My name's Goodwin," I said.

Kimball nodded. "Yes, I was expecting you. I'm through here for the day; we might as well go to the house and be comfortable." He spoke to the man in overalls. "Let that wait till tomorrow if you want to, Skinner, I won't be going up till afternoon." When he had finished wiping his hands he led me out and took his car, and I got in the roadster and drove back to the house.

He was decent and polite, no doubt about that, even if he did look like a foreigner and had made me nervous at lunch. He took me into a large room in front and steered me to a big comfortable leather chair and told the fat butler to bring us some highballs. When he saw me looking around he said that the house had been furnished by his father and himself after their personal tastes, since there had been no women to consider and they both disliked decorators.

I nodded. "Miss Barstow told me your mother died a long time ago."

I said it casually, without thinking, but I always have my eye on whoever I'm talking to, and I was surprised at what went over his face. It was a spasm, you couldn't call it anything else. It only lasted a fraction of a second, but for that moment something was certainly hurting him inside. I didn't know whether it was just because I had mentioned his mother or he really had a pain; anyhow, I didn't try it again.

He said, "I understand that you are investigating the death of Miss Barstow's father."

"Yes. At her request, in a way. Larry Barstow's father too, and Mrs. Barstow's husband, at the same time."

He smiled and his black eyes swerved to me. "If that is

your first question, Mr. Goodwin, it is neatly put. Bravo. The answer is no, I have no right to distinguish the dead man in that fashion. No right, that is, but my own inclination. I admire Miss Barstow—very much."

"Good. So do I. It wasn't a question, just a remark. What I really want to ask you about is what took place on the first tee that Sunday afternoon. I suppose you've told the story before."

"Yes. Twice to a detective whose name is Corbett, I believe, and once to Mr. Anderson."

"Then you ought to have it by heart. Would you mind telling it again?"

I sat back with my highball and listened without interrupting. I didn't use my notebook because I already had Larry's tale to check with and I could record any differences later. Manuel Kimball was precise and thorough. When he got through there was little left to ask, but there were one or two points I wasn't satisfied on, particularly one on which he differed from Larry. Manuel said that after Barstow thought a wasp had stung him he had dropped his driver on the ground and his caddy had picked it up; Larry had said that his father had hung onto the driver with one hand when he was opening his shirt to see what had happened to him. Manuel said he felt sure he was right but didn't insist on it if Larry remembered otherwise. It didn't seem of great importance, since the driver had in any event got back into the bag, and in all other respects Manuel's story tallied with Larry's.

Encouraged by his sending for more highballs, I spread the conversation out a little. He didn't seem to object. I learned that his father was a grain broker and went every day to his office in New York, on Pearl Street, and that he, Manuel, was considering the establishment of an airplane factory. He was, he said, a thoroughly skilled pilot, and he had spent a year at the Fackler works in Buffalo. His father had engaged to furnish the necessary capital, though he doubted the soundness of the venture and was entirely skeptical about airplanes. Manuel thought Larry Barstow showed promise of a real talent in structural design and hoped to be able to persuade him to take a share in the enterprise. He said:

"Naturally Larry is not himself just at present, and I'm not trying to rush him. No wonder, first his father's sudden death, and then the autopsy with its astonishing results.—By the way, Mr. Goodwin, of course everybody around here is wondering how Nero Wolfe—that's it, isn't it?—how he was able to predict those results in such remarkable detail. Anderson, the District Attorney, hints at his own sources of information—he did so to me the other day, sitting in the chair you're in now—but the truth of the matter is pretty generally known. At Green Meadow day before yesterday there were only two topics: who killed Barstow, and how Nero Wolfe found out. What are you going to do, disclose the answers to both riddles at the same dramatic moment?"

"Maybe. I hope so, Mr. Kimball. Anyway we won't answer that last one first.—No, thanks, none for me. With another of your elegant highballs I might answer almost anything. They won't come any better than that even after repeal."

"Then by all means have one. Naturally, like everybody else, I'm curious. Nero Wolfe must be an extraordinary man."

"Well, I'll tell you." I threw my head back to get the end of the highball, and with the slick ice-lumps sliding across my upper lip let the last rare drops trickle in, then suddenly came down with the glass and my chin at the same time. It was just one of my little tricks. All I saw was Manuel Kimball looking curious, and he had just said he was curious, so it couldn't be said that I had made any subtle discovery. I said, "If Nero Wolfe isn't extraordinary Napoleon never got higher than top-sergeant. I'm sorry I can't tell you his secrets, but I've got to earn what he pays me somehow even if it's only by keeping my mouth shut. Which reminds me." I glanced at my wrist. "It must be about your dinner time. You've been very hospitable, Mr. Kimball. I appreciate it, and so will Nero Wolfe."

"You're quite welcome. Don't hurry on my account. My father won't be home and I dislike eating alone. I'll run over to the club for dinner later."

"Oh," I said. "Your father won't be home? That throws me out a little. I had figured on finding a bite to eat in Pleasantville or White Plains and coming back for a little talk with him. In fact, I was just about to ask you for a favor: to tell him I was coming."

"I'm sorry."

"He won't be back tonight?"

"No. He went to Chicago on business last week. Your disappointment isn't the first one. Anderson and that detective have been wiring him every day, I don't exactly see why. After all, he barely knew Barstow. I imagine their telegrams won't start him back till he's through with his business. My father is like that. He finishes things."

"When do you expect him?"

"I hardly know. Around the fifteenth, he thought when he left."

"Well. That's too bad. It's just routine, of course, but any detective would want to complete the foursome, and since you can't do me the favor with your father that I wanted to ask, maybe you will do me another one. More routine. Tell me where you were between seven o'clock and midnight Monday evening, June fifth. That was the evening before the Barstow funeral. Did you go to the funeral? This was the evening before."

Manuel Kimball's black eyes were straight at me, concentrated, like a man trying to remember. "I went to the funeral," he said. "Yes, that was Tuesday. A week ago today. Oh yes. I think it was; yes, I'm sure. Skinner would know. I was in the clouds."

"In the clouds?"

He nodded. "I've been trying flying and landing at night. A couple of times in May, and again that Monday. Skinner would know; he helped me off and I had him wait till I got back to make sure the lights would be in order. It's quite a trick, very different from the daytime."

"What time did you go up?"

"Around six o'clock. Of course it wasn't dark until nearly nine, but I wanted to be ahead of the twilight."

"You got well ahead of it all right. When did you get back?"

"Ten or a little after. Skinner would know that too; we fooled around with the timer till midnight."

"Did you go up alone?"

"Completely." Manuel Kimball smiled at me with his lips, but it appeared to me that his eyes weren't co-operating. "You must admit, Mr. Goodwin, that I'm being pretty tolerant. What the devil has my flying Monday night or any other night got to do with you? If I wasn't so curious I might have reason to be a little irritated. Don't you think?"

"Sure." I grinned. "I'd be irritated if I was you. But anyway I'm much obliged. Routine, Mr. Kimball, just the damn routine." I got up and shook a leg to get the cuff of my trousers down. "And I am much obliged and I appreciate it. I should think it would be more fun flying at night than in the daytime."

He was on his feet too, polite. "It is. But do not feel obliged. It is going to distinguish me around here to have talked to Nero Wolfe's man."

He called the fat butler to bring my hat.

Half an hour later, headed south around the curves of the Bronx River Parkway, I was still rolling him over on my mind's tongue. Since there was no connection at all between him and Barstow or the driver or anything else, it could have been for no other reason than because he made me nervous. And yet Wolfe said that I had no feeling for phenomena! The next time he threw that at me I would remind him of my mysterious misgivings about Manuel Kimball, I decided. Granted, of course, that it turned out that Manuel had murdered Barstow, which I had to confess didn't seem very likely at that moment.

When I got home, around half-past eight, Wolfe had finished dinner. I had phoned from the drugstore on the Grand Concourse, and Fritz had a dish of flounder with his best cheese sauce hot in the oven, with a platter of lettuce and tomatoes and plenty of good cold milk. Considering my thin lunch at the Barstows' and the hour I was getting my knees under the table, it wasn't any too much. I cleaned it up. Fritz said it seemed good to have me busy and out working again.

I said, "You're darned right it does. This dump would be about ready for the sheriff if it wasn't for me."

Fritz giggled. He's the only man I've ever known who could giggle without giving you doubts about his fundamentals.

Wolfe was in his chair in the office, playing with flies. He hated flies and very few ever got in there, but two had somehow made it and were fooling around on his desk. Much as he hated them, he couldn't kill them; he said that while a live fly irritated him to the point of hatred, a killed one outraged his respect for the dignity of death, which was worse. My opinion was it just made him sick. Anyway, he was in his chair with the swatter in his hand, seeing how close to the fly he could lower it without the fly taking off. When I went in he handed me the swatter and I let them have it and raked them into the wastebasket.

"Thank you," Wolfe said. "Those confounded insects were trying to make me forget that one of the Dendrobiums chlorostele is showing two buds."

"No! Really?"

He nodded. "That one in half sunlight. The others have been moved over."

"One for Horstmann."

"Yes. Who killed Barstow?"

I grinned. "Give me a chance. The name just escapes me —I'll remember it in a minute."

"You should have written it down.—No, just your light. That's better. Did you get enough to eat?—Proceed."

That report was an in-between; I wasn't proud of it or ashamed of it either. Wolfe scarcely interrupted once throughout; he sat as he always did when I had a long story; leaning back, his chin on his chest, his elbows on the arms of the chair with his fingers interlaced on his belly, his eyes half closed but always on my face. Halfway through he stopped me to have Fritz bring some beer, then with two bottles and a glass within reach at the edge of the table he resumed his position. I went on to the end. It was midnight.

He sighed. I went to the kitchen for a glass of milk. When I got back he was pinching the top of his ear and looking sleepy.

"Perhaps you had an impression," he said.

I sat down again. "Vague. Pretty watery. Mrs. Barstow is just some kind of a nut. She might have killed her husband or she might not, but of course she didn't kill Carlo Maffei. For Miss Barstow you can use your own impression. Out. Her brother is out too, I mean on Maffei, his alibi for the fifth is so tight you could use it for a vacuum. Dr. Bradford must be a very interesting person, I would like to meet him some time. As for Manuel Kimball, I suppose there's no chance he killed Barstow, but I'll bet he runs over angels with his airplane."

"Why? Is he cruel? Does he sneer? Do his eyes focus badly?"

"No. But look at his name. He made me nervous. He looks like a Spaniard. What's he doing with the name Kimball?"

"You haven't seen his father."

"I know. Of course the bad news about the golf bag never being in his locker threw me off my stride and I was looking for something to kick."

"Bad news? Why bad?"

"Well, good Lord. We thought we had the membership of the Green Meadow Club to run through the sifter, and now we've got everybody that's been in Barstow's home at the university for the past nine months."

"Oh no. By no means. No known poison, exposed to the air, by being smeared on a needle for instance, will retain an efficacy sufficient to kill a man as Barstow was killed for more than a day or two. Probably only a few hours. It depends on the poison."

I grinned at him. "That's a help. What else did you read?"

"A few interesting things. Many tiresome ones. So the golf bag's itinerary is not bad news at all. Its later disappearance interests us only indirectly, for we never could have expected to come upon the driver. But who caused it to disappear and why?"

"Sure. But as far as that's concerned, who came to ask you to return the reward unopened and why? We already knew there's someone in that family with funny ideas."

Wolfe wiggled a finger at me. "It is easier to recognize a style from a sentence than from a single word. But as for that, the removal of the golf bag from the scene was direct, bold and forthright, while the visit to our office, though direct enough, was merely desperate."

I said, "Doctors know all about poisons."

"Yes. This one—this Dr. Bradford—is satisfactorily forthright. Three times today I was told that he was too busy to come to the telephone, and the indication was that that condition could be expected to continue. You are intending to resume in the morning?"

I nodded. "The club first, I thought, then the coroner, then back to town for Doc Bradford's office. I'm sorry old Kimball's gone; I'd like to clean up that foursome. You don't think Saul Panzer would enjoy a trip to Chicago?"

"It would cost a hundred dollars."

"That's not much of a chunk out of fifty grand."

Wolfe shook his head. "You're a spendthrift, Archie. And unnecessarily thorough. Let us first make sure no murderer can be found within the commuting area."

"Okay." I got up and stretched. "Good night, sir."

"Good night, Archie."

Chapter 11

There was a point on the public road from which the Green Meadow clubhouse could be seen, but at a considerable distance; to reach it you turned off the highway into a grove, and when you left that you were winding around a hollow. The clubhouse had a grove of its own, on top of a moderate hill; on one side were a bunch of tennis courts and an outdoor pool, everywhere else, in all directions, were smooth rolling fairways dotted with little tee plateaus, sand traps of various shapes and sizes, and the vivid velvet carpets of the putting greens. There were two courses of eighteen holes each; the Barstow foursome had started on the north course, the long one.

The club professional, who had dined with us at Wolfe's place Monday evening, wasn't there yet when I arrived and wasn't expected until eleven o'clock, so the only introduction I had to offer was Larry Barstow's phone call the preceding afternoon which had been received by the chief steward. He was nice enough and went with me out to the caddy master. Two of the caddies I wanted to see didn't come on weekdays, since the schools they attended weren't out yet, and the other two were out on the links somewhere with early morning matches. I monkeyed around for an hour trying to find someone for a page in the notebook, but as far as real information was concerned they were about as helpful as a bunch of Eskimos. I hopped in the roadster and beat it for White Plains.

The coroner's office was in the same building as Anderson's, where I had been six days previously trying to get Wolfe's money covered, and as I passed the door with *District Attorney* painted on the glass panel I stuck out my tongue at it. The coroner wasn't in, but by luck there was a doctor there signing papers and he was the one who had done the Barstow autopsy. Before leaving home in the morning I had telephoned Sarah Barstow, and now this doctor told me that he had had a phone call from Lawrence Barstow and had been told that I would visit the coroner's office as a representative of the Barstow family. I thought to myself, I'll have that Barstow brat fixing my flat tires before I get through with this.

But I came away as good as empty. Everything that the doctor could tell me I had read three days earlier in the newspapers except for a bunch of medical terms which the papers hadn't tried to print for fear of a typesetters' strike. I don't high-hat technical words, because I know there are a lot of things that can't be said any other way, but the doctor's lengthy explanation simply boiled down to this, that nothing conclusive could be said regarding the poison that had killed Barstow, because no one had been able to analyze it. Additional tissues had been sent to a New York laboratory but no report had been received. The needle had been taken by the District Attorney and was presumably being tested elsewhere.

"Anyway," I said, "there's no chance he died of old age or something? He was actually poisoned? He died a violent death?"

The doctor nodded. "Absolutely. Something remarkably virulent. Hæmolysis—"

"Sure. Just between you and me, what is your opinion of a doctor who would go up to a man who had just died like that and would say coronary thrombosis?"

He stiffened as if he had just got rigor mortis himself, only much quicker. "That is not a question for me to decide, Mr. Goodwin."

"I didn't ask you to decide anything, I just asked your opinion."

"I haven't got any."

"You mean you have, only you're going to keep it to remember me by. All right. Much obliged."

On my way out of the building I would have liked to stop in and ask Derwin for Ben Cook's telephone number or some such pleasantry, but I had too much on my mind. By the time I got back to the Green Meadow Club it was nearly noon and I had pretty well decided that life would be nothing but a dreary round until I had had the pleasure of meeting Dr. Bradford.

The two caddies were there. Their boss rounded them up for me, and I made a deal with them: I would get sandwiches, two apiece, bananas, ice cream, and root beer, and we would go over under a tree and eat, drink and be merry, provided they wouldn't expect me to pay for their lost time. They signed up and we collected the provisions from the lunch counter and found the tree.

One of them, a skinny pale kid with brown hair, had been Manuel Kimball's caddy and the other had been Peter Oliver Barstow's. This other was a chunky lad with snappy brown eyes and a lot of freckles; his name was Mike Allen. After we got arranged under the tree, before he took his first bite he said:

"You know, mister, we don't get paid."

"What do you mean, you work for fun?"

"We don't get paid all the time, only when we're out on a round. We're not losing any time. We couldn't get another match till after lunch anyhow."

"Oh. You don't say so. You're too darned honest. If you don't watch out you'll get a job in a bank. Go on and eat your sandwich."

While we chewed I got them onto the Barstow foursome. The way they rattled it off it was easy to see they hadn't gone over it more than a thousand times, with Anderson and Corbett of course, the other caddies, families and friends at home. They were glib and ready with an answer on every little detail, and that made it pretty hopeless to try to get anything fresh out of them, for they had drawn the picture so many times that they were now doing it with their eyes shut. Not that I really expected a damn thing, but I had long since learned from Wolfe that the corner the light doesn't reach is the one the dime rolled to. There was no variation worth mentioning from the versions I had got from Larry Barstow and Manuel Kimball. By the time the sandwiches and stuff were down I saw that the pale skinny kid was milked dry, so I sent him back to his boss. Chunky Mike I kept a while, sitting with him under the tree. He had some sense in him and he might have noticed something: for instance, how Dr. Bradford had acted when he arrived at the scene on the fourth fairway. But I didn't get a bite there. He only remembered that the doctor had been out of breath when he had run up with everyone waiting for him, and when he stood up after examining Barstow he had been white and calm.

I checked up on the golf bag. There was no uncertainty in him about that; he had positively put it in the front of Barstow's car, leaning against the driver's seat.

I said, "Of course, Mike, you were pretty excited. At a

time like that everybody is. Isn't there a chance you put it in
some other car?"

"No, sir. I couldn't. There was no other car there."

"Maybe it was someone else's bag you put in."

"No, sir. I'm not a dummy. When you're a caddy you get
so you glance at the heads to make sure all the clubs are in, and
after I leaned the bag against the seat I did that, and I
remember seeing all the new heads."

"New heads?"

"Sure, they were all new."

"What made them new? Do you mean Barstow had had
new heads put on?"

"No, sir, they were new clubs. The new bag of clubs his
wife gave him."

"What!"

"Sure."

I didn't want to startle him; I picked a blade of grass and
chewed on it. "How do you know his wife gave them to him?"

"He told me."

"How did he happen to tell you?"

"Well, when I went up to him he shook hands and said he
was glad to see me again, of course he was one my babies last
year—"

"For God's sake, Mike, wait a minute. What do you mean
he was one of your babies?"

The kid grinned. "That's what us fellows call it. When a
man likes us for a caddy and won't take another one he's our
baby."

"I see. Go on."

"He said he was glad to see me again, and when I took his
bag I saw they were all new Hendersons, genuine, and he said
he was glad to see I admired the new clubs his wife had given
him for his birthday."

There were a couple of bananas left and I handed him one
and he began peeling it. I watched him. After a minute I said:

"Do you know that Barstow was killed by a poison needle
shot out of the handle of a golf driver?"

His mouth was full. He waited till most of it was down
before he answered. "I know that's what they say."

"Why, don't you believe it?"

He shook his head. "They've got to show me."

"Why?"

"Well—" He took another bite and swallowed it. "I don't

believe you could do it. I've handled a lot of golf clubs. I just don't believe it."

I grinned at him. "You're a skeptic, Mike. You know what my boss says? He says that skepticism is a good watchdog if you know when to take the leash off. I don't suppose you happen to know when Barstow had a birthday?"

He didn't know that. I started to fish around a little more, here and there, but there didn't seem to be any more nibbles in that pool. Besides, the lunch hour was over, afternoon players were beginning to stroll up, and I saw Mike had his eyes on the caddy benches and was beginning to lose interest in me. I was about ready to scramble up and tell him the picnic was over, but he beat me to it. He was on his feet with a sudden spring, the kind young legs can make, and he tossed at me, "Excuse me, mister, that guy's my baby," and was off.

I gathered up the papers and banana skins and went to the clubhouse. There were a good many more people around than when I had arrived in the morning, and finally I had to send an attendant for the chief steward because I couldn't find him. He was busy, but he took time to show me where the library was and tell me to help myself. I looked around the shelves and in a minute had it spotted, the fat red *Who's Who in America*. I turned to the entry I had already read in Wolfe's office: BARSTOW, Peter Oliver, author, educator, physicist; *b*. Chatham, Ill., Apr. 9, 1875 . . .

I put the book back and went out to the lobby where I had seen some telephone booths, and called Sarah Barstow at her home and asked if I could drop in to see her for a minute. It was only a couple of miles out of my way returning to New York, and I thought I might as well clean this detail up. As I was going along the veranda to where I had parked the roadster I met Manuel Kimball. He was with some people, but when he saw me he nodded and I returned it, and I could guess what he was saying to the people with him because after I got past they turned to look at me.

Ten minutes later I was on the Barstow drive.

Small took me to a room in front that I hadn't been in the day before. In a little while Sarah Barstow came in. She looked pale and determined, and I realized that with my phone call I must have scared her some more without wanting to. I should have been a little more explanatory; I don't believe in pulling a dog's tail if there's anything else to do.

I got up. She didn't sit down.

"I'll only keep you a minute," I said. "I wouldn't have bothered you, only I ran across something that made me curious. Please tell me, was your father's birthday April ninth?"

She looked as if she was trying to breathe. She nodded.

"Did your mother give him a bag of golf clubs his last birthday?"

"Oh!" she said, and put her hand on the back of a chair.

"Listen, Miss Barstow. Buck up. I think you know Nero Wolfe wouldn't lie to you, and while he's paying me you can regard me as Nero Wolfe. We might try tricky questions on you, but we wouldn't tell you an honest lie. If you've been nursing the idea that the driver your father killed himself with was in the bag when your mother gave it to him on his birthday, forget it. We have reason to know it couldn't have been. Impossible."

She just looked at me with her lips working but not opening. I don't believe she would have been able to stand without her hand on the chair. She had a good hold on it.

I said, "Maybe I'm telling you something and maybe I'm not. But I've brought this right to you as soon as I found it out, and I'm giving it to you straight. If it's any help to you, you're welcome, and how about making it fifty-fifty? I could use a little help too. Was that what was eating you, that birthday present? Was that the reason for all the fol-de-rol?"

She got her tongue working at last but all she said was, "I don't believe you would lie to me. It would be too cruel."

"I wouldn't. But even if I would, I know about the birthday present anyhow, so you can answer my simple question without running a temperature. Was that what was eating you?"

"Yes," she said. "That—and—yes, it was that."

"What else was it?"

"Nothing. My mother—"

"Sure." I nodded. "Your mother got goofy sometimes and got ideas about your father, and she gave him a golf bag on his birthday. What else?"

"Nothing." She took her hand off the chair, but put it back again. "Mr. Goodwin. I think—I'll sit down."

I went and took her arm and shoved the chair back a little with my foot, and held onto her until she got seated. She shut her eyes and I stood and waited till she opened them again.

"You're right," she said. "I ought to buck up. I'm no good.

It has been a strain. Not only this, a long while. I always thought my mother was a wonderful woman, I still think so, I know she is. But it is so ugly! Dr. Bradford says he believes that now, since Father is dead, Mother will be completely cured and will never again have any—difficulties. But much as I love my mother, that is too high a price. I think we would be better off without modern psychology, everything it tells us is so ugly. It was at my father's suggestion that I studied it."

"Anyway, this is one thing off your mind."

"Yes. I can't appreciate it yet, but I will. I ought to thank you, Mr. Goodwin, I'm sorry. You say that my mother had nothing—that she couldn't—"

"I say that the driver that killed your father wasn't anywhere on April ninth. It didn't exist until at least a month later."

"How sure are you?"

"Just damn sure."

"Well. That's a good deal." She tried to smile at me, and I admired her nerve, for it was easy to see that she was so near gone from worry and grief and loss of sleep that you might as well have expected a guffaw from Job. Anyone with an ounce of decency in him would have got up and left her alone with the good news I'd brought her; but business is business, and it wouldn't have been right to pass up the chance that she was unstrung enough to loosen up at a vital point. I said:

"Don't you think you might tell me who took the golf bag from the car and where it is now? Now that we know that the driver is not the one that was in it when your mother gave it to him?"

She said without hesitation, "Small took it from the car."

My heart jumped the way it did when I saw Wolfe's lips push out. She was going to spill it! I went right on without giving her time to consider, "Where did he take it to?"

"Upstairs. To Father's room."

"Who took it away from there?"

"I did. Saturday evening, after Mr. Anderson came. It was Sunday that the men searched the house for it."

"Where did you put it?"

"I drove to Tarrytown and got on the ferry and dropped it in the middle of the river. I filled it full of stones."

"You're lucky they weren't tailing you. Of course you examined the driver. Did you take it apart?"

"I didn't examine it. I—was in a hurry."

"You didn't examine it? You mean you didn't even take it out and look at it?"

"No."

I stared at her. "I've got a better opinion of you. I don't believe you're such an awful fool. You're stringing me."

"No. No, I'm not, Mr. Goodwin."

I still stared. "You mean you actually did all that? Without even looking at the driver? Leave it to a woman! What were your brother and Bradford doing, playing billiards?"

She shook her head. "They had nothing to do with it."

"But Bradford says that your mother will be all right now that your father's dead."

"Well? If that is his opinion—." She stopped; the mention of her mother had been a mistake, it had her down again. After a minute she looked up at me, and for the first time I saw tears in her eyes. Two hung there. "You wanted me to go fifty-fifty, Mr. Goodwin. That's my share."

Something about her, the tears maybe, made her look like nothing but a kid, trying to be brave. I reached down and patted her on the shoulder and said:

"You're a good sport, Miss Barstow. I'll let you alone."

I went to the hall and got my hat and left.

BUT, I thought, in the roadster again headed south down the highway. Plenty of BUT. Part of it was that as much as I respected filial devotion and as much as I liked Sarah Barstow, it would have been a real satisfaction to put her across my knees and pull up her skirts and give her a swell fanning, for not taking a look at that driver. I had to believe her and I did believe her. She hadn't made that up. Now the driver was gone for good. With a lot of luck and patience it might have been grappled out of the river, but it would have cost more money than Nero Wolfe was apt to let go of. It was just simply good-bye driver. As I went through White Plains it was a temptation to leave the Parkway and run over to the District Attorney's office and say to Anderson, "I'll bet you ten dollars that the golf bag containing the driver that killed Barstow is at the bottom of the Hudson River halfway between Tarrytown and Nyack." It wouldn't have been a bad idea at that, for he might have sent a couple of boats out and found it. But as things turned out it was just as well I didn't.

I had had it in mind to go back to New York by another route, Blueberry Road, and just for curiosity take a look at the spot where Carlo Maffei's body had been found; not that I expected to discover that the murderer had left his scarfpin or automobile license lying around, just thinking that it never hurts a spot to look at it. But dropping in on Sarah Barstow had used up some time, and I wanted to make a call in the city. So I took the quickest way in.

On upper Park Avenue I stopped at a drugstore and phoned Wolfe. He had called Bradford's office once more, around eleven-thirty, but it had been the same story, too busy to come to the phone. He told me to go to it. I thought to myself, if he's busy now he's going to be positively rushed before we get through with him. It took me less than ten minutes to get to Sixty-ninth Street, and I parked around the corner.

Dr. Nathaniel Bradford certainly had an office. The entrance hall was wide enough to have a row of Brazilian ferns along each side, and the anteroom was big and grand. The lights and rugs and pictures and chairs made it plain, but not noisy, that everything done in that place was on a high level, including making out the patients' bills. But the chairs were all empty. The girl in starched white at a desk over in a corner told me that Dr. Bradford was not in. She seemed surprised that I didn't know that, just as I would know that Central Park begins at Fifty-ninth Street, and asked if I was a former patient. Then she said that the doctor was never in his office in the afternoon before four-thirty, and that he never saw anyone except by appointment. When I said that that was what I wanted to see him for, to make an appointment, she raised her eyebrows. I went back to the street.

At first I thought I would wait around for him, but it was only a little after three, so I went and sat in the roadster and let my mind out for a stroll to see if it would run across an idea for passing the time. In a few minutes it did, a pretty one. I went to a restaurant on Park Avenue to look at a telephone book, and then went back to the car and stepped on the starter and started along Sixty-ninth Street, and at Fifth Avenue turned downtown. At Forty-first Street I headed east.

As usual every car along the curb was laying its head on the next one's tail, and I had to go nearly to Third Avenue to find a space where I could edge the roadster in. I walked back almost two crosstown blocks, and found that the number I was looking for was one of the new office buildings a mile high. The directory said that my meat was on the twentieth floor.

The elevator shot me up and I found it on a door down the corridor: *Metropolitan Medical Record*.

It was a young man, not a girl, at the desk in the outside room; that was nice for a change. I said to him:

"I'd like to ask a favor, if you're not too busy to help me out a little. Would you have any record showing the meetings of medical associations and so on held in New York on June fifth?"

He grinned. "The Lord knows I'm not busy. Yes, sir, we have. Of course. Just a minute. June fifth?"

He went to a stack of magazines on a shelf and took off the top one. "This is our last issue, it would have it." He began flipping the pages and stopped around the middle and looked at it. I waited. "Nothing on the fifth, I'm afraid—Oh yes, here it is. Most of the big meetings come later. On the fifth the New York Neurological Society was at the Knickerbocker Hotel."

I asked if I could look at it and he handed it to me. I ran through the paragraph. "I see. This is a notice of the meeting. Of course it was printed before the meeting took place. You wouldn't have anything later? A report, a write-up?"

He shook his head. "There'll be one in our next issue I suppose. Was it something particular you wanted? The daily papers may have run it."

"Maybe. I haven't tried them. What I'm looking for is a report of Dr. Bradford's paper. As a matter of fact, all I want is to make sure he was there. You wouldn't know?"

He shook his head. "But if all you want to know is whether he was there or not, why don't you ask him?"

I grinned. "I hate to bother him. But of course it's quite simple, I happened to be in the neighborhood and thought that by dropping in here I could save time."

He said, "Wait a minute," and disappeared through a door to an inner office. He didn't take much more than the minute he mentioned. When he came back he told me, "Mr. Elliot says that Dr. Bradford was at the meeting and delivered his paper."

Elliot, he said, was the editor of the *Record*. I asked if I could speak to him. The young man disappeared through the door again, and after a moment it opened once more and a big red-faced man in his shirt sleeves came through. One of the brusque breezy kind. "What's all this? What's this about?"

I explained. He wiped his forehead with his handkerchief

and said that he had attended the meeting and that Dr.
Bradford had delivered his most interesting paper to applause.
He was writing it up for the August *Record*. I questioned him,
and he took it very nicely. Yes, he meant Dr. Nathaniel
Bradford whose office was on Sixty-ninth Street. He had
known him for years. He couldn't say at what hour Bradford
had arrived at the hotel, but it had been a dinner meeting and
he had seen Bradford at his table as early as seven and on the
speaking platform as late as ten-thirty.

I guess I went out without thanking him. Driving back
uptown I was sore as a pup. Of course it was Bradford I was
sore at. What the devil did he mean by fooling around at a
meeting reading a paper on neurology when I had him all set
up in Westchester County sticking a knife into Carlo Maffei?

I supposed it would have taken me about a year to get
introduced to Dr. Nathaniel Bradford if I hadn't been so sore
when I got back to his office. There were two patients waiting
this time. The doctor was in. I asked the girl at the desk for a
piece of paper and sat down and held it on a magazine and
wrote on it:

> *Dr. Bradford: For the last few days I've been sure
> you were a murderer but now I know you are just an
> old fool. The same goes for Mrs. Barstow and her son
> and daughter. It will take me about three minutes to
> tell you how I know.*
>
>   *Archie Goodwin*
>   *For Nero Wolfe*

By the time the two patients had been taken care of some
more had come in, and I went over to the girl and told her I
was next. She got impatient and began explaining to me what
an appointment was. I said:

"It wouldn't break any furniture if you just handed him
this note. Honest, I'm in a hurry. Be human. I've got a sister at
home. Don't read it yourself because there's a swear-word in
it."

She looked disgusted, but she took the note and went
away with it through the door where the patients had gone.
After a while she came back and stood on the threshold and
said my name. I took my hat along with me because there had
been time enough to call a cop.

One look at Dr. Bradford was enough to show me that I
had been wasting a lot of pleasant suspicions which might have

Introducing the first and only complete hardcover collection of Agatha Christie's mysteries

Now you can enjoy the
greatest mysteries ever written
in a magnificent
Home Library Edition.

Discover Agatha Christie's world of mystery, adventure and intrigue

Agatha Christie's timeless tales of mystery and suspense offer something for every reader—mystery fan or not—young and old alike. And now, you can build a complete hardcover library of her world-famous mysteries by subscribing to The Agatha Christie Mystery Collection.

This exciting Collection is your passport to a world where mystery reigns supreme. Volume after volume, you and your family will enjoy mystery reading at its very best.

You'll meet Agatha Christie's world-famous detectives like Hercule Poirot, Jane Marple, and the likeable Tommy and Tuppence Beresford.

In your readings, you'll visit Egypt, Paris, England and other exciting destinations where murder is always on the itinerary. And wherever you travel, you'll become deeply involved in some of the most ingenious and diabolical plots ever invented ... "cliff-hangers" that only Dame Agatha could create!

It all adds up to mystery reading that's so good ... it's almost criminal. And it's yours every month with The Agatha Christie Mystery Collection.

Solve the greatest mysteries of all time. The Collection contains all of Agatha Christie's classic works including *Murder on the Orient Express, Death on the Nile, And Then There Were None, The ABC Murders* and her ever-popular whodunit, *The Murder of Roger Ackroyd.*

Each handsome hardcover volume is Smythe sewn and printed on high quality acid-free paper so it can withstand even the most murderous treatment. Bound in Sussex-blue simulated leather with gold titling, The Agatha Christie Mystery Collection will make a tasteful addition to your living room, or den.

Ride the Orient Express for 10 days without obligation.
To introduce you to the Collection, we're inviting you to examine the classic mystery, *Murder on the Orient Express*, without risk or obligation. If you're not completely satisfied, just return it within 10 days and owe nothing.

However, if you're like the millions of other readers who love Agatha Christie's thrilling tales of mystery and suspense, keep *Murder on the Orient Express* and pay just $9.95 plus postage and handling.

You will then automatically receive future volumes once a month as they are published on a fully returnable, 10-day free-examination basis. No minimum purchase is required, and you may cancel your subscription at any time.

This unique collection is not sold in stores. It's available only through this special offer. So don't miss out, begin your subscription now. Just mail this card today.

☐ Yes! Please send me *Murder on the Orient Express* for a 10-day free-examination and enter my subscription to <u>The Agatha Christie Mystery Collection</u>. If I keep *Murder on the Orient Express*, I will pay just $9.95 plus postage and handling and receive one additional volume each month on a fully returnable 10-day free-examination basis. There is no minimum number of volumes to buy, and I may cancel my subscription at any time.   07013

☐ I prefer the deluxe edition bound in genuine leather for $24.95 per volume plus shipping and handling, with the same 10-day free-examination.   07054

Name_____

Address_____

City_____ State_____ Zip_____

AS1

Send No Money...
But Act Today!

BUSINESS REPLY CARD

FIRST CLASS   PERMIT NO. 2274   HICKSVILLE, N.Y.

Postage will be paid by addressee:

The Agatha Christie
Mystery Collection
Bantam Books
P.O. Box 957
Hicksville, N.Y. 11802

been avoided if I had happened to catch sight of him somewhere. He was tall and grave and correct, the distinguished old gentleman type, and he had whiskers! There may have been a historical period when it was possible for a guy with whiskers to pull a knife and plunge it into somebody's back, but that was a long time ago. Nowadays it couldn't be done. Bradford's were gray, so was his hair. To tell the truth, as tight as his alibi for June fifth had been made by my trip to Forty-first Street, I had been prepared to try to find a leak in it until I got a look at him.

I went over to where he sat at his desk, and stood there. He just looked at me until the door had closed behind the girl, then he said:

"Your name is Goodwin. Are you a genius too?"

"Yes, sir." I grinned. "I caught it from Nero Wolfe. Sure, I remember he told Miss Barstow he was a genius, and of course she told you. Maybe you thought it was only a joke."

"No. I kept an open mind. But whether you are a genius or merely an impertinent ass, I can't keep my patients waiting for you. What is this note you sent me, bait? I'll give you three minutes to justify it."

"That's plenty. I'll put it this way: Nero Wolfe discovered certain facts. From those facts he reached a certain conclusion as to the cause and manner of Barstow's death. When the autopsy verified his conclusion it also verified his facts; that is, it made them an inseparable part of the picture, and whoever killed Barstow has got to fit those facts. Well, the Barstows don't fit, none of them. You don't either. You're a washout."

"Go on."

"Go on?"

"That's a good general statement. Specify."

"Oh no." I shook my head. "That's not the way us geniuses work, you can't shake us empty like a bag of peanuts. For one thing, it would take a lot longer than three minutes. For another, what do you expect for nothing? You've got a nerve. Something happens to get you into such a state that you can't tell coronary thrombosis from an epileptic fit, and to keep you on such an edge for days that you're afraid to go to the telephone, and it's all right for Nero Wolfe to spend his time and money chasing the clouds away for you and turning on the sunshine, but he mustn't make a nuisance of himself. I've got to send you in a trick note just to have the honor of looking at your whiskers. You've got a nerve."

"Dear me." Dr. Bradford was swearing. "Your indignation is eloquent and picturesque, but it demonstrates nothing but indignation." He looked at his watch. "I don't need to tell you, Mr. Goodwin, that I'm tremendously interested. And while I shall continue to regard the vocation of raking scandal out of graveyards as an especially vile method of making a living, I shall certainly be vastly grateful to you and Nero Wolfe if the general statement you have made can be substantiated. Can you return here at half-past six?"

I shook my head. "I'm just a messenger. Nero Wolfe dines at seven o'clock. He lives on West Thirty-fifth Street. He invites you to dine with him this evening. Will you?"

"No. Certainly not."

"All right. That's all." I was fed up with the old pillar, moss and all. "If you get a rash from your curiosity itching don't blame us. We don't really need anything you're likely to have, we just like to clean up as we go along. My three minutes are up."

I turned to go. I didn't hurry, but I got to the door with my hand on the knob.

"Mr. Goodwin."

I kept my hand on the knob and looked around at him.

"I accept Mr. Wolfe's invitation. I shall be there at seven."

I said, "Okay, I'll give the girl the address," and went on out.

Chapter 12

I've sometimes wondered how many people there were in New York from whom Nero Wolfe could have borrowed money. I suppose more than a thousand. I made it a severe test to narrow it down. Of course there were more than that who felt grateful to him, and as many more who had reason to hate him, but there's a special kind of attitude a man has to have toward you before you can bump him for a loan and get something more substantial than a frown and a stammer for your trouble; a mixture of trust and goodwill, and gratitude without any feeling of obligation to make it unpleasant. At least a thousand. Not that Wolfe ever took advantage of it. I remember a couple of years ago we were really hard up for cash for a while, and I made a suggestion regarding a multimillionaire who didn't owe Wolfe much more than his life. Wolfe wouldn't consider it. "No, Archie, nature has arranged that when you overcome a given inertia the resulting momentum is proportionate. If I were to begin borrowing money I would end by devising means of persuading the Secretary of the Treasury to lend me the gold reserve." I told him that as things stood we could use it and more too, but he wasn't listening.

After that Wednesday evening dinner I could have added Dr. Nathaniel Bradford to the thousand. Wolfe got him completely, as he always got everyone when he cared to take the trouble. Between six and seven, before Bradford arrived, I had made a condensed report of the events of the day, and at the dinner table I had seen at once that Wolfe agreed with me in erasing Bradford right off the slate. He was easy and informal, and to my practiced eye he always kept on a formal basis with a man as long as there was a chance in his mind that the man was headed for the frying-pan at Sing Sing or a cell at Auburn, with Wolfe furnishing the ticket.

At dinner they discussed rock gardens and economics and Tammany Hall. Wolfe drank three bottles of beer and Bradford a bottle of wine; I stuck to milk, but I had had a shot of rye upstairs. I had told Wolfe of Bradford's observation about a vile vocation and threw in my opinion of him. Wolfe had said, "Detach yourself, Archie, personal resentment of a general statement is a barbarous remnant of a fetish-superstition." I had said, "That's just another of your flossy remarks that don't mean anything." He had said, "No. I abhor meaningless remarks. If a man constructs a dummy, clothes and paints it in exact outward resemblance to yourself, and proceeds to strike it in the face, does your nose bleed?" I had said, "No, but his will before I get through with him." Wolfe had sighed into my grin, "At least you see that my remark was not meaningless."

In the office after dinner Wolfe said to Bradford that there were things he wanted to ask him but that he would begin by telling him. He gave him the whole story: Maffei, the clipped newspaper, the question about the golf club that stopped Anna Fiore, the game with Anderson, the letter Anna got with a hundred bucks. He told it straight and complete, and then said, "There, Doctor. I asked you for no pledge beforehand, but I now request you to keep everything I have said in confidence. I ask this in my own interest. I wish to earn fifty thousand dollars."

Bradford had got mellow. He was still trying to make Wolfe out, but he was no longer nursing any hurtful notions, and the wine was making him suspect Wolfe of being an old friend. He said, "It's a remarkable story. Remarkable. I shall mention it to no one of course, and I appreciate your confidence. I can't say that I have digested all the implications, but I can see that your disclosure of the truth regarding Barstow was a necessary part of the effort to find the murderer of the man Maffei. And I can see that you have relieved Sarah and Larry Barstow of an intolerable burden of fear, and myself of a responsibility that was becoming more than I had bargained for. I am grateful, believe me."

Wolfe nodded. "There are subtleties, certainly. Naturally some of them escape you. All that we have actually proven is that of you four—Mrs. Barstow, her son and daughter, and yourself—none of you killed Carlo Maffei, and that the fatal driver was not in the golf bag on April ninth. It is still possible that any one of you, or all of you in conspiracy, killed Barstow. That theory would only require a colleague to dispose of Maffei."

Bradford, suddenly a little less mellow, stared. But the stare soon disappeared and he was easy again. "Rot. You don't believe that." Then he stared again. "But as a matter of fact, why don't you?"

"We'll come to that. First let me ask, do you think my frankness has earned a similar frankness from you?"

"I do."

"Then tell me, for example, when and how Mrs. Barstow previously made an attempt on her husband's life."

It was funny to watch Bradford. He was startled, then he went stiff and quiet, then he realized he was giving it away and tried to dress up his face in natural astonishment. After all that he said, "What do you mean? That's ridiculous!"

Wolfe wiggled a finger at him. "Easy, Doctor. I beg you, do not suspect me of low cunning. I am merely seeking facts to fit my conclusions. I see I had better first tell you why I have dismissed from my mind the possibility of your guilt or that of the Barstows. I cannot feel such a guilt. That is all. Of course I can rationalize my feeling, or lack of it. Consider the requirements: a wife or son or daughter who plans the murder of the father with great deliberation, shrewdness and patience. The lengthy and intricate preparation of the tool. If the wife or daughter, a fellow conspirator who killed Maffei. If the son, the same requirement, since he did not do it himself. Archie Goodwin went there, and he could not spend hours in such a household without smelling the foul odor that it would generate and without bringing the smell to me. You also would have required an accomplice for Maffei. I have spent an evening with you. Though you might murder, you would not murder like that, and you would trust no accomplice whatever. That is the rationalization; it is the feeling that is important."

"Then why—"

"No, let me. You, a qualified and competent observer, certified a heart attack when the contrary evidence must have been unmistakable. That is adventurous conduct for a reputable physician. Of course you were shielding someone. The statement of Miss Barstow indicated whom. Then on finding Barstow dead you must have immediately conjectured that his wife had killed him, and you would not reach so shocking a conclusion without good reason, surely not merely because Mrs. Barstow had in her neurotic moments wished her husband dead. If that constituted murder, what kitchen in this country could shut its door to the hangman? You had better reason, knowledge either of her preparations for this crime or for a previous attempt on her husband's life. Since our facts make the former untenable, I assume the latter, and I ask you simply, when and how did she make the attempt? I ask you only to complete the record, so that we may consign these aspects of the case to the obscurity of history."

Bradford was considering. His mellowness was gone and he was leaning forward in his chair as he followed Wolfe's exposition. He said, "Have you sent someone to the university?"

"No."

"They know about it there. You really guessed it then. Last November Mrs. Barstow shot a revolver at her husband. The bullet went wide. Afterward she had a breakdown."

Wolfe nodded. "In a fit, of course.—Oh, don't object to the word; whatever you may call it, was it not a fit? But I am still surprised, Doctor. From a temporary fit of murderous violence, is it permissible to infer a long-premeditated diabolical plot?"

"I made no such inference." Bradford was exasperated. "Good God, there I was with my best and oldest friend lying dead before me, obviously poisoned. How did I know with what he was poisoned, or when or how? I did know what Ellen —Mrs. Barstow—had said only the evening before. I went by my feelings too, as you say you do, only mine were wrong. I got him safely and quietly buried, and I had no regrets. Then when the autopsy came with its amazing results I was too bewildered, and too far in, to act with any intelligence. When Mrs. Barstow proposed to offer the reward I opposed it unsuccessfully. In one word, I was in a funk."

I hadn't noticed Wolfe pushing the button, but as Bradford finished Fritz was on the threshold. "Some port for Dr. Bradford. A bottle of the Remmers for me. Archie?"

"Nothing, thanks."

Bradford said, "I'm afraid none for me, I should be going. It's nearly eleven and I'm driving to the country."

"But, Doctor," Wolfe protested, "you haven't told me the one thing I want to know. Another fifteen minutes? So far you have merely verified a few unimportant little surmises. Don't you see how shrewdly I have labored to gain your confidence and esteem? To this end only, that I might ask you, and expect a full and candid reply: who killed your friend Barstow?"

Bradford stared, discrediting his ears.

"I'm not drunk, merely dramatic," Wolfe went on. "I am a born actor, I suppose; anyway, I think a good question deserves a good setting. My question is a good one. You see, Doctor, you will have to shake the dust from your mind before you can answer me adequately—the dust remaining from your hasty and unkind inference regarding your friend Mrs. Barstow. From that and your funk. Understand that it really is true, despite the anxieties you have harbored for many months, that Mrs. Barstow did not kill her husband. Then who did? Who, with the patience of a devil and the humor of a fiend, prepared that lethal toy for his hand? I believe you were Barstow's oldest and closest friend?"

Bradford nodded. "Pete Barstow and I were boys together."

"A mutual confidence was sustained? Though superficial interests separated you intermittently, you presented a common front to life?"

"You put it well," Bradford was moved, it showed in his voice. "A confidence undisturbed for fifty years."

"Good. Then who killed him? I'm really expecting something from you, Doctor. What had he ever said or done that he should die? You may never have heard the story whole, but surely you must have caught a chapter of it, a paragraph, a sentence. Let the past whisper to you; it may be the distant past. And you must discard reluctance; I am not asking you for an indictment; the danger here is not that the innocent will be harassed but that the guilty will go free."

Fritz had brought the beer and the port, and the doctor was leaning back in his chair again, glass in hand, with his eyes on the red rich juice. He jerked his head up and nodded at Wolfe and then resumed his contemplation. Wolfe poured himself some beer, waited for the foam to subside, and gulped it down. He always thought he had a handkerchief in the breast pocket of his coat but rarely did, so I went to a drawer where I kept a stack for him and got one and handed it to him.

"I'm not listening to whispers from the past," Bradford finally said. "I'm being astonished, and impressed, that there are none, of the kind you mean. Also I'm seeing another reason why I so readily concluded that Mrs. Barstow—was responsible. Or rather, irresponsible. It was because I knew, or felt, unconsciously, that no one else could have done it. I see now more clearly than I ever did what an extraordinary person Pete Barstow was. As a boy he was scrappy, as a man he fought for every right he believed in, but I'll swear there wasn't a man or woman alive who could have wished him serious harm. Not one."

"Except his wife."

"Not even she. She shot at him from ten feet and missed him."

"Well." Wolfe sighed, and gulped another glass of beer. "I'm afraid I have nothing to thank you for, Doctor."

"I'm afraid not. Believe me, Mr. Wolfe, I'd help you if I could. It is curious, what is happening inside of me at this moment; I would never have suspected it. Now that I know Ellen is out of it, I am not sure I disapprove of the reward she offered. I might even increase it. Am I vindictive, too, then? For Pete, maybe; I think he might have been for me."

It was altogether a bum evening, as far as I was concerned. For the last ten minutes I was half asleep and didn't hear much. It was beginning to look to me as if Wolfe was going to have to develop a feeling for a new kind of phenomenon: murder by eeny-meeny-miny-mo. That was the only way that needle could have got into Barstow, since everybody was agreed that no one had wanted it there.

It was a bum evening, but I got a grin out of it at the end. Bradford had got up to go and walked toward Wolfe's chair to tell him good night. I saw him hesitating. He said, "There's a little thing on my mind, Mr. Wolfe. I—I owe you an apology. In my office this afternoon I made a remark to your man, a quite unnecessary remark, something about raking scandal out of graveyards—"

"But I don't understand. Apology?" Wolfe's quiet bewilderment was grand. "What had your remark to do with me?"

Of course Bradford's only out was the door.

After seeing the distinguished old gentleman to the entrance and sliding the night bolt in, I went to the kitchen for a glass of milk on my way back to the office. Fritz was there and I told him he had wasted enough good port for one evening, he might as well shut up shop. In the office Wolfe was leaning back in his chair with his eyes shut. I sat down and sipped away at the milk. When it was all gone I was pretty well bored and began talking just for practice.

"It's like this, ladies and gentlemen. The problem is to discover what the devil good it does you to use up a million dollars' worth of genius feeling the phenomenon of a poison needle in a man's belly if it turns out that nobody put it there. Put it this way: if a thing gets where no one wants it, what happened? Or this way: since the golf bag was in the Barstow home for the twenty-four hours preceding the killing, how about finding out if one of the servants has got funnier ideas even than Mrs. Barstow? Of course, according to Sarah's information there's no chance of it, and another objection is that it doesn't appeal to me. Lord, how I hate tackling a bunch of servants. So I guess I'll drop in on the Barstows in the morning and go to it. It looks like it's either that or quit and kiss the fifty grand good-bye. This case is a lulu all right. We're right where we started. I wouldn't mind so much if there was anyone to help me out on it, if only I didn't have to do all the thinking and planning for myself, in addition to running around day after day and getting nowhere—"

"Continue, Archie." But Wolfe didn't open his eyes.

"I can't, I'm too disgusted. Do you know something? We're licked. This poison needle person is a better man than

we are. Oh, we'll go on for a few days fooling around with
servants and trying to find out who put the ad in the paper for
the metal-worker and so on, but we're licked as sure as you're
full of beer."

His eyes opened. "I'm going to cut down to five quarts a
day. Twelve bottles. A bottle doesn't hold a pint. I am now
going to bed." He began the accustomed preparations for
rising from his chair. He got up. "By the way, Archie, could
you get out fairly early in the morning? You might reach the
Green Meadow Club before the caddies depart with their
babies. That is the only slang epithet you have brought me
recently which seems to me entirely apt. Perhaps you could
also kidnap the two who are attending school. It would be
convenient if all four of them were here at eleven. Tell Fritz
there will be guests at lunch. What do boys of that age eat?"

"They eat everything."

"Tell Fritz to have that."

As soon as I had made sure that he could still get into the
elevator, I went on upstairs and set my alarm for six o'clock
and hit the hay.

In the morning, rolling north along the Parkway again, I
wasn't singing at the sunshine. I was always glad to be doing
something, but I was not so liable to burst from joy when I
suspected that my activity was going to turn out to be nothing
but discarding from a bum hand. I didn't need anybody to tell
me that Nero Wolfe was a wonder, but I knew this gathering in
the caddies was just a wild stab, and I wasn't hopeful. As a
matter of fact, it seemed to me more likely than ever that we
were licked, because if this was the best Wolfe could do—

It was a motor cop. With the northbound half of the
Parkway empty at that hour of the morning I had been going
something above fifty without noticing, and this bicycle Cos-
sack waved me over. I pulled alongside the curb and stopped.
He asked for my license and I handed it to him, and he got out
his book of tickets.

I said, "Sure I was going too fast. It may not interest you, I
don't know, but I'm headed for Anderson's office in White
Plains—the District Attorney—with some dope on the Barstow case. He's in a hurry for it."

The cop just had his pencil ready. "Got a badge?"

I handed him one of my cards. "I'm private. It was my
boss, Nero Wolfe, that started the party."

He handed the card and the license back. "All right, but
don't begin jumping over fences."

I felt better after that. Maybe luck was headed our way
after all.

I got the two caddies at the club without any trouble, but
it took over an hour to round up the other two. They went to
different schools, and while one of them didn't need any
persuading to go for a ride to New York, the other one must
have been trying to qualify for teacher's pet or a Rhodes
scholarship. At first I kidded him, and when that didn't work I
switched to the ends of justice and the duties of a good citizen.
That got him, and the woman in charge of the school, too. I
suspected I wouldn't care an awful lot for his companionship,
so I put him and another one in the rumble seat, and with the
other two in with me I found the trail back to the Parkway and
turned south. I kept the speedometer down to forty thence-
forth, for I knew I couldn't expect Anderson to do me nothing
but favors.

We arrived at a quarter to eleven, and I took the boys to
the kitchen and fed them sandwiches, for the lunch hour was
one. I wanted to take them up and show them the orchids,
thinking it wouldn't hurt them any to get impressed, but there
wasn't time. I got their names and addresses down. One of
them, the pale skinny kid who had caddied for Manuel
Kimball, had a dirty face and I took him to the bathroom for a
wash. By the time Wolfe appeared I was beginning to feel like
a boy scout leader.

I had them arranged on chairs in a row for him. He came
in with a bunch of Cymbidiums in his hand which he put into a
vase on his desk, then he got into his chair and flipped the
mail. He had told the boys good morning as he entered; now
he turned and settled himself comfortably and looked them
over one by one. They were embarrassed and shifted around.

"Excuse me, Archie. Bad staging." He turned to the boy
at the end, one with red hair and blue eyes. "Your name, sir?"

"William A. Riley."

"Thank you. If you will move your chair over there, near
the wall—much better.—And your name?" When he had got
all their names and scattered them around he said, "Which one
of you expressed doubt that Peter Oliver Barstow was killed
by a needle shot from the handle of a golf driver?—Come, I'm
only trying to get acquainted; which one?"

Chunky Mike spoke up. "That was me."

"Ah. Michael Allen. Michael, you are young. You have learned to accept the commonplace, you must yet learn not to exclude the bizarre.—Now, boys, I'm going to tell you a story. Please listen, because I want you to understand it. This happens to be a true story. There was a meeting in a public hall of a hundred psychologists. A psychologist is—by courtesy —a man trained to observe. It had been arranged, without their knowledge, that a man should run into the hall and down the aisle, followed by another man waving a pistol. A third man ran in by another door. The second man shot at the first man. The third man knocked the second man down and took the pistol from him. They all ran out by different doors. One of the psychologists then arose and stilled the clamor, and announced that the events had been prearranged, and asked each of his colleagues to write down immediately a complete detailed report of the whole affair. They did so, and the reports were examined and compared. Not one was entirely correct. No two agreed throughout. One even had the third man shooting at the first man."

Wolfe stopped and looked around at them. "That's all. I'm not a good story-teller, but you may have caught the point. Do you see what I'm getting at?"

They nodded.

"You do. Then I shall not insult your intelligence with an exposition. Let us go on to our own story. We shall sit here and discuss the death of Peter Oliver Barstow, more particularly the events on the first tee which led up to it. At one o'clock we shall have lunch, then we shall return here and resume. We shall discuss all afternoon, many hours. You will get tired, but not hungry. If you get sleepy you may take a nap. I state the program thus in full so that you may know how elaborate and difficult an undertaking confronts us. Mr. Goodwin has heard two of your stereotypes; I fancy the other two are practically identical. A stereotype is something fixed, something that harbors no intention of changing. I don't expect you boys to change your stories of what happened on that first tee; what I ask is that you forget all your arguments and discussions, all your recitals to families and friends, all the pictures that words have printed on your brains, and return to the scene itself. That is vitally important. I would have left my house and journeyed to the scene myself to be with you there, but for the fact that interruptions would have ruined our efforts. By our imaginations we must transfer the scene here. Here we are, boys, at the first tee.

"Here we are. It is Sunday afternoon. Larry Barstow has engaged two of you; two of you are with the Kimballs, carrying their bags. You are on familiar ground, as familiar to you as the rooms of your own homes. You are occupied with activities so accustomed as to have become almost automatic. The straps of the bags are on your shoulders. You, Michael Allen, when you see Mr. Barstow, your last season's baby, at a distance from the tee practicing with a mashie, you do not need to be told what to do; you join him, pick up his bag, hand him a club perhaps—"

Mike was shaking his head.

"No? What do you do?"

"I begin chasing balls."

"Ah. The balls he was hitting with the mashie."

"Yes, sir."

"Good. What were you doing, William Riley, while Michael was chasing balls?"

"I was chewing gum."

"Exclusively? I mean, was that the utmost of your efforts?"

"Well, I was standing holding old Kimball's bag."

Listening to him start, I was thinking that Wolfe's long words would get the kids so tied up that pretty soon they would just go dead on him, but it worked the other way. Without telling them so he had given them the feeling that he was counting on them to help him show how dumb the hundred psychologists had been, and they weren't going to get licked at it because it took long words to do it.

He went along inch by inch, now with this boy, now with that, sometimes with all of them talking at once. He let them get into a long discussion of the relative merits of various brands of clubs, and sat with his eyes half closed pretending he enjoyed it. He questioned them for half an hour regarding the identities and characteristics of the other caddies and golfers present, those belonging to the matches which immediately preceded the Barstow foursome at the tee. Every time one of the boys bolted ahead to the actual teeing off Wolfe called him back. Among all the irrelevancies I could see one thing, perhaps the main thing, he was doing: he wasn't losing sight for a single instant of each and every club in each and every bag.

For lunch Fritz gave us two enormous chicken pies and four watermelons. I did the serving, as usual when there was company, and by speeding up with my knife and fork I barely managed to get my own meal in by the time the casseroles were empty. The watermelons were simple; I gave a half to each of the boys and the same for Wolfe and myself, and that left one for Fritz. I suspected he wouldn't touch it but thought there might be use for it later on.

After lunch we resumed where we had left off. It was wonderful the way Wolfe had long since opened those boys' minds up and let the air in. They went right ahead. They had forgotten entirely that someone was trying to get something out of them or that they were supposed to be using their memories; they were just like a bunch of kids talking over the ball game they had played the day before, only Wolfe was on top of them every minute not letting them skip a thing and all the time making them go back, and back again. Even so they were making progress. Larry Barstow had made his drive, and Manuel Kimball had made his.

When the break came it was so simple and natural, and went along so easy with all the rest of it, that for a minute I didn't realize what was happening. Wolfe was saying to Chunky Mike:

"Then you handed Barstow his driver. Did you tee up his ball?"

"Yes, sir.—No—I couldn't, because I was over hunting a ball he had put in the rough with his mashie."

"Exactly, Michael, you told us before you were hunting a ball. I wondered then how you could have teed up for Barstow."

William Riley spoke. "He teed up himself. The ball rolled off and I fixed it for him."

"Thank you, William.—So you see, Michael, you did not tee up for him. Wasn't the heavy golf bag a nuisance while you were hunting the lost ball?"

"Naw, we get used to it."

"Did you find the ball?"

"Yes, sir."

"What did you do with it?"

"Put it in the ball pocket."

"Do you state that as a fact or an assumption?"

"I put it in. I remember."

"Right away?"

"Yes, sir."

"Then you must have had the bag with you while you were hunting the ball. In that case, you could not have handed Barstow his driver when he teed off, because you weren't there. He could not have removed it from the bag himself, because the bag wasn't there. Had you perhaps handed him the driver previously?"

"Sure. I must have."

"Michael! We need something much better than *must have*. You did or you didn't. Remember that you are supposed to have told us—"

William Riley butted in: "Hey! Mike, that's why he borrowed old Kimball's driver, because you were off looking for the ball."

"Ah." Wolfe shut his eyes for a tenth of a second and then opened them again. "William, it is unnecessary to shout. Who borrowed Mr. Kimball's driver?"

"Barstow did."

"What makes you think so?"

"I don't think so, I know. I had it out ready to hand to old Kimball, and Barstow's ball rolled off his tee and I fixed it for him, and when I stood up old Kimball was saying to Barstow, 'Use mine,' and Barstow reached out and I handed old Kimball's driver to him."

"And he used it?"

"Sure. He drove right away. Mike didn't come back with the bag until after old Kimball had drove too."

I was having all I could do to stay in my chair. I wanted to do a dance like *Spring on the Mountaintop* that I'd seen in the movies, and pin a bunch of orchids on William Riley, and throw my arms halfway around Wolfe which was as far as they would go. I was afraid to look at Wolfe for fear I would grin so hard and wide I'd burst my jaw.

He was after the pale skinny kid and the one that wanted to be a good citizen, but neither of them remembered anything about Barstow borrowing the driver. The skinny one said he had his eyes glued far out on the fairway, spotting the place where Manuel Kimball had pulled his drive into the bushes, and the good citizen just didn't remember. Wolfe turned to Chunky Mike. Mike could not say positively that Barstow's driver had been in the bag when he had had it with him hunting the ball, but he could not remember handing it to Barstow, and he could not remember receiving it back and returning it to the bag. During all this William Riley was straining his politeness to keep still. Finally Wolfe got back to him:

"Excuse me, William. Do not think I doubt your memory or your fidelity to truth. Corroboration is always helpful. And it might be thought a little curious that you had forgotten so informing a detail."

The boy protested, "I hadn't forgotten it, I just didn't happen to think of it."

"You mean that you have not included that incident in any of your recitals to your friends?"

"Yes, sir."

"Good, William. I put my question badly, but I see that you have the intelligence to stick to the main clause. Possibly you mentioned the incident to Mr. Anderson?"

The boy shook his head. "I haven't seen Mr. Anderson. The detective came and asked me a few questions, not much."

"I see." Wolfe sighed, deep and long, and pushed the button. "It is tea time, messieurs."

Of course for Wolfe that meant beer. I got up and collected the boys and herded them into the kitchen; sure enough, the watermelon was intact. I cut it into four quarters and passed it around. Fritz, having been to answer Wolf's bell, was arranging a glass and two bottles on a tray; but as he went down the hall I noticed that he turned toward the stairs instead of the office. I glanced at my wrist. It was two minutes to four. The son-of-a-gun had saved his schedule! I left the boys with the melon and hurried out and caught him on his way to the elevator. He said:

"Give the boys my thanks, pay them adequately but not generously, for I am not a generous man, and take them home. Before you leave, telephone the office of E. D. Kimball and learn when he is expected to return from Chicago. He is probably still alive, since he had either the shrewdness or the luck to remove himself a thousand miles from his destiny. If by any chance he has returned get him here at once; on that there must be no delay."

"Yes, sir. And don't you think that if this news got to Mr. Anderson it would only confuse and upset him? Hadn't I better try to persuade the boys to keep it in the family?"

"No, Archie. It is always wiser, where there is a choice, to trust to inertia. It is the greatest force in the world."

When I got back to the kitchen Fritz was cutting an apple pie.

Chapter 13

After I had finished delivering the caddies here and there all over Westchester, I certainly would have loved to run over to Kimball's place and say to Manuel, "Would you mind telling me whether your father keeps his golf bag in his locker at the club and whether you have a key to it?" I had an idea he would recognize that as a question that couldn't be answered just by lifting his eyebrows. I already had him down for two thousand volts. But I realized that if it was him we had a big advantage in his ignorance of what we had found out, and I also realized that if I expected Manuel Kimball to be arrested and convicted of murder there would have to be a little more evidence than the fact that he made me nervous.

I had another temptation, to stop in at Anderson's office and offer to bet him ten thousand dollars that nobody had murdered Peter Oliver Barstow. Wolfe had certainly started a game of hide-and-seek. For two days he and I had been the only two people alive, except the man that did it, who knew that Barstow had been murdered; now we were the only two, with the same exception and the caddies, who knew that he had been killed by accident.

I did go to the Green Meadow Club, after getting the last caddy delivered; it was close by. I went intending to go into the locker question a little, but after I arrived I got cold feet. It might ruin everything if it became known that we had the faintest interest in lockers, since it was common knowledge that Barstow's bag had never been in his. So I just had a little talk with the caddy master and said hello to the chief steward. Maybe I was hoping to get another eyeful of Manuel Kimball, but I didn't see him anywhere.

E. D. Kimball, as his son had told me, had a grain

brokerage office on Pearl Street. When I had telephoned there a little after four o'clock I had been told that Kimball was expected back from Chicago the next day, Friday, on the Century. If it hadn't been for that I think I would have tried to start something there in Westchester that evening, if it had been nothing more than to wait till dark and sneak over to the Kimball place and peek in at the windows; but with Kimball on the way there was nothing to do but wait. I went on home.

After dinner that evening Wolfe had me take my notebook and read to him again about my visit to Manuel Kimball, also everything that Sarah and Larry Barstow had said about him, though that wasn't much. We had a general discussion and got our minds to fit; we even considered the possibility that the lending of the driver had been planned and that old Kimball had murdered Barstow, but of course that was out, that was nothing but drivel. I took a few cracks at Manuel, but when Wolfe put it up to me seriously I had to say that not only was there no evidence against Manuel, there wasn't even any reason to suspect him. As far as I knew, it was no more likely to be him than any other member of the Green Meadow Club who had had opportunity to get at the Kimball locker.

"All the same," I insisted, "if he was my son I'd send him on a trip around the world and build a fence across the Pacific Ocean so he couldn't get through."

Before we went to bed Wolfe outlined again my program for the following day. I didn't care much for the first number on it, but of course he was right; the caddies were sure to talk, and the talk would get to Anderson, and it wouldn't hurt us any to get there first since the information was certain to reach him anyhow. I could perform that errand of mercy and still get to Kimball's office almost as soon as he arrived from Grand Central.

So early the next morning found me in the roadster bound for White Plains again. I was hoping the same motor cop would trip me up, it would have been so neat, since I could have handed him the same yarn as the day before and maybe this time have had the pleasure of an escort to the courthouse. But I made it from Woodlawn to the Main Street bridge without seeing anything more exciting than a squirrel running up a tree.

I was creeping along Main Street behind three lumbering buses like a pony following the elephants in a circus parade, when an idea struck me. I liked it. Wolfe seemed to have the notion that all he needed to do to have anybody call at his office from the Dalai Lama to Al Capone was to tell me to go and get him, but I knew from long experience that you never knew when you were going to run up against someone with as many feet as a centipede and all of them reluctant. And here was I, not only supposed to haul a prominent grain broker out of his office immediately upon his return from a week's absence, but also headed for a revelation to the District Attorney that would probably result in my having the pleasure of meeting H. R. Corbett or some other flatfooted myrmidon in the anteroom of E. D. Kimball's office—and wouldn't that have been nice? So I parked the roadster in the first available spot and went to a telephone, and called up Wolfe and told him we were putting the soup before the cocktail. He was a little stubborn and gave me an argument, because he was full of the idea that it would pay us to hand Anderson something before he inevitably got hold of it himself, but when he saw that I intended to go on talking right up to a dollar's worth he said all right, I could return to New York and proceed to Pearl Street and wait for my victim.

On the way back I reflected that it was just as well the motor cop hadn't favored me with his attention after all.

When I got to the number on Pearl Street and left the elevator at the tenth floor, I discovered that E. D. Kimball & Company wasn't only selling chicken feed to backyard poultry kings. It had a suite that took up half the floor, with its name on doors everywhere and a double one covered with the names of exchanges all over the country for an entrance. The clock on the wall said a quarter to ten; if the Century was on time it was already at Grand Central, and Kimball might be expected in fifteen or twenty minutes.

I spoke to a girl at a desk, and after using the telephone she took me to an inside room and left me with a square-jawed guy who had his feet on the window sill looking at the morning paper. He said, "Just a minute," and I sat down. After a little he threw the paper on his desk and turned around.

"Mr. E. D. Kimball will be here pretty soon," I said. "I know he'll be busy catching up with the week he's been away. But before he gets started on that I need ten minutes with him on an urgent personal matter. I'm a private detective; here's my card. He never heard of me; I work for Nero Wolfe. Can you fix it for me?"

"What do you want? Tell me what you want."

I shook my head. "It really is personal, and it's damn urgent. You'll just have to trust my honest young face. If you think it's a racket phone the Metropolitan Trust Company at Thirty-fourth Street. They'll tell you that I make a little change in my spare time tending baby carriages."

Square jaws grinned. "I don't know. Mr. Kimball has a dozen appointments, the first one is ten-thirty. I'm his secretary, I know more about his business than he does. You'd better tell me."

"I'm sorry, it has to be him."

"All right, I'll see what I can do. Go on out front—no, wait here. Want to look at the paper?"

He tossed me the paper and got up and gathered some mail and stuff together and left the room with them. At a quick early breakfast I had taken a glance at the front page but hadn't had time for more. Turning through, I saw that the Barstow case was already back to page seven, and not much of it there. Anderson was saying that "progress was being made in the investigation." Dear old progress, I thought, you haven't changed a bit since I saw you last except you're covered with wrinkles and your teeth are falling out. The coroner had nothing definite on the poison, but soon would have. There had never been, in any paper that I had seen, any hint of a suspicion that it was a family job; and now, I thought, there never would be. But this piece took another little crack at Dr. Bradford, and I knew it would be a long time before he would be able to look coronary thrombosis in the face without swallowing hard. I turned to the sports page.

The door opened, and the secretary was there.

"Mr. Goodwin. This way."

In the next room but one, a big room with windows on two sides, a lot of old furniture and a ticker going in a corner, a man sat at a desk. He was smooth-shaven, his hair was turning gray, and while he wasn't fat there was size to him. He looked worried but amused, as if someone had just told him a funny story but he had a toothache. I wondered whether it was the worry or the amusement that came from what the secretary had told him about me, but found out on acquaintance that it was neither one, he always looked that way.

The secretary said, "This is the man, Mr. Kimball."

Kimball grunted and asked me what I wanted. I said that my business was strictly personal. Kimball said, "In that case you'd better take it up with my secretary so I won't have the bother of turning it over to him." He laughed and the secretary smiled and I grinned.

I said, "I only asked for ten minutes, so if you don't mind I'll get started. Nero Wolfe would like to have you call at his office this morning at eleven o'clock."

"Goodness gracious!" The amusement was on top. "Is Nero Wolfe the King of England or something?"

I nodded. "Something. I'll tell you, Mr. Kimball, you'll get this quicker and easier if you let me do it my own way. Just humor me. On Sunday, June fourth, Peter Oliver Barstow died suddenly while he was playing golf with his son and you and your son. On Thursday the eighth you left for Chicago. On Sunday the eleventh the results of an autopsy were announced. I suppose it was in the Chicago papers?"

"Oh, that's it." The worry had ascended. "I knew that would be a nuisance when I got back. I read a lot of poppycock about poison and a needle and whatnot." He turned to his secretary. "Blaine, didn't I write you this would be a nuisance when I returned?"

The secretary nodded. "Yes, sir. You have an appointment at eleven-thirty with a representative of the Westchester District Attorney. I hadn't had time to mention it."

I kept my grin inside. "It's not poppycock, Mr. Kimball. Barstow was killed by a poisoned needle shot out of the handle of a golf driver. That's wrapped up. Now come with me a minute. Here you are at the first tee, ready to shoot. All four of you with your caddies.— No, don't wander off somewhere, stay with me, this is serious. Here you are. Larry Barstow drives. Your son Manuel drives. Peter Oliver Barstow is ready to drive; you are standing near him; remember? His ball rolls off its tee and your caddy fixes it because his caddy is off hunting a ball. Remember? He is ready to drive but hasn't got his driver because his caddy is off with his bag. You say, 'Use mine,' and your caddy straightens up from fixing his ball and hands him your driver. Remember? He drives with your driver, and then jumps and begins rubbing his belly because a wasp stung him. It was that wasp that came out of your driver that killed him. Twenty minutes later he was dead."

Kimball was listening to me with a frown, with the worry and amusement both gone. He went on frowning. When he finally spoke all he said was, "Poppycock."

"No," I said. "You can't make it poppycock just by

pronouncing it. Anyway, poppycock or not, it was your driver Barstow used on the first tee. You remember that?"

He nodded. "I do. I hadn't thought of it, but now that you remind me I recall the scene perfectly. It was just as you—"

"Mr. Kimball!" The secretary was secretarying. "It would be better perhaps if you—that is, upon reflection—"

"Better if I what? —Oh. No, Blaine. I knew this would be a nuisance, I knew it very well. Certainly Barstow used my driver. Why shouldn't I say so? I barely knew Barstow. Of course the poisoned needle story is a lot of poppycock, but that won't keep it from being a nuisance."

"It'll be worse than a nuisance, Mr. Kimball." I hitched my chair toward him. "Look here. The police don't know yet that Barstow used your driver. The District Attorney doesn't know it. I'm not suggesting that you hide anything from them, they'll find it out anyway. But whether you think the poisoned needle is poppycock or not, they don't. They know that Barstow was killed by a needle that came out of his driver on the first tee, and when they find out that it was your driver he used, what are they going to do? They won't arrest you for murder just like that, but they'll have you looking in the dictionary for a better word than nuisance. My advice is, see Nero Wolfe. Take your lawyer along if you want to, but see him quick."

Kimball was pulling at his lip. He let his hand fall. At length he said, "Goodness gracious."

"Yes, sir, all of that."

He looked at his secretary. "You know, Blaine, I have no respect for lawyers."

"No, sir."

Kimball got up. "This is a fine to-do. I have told you before, Blaine, that there is just one thing in the world I am good at. Trading. I am a good trader, and that is surprising when you consider how soft I am really. Soft-hearted. With the more personal aspects of life I do not know how to deal." He was moving back and forth behind his desk. "Yes, this appears to be more than a nuisance. Goodness gracious. What would you do, Blaine?"

I glared at the secretary. He hesitated. "If you care to go to see this Nero Wolfe, I could go with you. If I were you I would take a lawyer."

"What appointments have I?"

"The usual sort of thing, nothing important. At eleven-thirty the man from the Westchester District Attorney."

"Oh, I would miss him. Well, tell him anything. How's the ticker?"

"Firm at the opening. Cotton easing off."

Kimball turned to me. "Where is this Nero Wolfe? Bring him here."

"Impossible, Mr. Kimball. He is—" But Wolfe had once found out that I had told a man he was infirm, and I didn't want that to happen again. "He is an eccentric genius. It's only up on Thirty-fifth Street. I've got my car down below and I'd be glad to run you up."

Kimball said, "I've only met one genius in my life; he was an Argentine cowboy. A *gaucho*. All right. Wait for me in the front office."

Back in the front room I had first entered, I sat on the edge of a chair. Meeting E. D. Kimball and looking at him and talking with him had somehow cleared my mind. I saw plainly what I should have realized the night before, that the minute it came out that it was Kimball's driver that had been turned into what Wolfe called a lethal toy, and the minute Kimball himself arrived on the scene, we were probably turning into the home-stretch. It was the same as if you found a man murdered and by some kind of hocus-pocus were able to bring him back to life long enough to ask him who killed him, and get his answer. That's what E. D. Kimball was, a man who had been murdered and was still living. I had to get him up to Wolfe's place and lock the door, and get him there quick, before Corbett got a chance at him—or, as far as that was concerned, anyone else. Anyone at all. How did I know but what it was the secretary, Square-jaw Blaine, who had had that driver made and found opportunity to get it into Kimball's bag? At that moment, as I sat there on the edge of the chair, Blaine might be sticking a knife into Kimball as he had into Carlo Maffei. . . .

It was ten-fifty. I got up and began walking up and down the linoleum. Anderson's man—I was sure it would be Corbett—was due at half past eleven, and he might take it into his thick head to come early and wait. I had just decided to ask the girl at the desk to phone into Blaine for me, when the inner door opened and Kimball appeared with his hat on. I was pretty glad to see him. He nodded at me and I jumped to the entrance door to open it for him.

As we got into the elevator I observed, "Mr. Blaine isn't coming."

Kimball shook his head. "He's needed here more than I need him. I like your face. I find I usually do like a man's face, and it pays every time. Trust is one of the finest things in the world, trust in your fellow man."

Yes, I thought to myself, I'll bet a successful trader like you can use up lots of trust.

It was only half a block to where I had parked the roadster. I cut across as far west as I could get to avoid the traffic, and it was still short of eleven-fifteen when I was ushering Kimball in ahead of me at Wolfe's door.

I took Kimball to the front room and asked him to wait there a minute, then returned to the entrance and made sure the latch was caught. Then I went to the kitchen. Fritz was making cherry tarts; a pan was just out of the oven and I nabbed one and stuffed it in and darned near burned my tongue off. I told Fritz, "One guest for lunch and don't put any poison in it. And be careful who you let in; if there's any doubt, call me."

In the office, Wolfe was at his desk. As soon as I saw him I stopped, exasperated, for he was cleaning house. He had only one drawer in his desk, a wide shallow one in the middle, and since he had begun having his beer in bottles instead of brought up from the basement in a pitcher, he had formed the habit, every time he opened a bottle, of pulling the drawer out and dropping the bottle cap in there. Fritz wasn't supposed to open any drawers in the office, and I knew Wolfe had some sort of a nutty notion that he was saving the bottle caps for something so I had let them alone. Now, when I entered, he had the drawer half out and was scattering the caps all over the desk, arranging them in piles.

I said, "Mr. E. D. Kimball is in the front room. Do you want him to come in and help you?"

"The devil." Wolfe looked around at his piles, and at me helplessly. He sighed. "Can't he wait a while?"

"Of course, sure. How would next week do?"

He sighed again. "Confound it. Bring him in."

"With that junk scattered all over the desk?—Oh, all right, I told him you're eccentric." I had kept my voice lowered; now I lowered it some more to let him know how Kimball had shaped up and what I had said to him. He nodded, and I went to get Kimball.

Kimball had his worried-amused look back on again. I introduced him and pulled a chair around for him, and after they had exchanged a few words I said to Wolfe, "If you won't need me, sir, I'll get on to those reports." He nodded, and I got fixed at my desk with papers all around and half underneath a pad which I used for a notebook on such occasions. I had got my signs so abbreviated that I could get down every word of some pretty fast talk and still give the impression to a careless eye that I was just shuffling around looking for last week's delicatessen bill.

Wolfe was saying, "You are perfectly correct, Mr. Kimball. A man's time is his own only by sufferance. There are many ways in which he may be dispossessed: flood, famine, war, marriage—not to speak of death, which is the most satisfactory of all because it closes the question finally."

"Goodness gracious." Kimball was fidgety. "I do not see why that should make it satisfactory."

"You came very near finding out, a week ago last Sunday." Wolfe wiggled a finger at him. "You are a busy man, Mr. Kimball, and you have just returned to your office after a week's absence. Why, under those circumstances, did you take time this morning to come to see me?"

Kimball stared at him. "That's what I want you to tell me."

"Good. You came because you were confused. That is not a desirable condition for a man in the extreme of danger, as you are. I see no indication in your face of alarm or fear, merely confusion. That is astonishing, knowing as I do what Mr. Goodwin has told you. He has informed you that on June fourth, twelve days ago, it was nothing but inadvertence that killed Peter Oliver Barstow, and the same inadvertence saved your life. You met his statement with incredulity, crudely expressed. Why?"

"Because it's nonsense." Kimball was impatient. "Rubbish."

"Before, you said poppycock. Why?"

"Because it is. I didn't come here to argue about that. If the police get into difficulties trying to explain something they don't happen to understand and want to make up any sort of a fancy tale to cover themselves, that's all right, I believe in letting every man handle his own business his own way, but they don't need to expect me to take any stock in it, and they can leave me out of it. I'm a busy man with something better to do. You're wrong, Mr. Wolfe, I didn't come to see you because I was confused, and I certainly didn't come to give you a chance to try to scare me. I came because the police apparently are trying to mix me up in a fancy tale that might give me a lot of trouble and publicity I don't want, and your man gave me to understand you could show me how to avoid it. If you can, go ahead and I'll pay you for it. If you can't, say so, and I'll find better advice."

"Well." Wolfe leaned back in his chair and let his half-shut eyes study the broker's face. Finally he shook his head. "I'm afraid I can't show you how to escape trouble, Mr. Kimball. I might with good fortune show you how to escape death. Even that is uncertain."

"I have never expected to escape death."

"Do not quibble. I mean of course unpleasant and imminent death. I shall be frank with you, sir. If I do not at once bid you good day and let you depart on your business, it is not because of my certain knowledge that you are confronting death like a fool. I refrain from contributing to certain Christian enterprises because I think that no man should be saved by coercion. But here I am guided by self-interest. Mrs. Barstow has offered a reward of fifty thousand dollars for the discovery of her husband's murderer. I intend to discover him; and to do so I need only learn who it was that tried to kill you on June fourth and will proceed to do so within a reasonable time if means are not found of preventing him. If you will help me, it will be convenient for both of us; if you will not, it may well be that only through some misstep or mischance in his successful second attempt shall I be able to bring him to account for his abortive first one. Naturally it would be all the same to me."

Kimball shook his head. But he didn't get up; instead, he was settling into his chair. Still he showed no sign of alarm, he merely looked interested. He said, "You're a good talker, Mr. Wolfe. I don't think you're going to be of any use to me, since you seem to like fancy tales as well as the police, but you're a good talker."

"Thank you. You like good talking?"

Kimball nodded. "I like everything good. Good talking, and good trading, and good manners, and good living. I don't mean high living, I mean good. I've tried to live a good life myself, and I like to think everyone else does. I know some can't, but I think they try to. I was thinking of that in the car a little while ago, riding up here with your man. I'm not saying that the tale he told me made no impression on me at all; of course it did. When I told him it was poppycock I meant it, and I still mean it, but nevertheless it got me thinking. What if somebody had tried to kill me? Who would it be?"

He paused, and Wolfe murmured at him, "Well, who would it be?"

"Nobody." Kimball was emphatic.

I thought to myself, if this guy turns out like Barstow, so lovable a mosquito wouldn't bite him, I'm through.

Wolfe said, "I once met a man who had killed two other men because he had been bettered in a horse trade."

Kimball laughed. "I'm glad he wasn't in grain. If his method of averaging down was universal I would have been killed not once, but a million times. I'm a good trader, it's the one thing I'm proud of. What I love is wheat. Of course what you love is a fancy tale and a good murder, and that's all right, that's your business. What I love is wheat. Do you know there are seven hundred million bushels of wheat in the world? And I know where every one of them is this minute. Every one."

"You probably own a hundred or so yourself."

"No, not one. I'm out. Tomorrow I'll be back in, or next week.—But I was saying, I'm a good trader. I've come out on top in a good many deals, but no one has any kick coming, I've stuck to the rules. That's what I was thinking on the way riding up here. I don't know all the details of this Barstow business, just what I've read in the papers. As I understand it, they haven't found the driver. I don't believe it ever existed. But even if they found it, and even if I did lend mine to Barstow on the first tee, I still would have a hard time believing anyone intended it for me. I've stuck to the rules and played fair, in my business and in my private life."

He paused. Wolfe murmured, "There are many kinds of injuries, Mr. Kimball. Real, fancied, material, spiritual, trivial, fatal—"

"I've never injured anyone."

"Really? Come now. The essence of sainthood is expiation. If you will permit it, take me. Whom have I not injured? I don't know why your presence should stimulate me to confession, but it does. Forget the Barstow murder, since to you it is poppycock; forget the police; we shall find means of preventing their becoming a nuisance to you. I enjoy talking with you; unless your affairs are really pressing. I would not keep you from anything urgent."

"You won't." Kimball looked pleased. "When anything's urgent I attend to it. The office has got along without me for a week; an hour more won't hurt them."

Wolfe nodded approvingly. "Will you have a glass of beer?"

"No, thanks. I don't drink."

"Ah." Wolfe pressed the button. "You're an extraordinary man, sir. You have learned to abstain, and you are at the same time a good business man and a philosopher.—One glass, Fritz.—But we were speaking of injuries, and I was hovering on confession. Whom have I not injured? That of course is rhetorical; I would not pose as a ruffian; and I suffer from a romantic conscience. Even so, making all allowances, it is not easy for me to understand why I am still alive. Less than a year ago a man sitting in the chair you now occupy promised to kill me at his earliest convenience. I had pulled the foundations of his existence from under him from purely mercenary motives. There is a woman living not twenty blocks from here, and a remarkably intelligent one, whose appetite and disposition would be vastly improved by news of my death. I could continue these examples almost to infinity. But there are others more difficult to confess and more impossible to condone.—Thank you, Fritz."

Wolfe removed the opener from the drawer and opened a bottle and dropped the cap into the drawer before he closed it again. Then he filled a glass and gulped it down. Kimball was saying, "Of course every man has to take the risks of his profession."

Wolfe nodded. "That's the philosopher in you again. It is easy to see, Mr. Kimball, that you are a cultured and an educated man. Perhaps you will understand the obscure psychology which prompts—well, me, for instance—to persist in an action which deserves unqualified condemnation. There is a woman under this roof at this moment, living on the top floor of this building, who cannot wish me dead only because her heart is closed to venom by its own sweetness. I torture her daily, hourly. I know I do and that knowledge tortures me; still I persist. You can guess at the obscurity of the psychology and the depth of the torture when I tell you that the woman is my mother."

I got it all down as he said it, and I almost glanced up at him in surprise, he said it so convincingly, with little emotion in his voice but the impression that the feeling underneath was

so overwhelming that it was kept down only by a determined
will. For a second he darned near had me feeling sorry for his
mother though it was I who, balancing the bank account each
month, checked off the debit item for his remittance to her at
her home in Budapest.

"Goodness gracious," Kimball said.

Wolfe downed another glass of beer and slowly shook his
head from side to side. "You will understand why I can recite a
category of injuries. I can justly claim familiarity."

It seemed to me that Kimball wasn't going to take the
hint. He was looking sympathetic and self-satisfied. In fact, he
smirked. "I'm wondering why you think I'm an educated
man."

Wolfe's eyebrows went up. "Isn't it obvious?"

"It's a compliment if you think so. I quit school—out in
Illinois—when I was twelve, and ran away from home. It
wasn't much of a home, with an uncle and aunt. My parents
were dead. I haven't been in a school since. If I'm educated
it's self-education."

"Not the worst kind." Wolfe's voice was low and quiet, not
much more than a murmur; the voice that he used to say "go
on" without saying it. "You are another proof of it, sir. And
New York is itself an education for a lad of that age if he had
spirit and character."

"Probably. It might be, but I didn't come to New York. I
went to Texas. After a year on the Panhandle, to Galveston,
and from there to Brazil and the Argentine."

"Indeed! You did have spirit; and your education is
cosmopolitan."

"Well, I covered a lot of territory. I was in South America
twenty years, mostly in the Argentine. When I came back to
the States I nearly had to go to school again to learn English.
I've lived—well, I've lived a lot of funny ways. I've seen a lot
of rough stuff and I've taken part in it, but wherever and
whatever it was I always did one thing, I always stuck to the
rules. When I came back to the States I was selling beef, but
gradually I worked into grain. That was where I found myself;
grain takes a man not afraid to guess and ready to ride his guess
the way a *gaucho* rides a horse."

"You were a *gaucho*?"

"No, I've always been a trader. It was born in me. Now I
wonder if you would believe this. Not that I'm ashamed of it;
sitting in my office sometimes, with a dozen markets waiting

to see which way I'm going to jump, I remember it and I'm proud of it. For two years I was a rope peddler."

"Not really."

"Yes. Three thousand miles a season in the saddle. I still show it when I walk."

Wolfe was looking at him admiringly. "A real nomad, Mr. Kimball. Of course you weren't married then."

"No. I married later, in Buenos Aires. I had an office then on the Avenida de Mayo—"

He stopped. Wolfe poured another glass of beer. Kimball was looking at him, but his eyes were following the movement without seeing it, for obviously the vision was inside. Something had pulled him up short and transported him to another scene.

Wolfe nodded at him and murmured, "A memory—I know—"

Kimball nodded back. "Yes—a memory. That's a funny thing. Goodness gracious. It might almost seem as if I had thought of that on account of what you said about injuries. The different kinds, fancied injuries. Fatal injuries. But this wasn't one at all, the only injury was to me. And it wasn't fancied. But I have a conscience too, as you said you have, only I don't think there's anything romantic about it."

"The injury was to you."

"Yes. One of the worst injuries a man can suffer. It was thirty years ago, and it's still painful. I married a girl, a beautiful Argentine girl, and we had a baby boy. The boy was only two years old when I came home from a trip a day too early and found my best friend in my bed. The boy was on the floor with his toys. I stuck to the rules; I've told myself a thousand times that if I had it to do over I'd do it again. I shot twice—"

Wolfe murmured, "You killed them."

"I did. The blood ran onto the floor and got on one of the toys. I left the boy there—I've often wondered why I didn't shoot him too, since I was sure he wasn't mine—and went to a café and got drunk. That was the last time I drank—"

"You came to the States—"

"A little later, a month later. There was no question of escaping, you don't have to run away from that in the Argentine, but I wound things up and left South America for good, and I've only been back once, four years ago."

"You brought the boy with you?"

"No. That's what I went back for. Naturally I didn't want
him, my wife's family took him. They lived out on the pampa,
that's where I got her from. The boy's name was Manuel, and
that had been my friend's name; I had suggested naming him
after my friend. I came back alone, and for twenty-six years I
lived alone, and I found the market a better wife than the one I
had tried. But I suppose there was a doubt in me all the time,
or maybe as a man gets older he softens up. Maybe I just got
lonely, or maybe I wanted to persuade myself that I really had
a son. Four years ago I got things in shape and went to Buenos
Aires. I found him right away. The family had gone broke
when he was young and they were mostly dead, and he had
had a hard time of it, but he had made good. When I found
him he was one of the best aviators in the Argentine army. I
had to persuade him to break away. For a while he tried my
office, but he wasn't cut out for it, and he's going into the
airplane business with my money. I bought a place up in
Westchester and built a new house on it, and I only hope when
he gets married he won't take any trips that end the way mine
did."

"Of course he knows—about his mother?"

"I don't think so. I don't know, it's never been mentioned.
I hope not. Not that I've got any remorse about it; if I had it to
do over I'd do it again. I don't pretend, even to him, that
Manuel is exactly the son I would want to get if I could just file
a buy order; after all, he's Argentine and I'm Illinois. But his
name's Kimball and he's got a head on him. He'll get an
American girl, I hope, and that will even it up."

"Indubitably." Wolfe had left his beer untasted so long
that the foam was gone, leaving it as still as tea. He reached for
the glass and gulped it. "Yes, Mr. Kimball, you proved your
point; the injury was to you. But you—let us say—took care of
it. If there was an injury to the boy you are repairing it
handsomely. Your confession is scarcely as damaging as mine;
I perforce admit culpability; as Mr. Goodwin would say, I have
no out. But if the boy feels the injury?"

"No."

"But if by chance he does?"

I saw Kimball's eyes fall. It was sometimes not easy to
meet Wolfe's eyes, but Kimball the trader should have been
impervious to any eye. He wasn't. He didn't try it again.
Abruptly he got up and, standing, said:

"He doesn't. I took no such advantage of your confession, Mr. Wolfe."

"You may, sir." Wolfe didn't stir. "You are welcome to all advantages. Why not be frank? There is no danger in me to the innocent." He looked at his watch. "In five minutes there will be lunch. Lunch with me. I do not pretend to be your friend, but certainly for you or yours I have no ill-will. Thirty years ago, Mr. Kimball, you faced a bitter disappointment and acted upon it with energy; have you lost your nerve? Let us see what might be done. Lunch with me."

But Kimball wouldn't. As a matter of fact, it seemed to me that for the first time he looked scared. He wanted to get away from there. I didn't quite get it.

Wolfe tried some more to persuade him to stay, but Kimball wasn't having any. He quit looking scared and got polite. He said goodness gracious, he had no idea it was so late, and that he was sorry Wolfe was able to suggest nothing to prevent the police from making a nuisance of themselves, and that he trusted Wolfe would consider their conversation confidential.

I went to the door with him. I offered to drive him back downtown, but he said no, he could get a taxi at the corner. From the stoop I watched him shoving off, and he was right, you could see he had been in a saddle enough to bend his knees out.

When I got back to the office Wolfe wasn't there, so I went on to the dining-room. He was getting himself set in front of his chair, with Fritz behind ready to push it. After he had got fixed I sat down. I had never known him to discuss business during a meal, but I was thinking that day he might. He didn't. However, he did violate a custom; ordinarily he loved to talk as he ate, leisurely and rambling on any subject that might happen to suggest itself, as much to himself as to me, I suspected, though I think I was always a good audience. That day he didn't say a word. In between his bites I could see his lips pushing out and pulling back again. He didn't even remember to commend Fritz for the dishes; so as Fritz cleared away for the coffee I tossed a wink at him and he nodded back with a solemn smile, as much as to say that he understood and would bear no grudge.

In the office after lunch Wolfe got into his chair, still silent. I straightened up the papers on my desk and removed from the pad the sheets that I had used and clipped them together. Then I sat down and waited for the spirit to move him. After a while he pulled a sigh that would have fed a blacksmith's bellows all afternoon, shoved his chair back so he could get the drawer of his desk open, and began raking the piles of bottle caps into the drawer. I watched him. When it was finished and the drawer shut he said:

"Mr. Kimball is an unhappy man, Archie."

I said, "He's a slicker."

"Perhaps. Nevertheless, unhappy. He is beset from many sides. His son wants to kill him, and intends to. But if Kimball admits that fact, even to himself, he is done for and he knows it. His son, and through his son the future Kimballs, are now all he has to live for. So he cannot admit it and will not. But if he doesn't admit it, and not only admit it but do something about it, again he is done for, for shortly he will die and probably in a thoroughly disagreeable manner. The dilemma is too much for him, and no wonder, for it has additional complications. He wants help, but he dares not ask for it. The reason he dares not ask for it is that like all mortal fools he hopes against all hope. What if—he does not admit this, but no man is so poor that he cannot afford a *what if*—what if his son did attempt to kill him and by mischance killed Barstow instead? Might the son not take that mischance as an omen? Might he not be persuaded—the father could even discuss it with him, man to man—might he not be persuaded to make a sensible trade with destiny and give his father's life for the one he has inadvertently taken? That way Kimball could live to see a grandchild on his knee. In the meantime, until that trade, which would be the most triumphant one of his career, could be consummated, there would be great and constant danger. It would be enough to frighten a younger and an honester man. But he dares not ask for help, for in doing so he would expose his son to a peril as great as the one that confronts himself. It is an admirable dilemma; I have rarely seen one with so many horns and all of them so sharp. It so confused Kimball that he did something which I suspect has been rare with him; he acted like a fool. He exposed his son without gaining any protection for himself. The facts behind the fear he blurted out; the fear itself he denied."

Wolfe stopped. He leaned back in his chair and let his chin fall and laced his fingers on his belly.

"Okay," I said. "Okay for Kimball. Now Manuel. I told you he made me nervous. But aside from that, shall I take the typewriter and make a list of all the swell proof we have that he killed Barstow?"

"Confound it." Wolfe sighed. "I know, the picture must be varnished. The can is empty, Archie. In fact, the can itself is gone. There is nothing."

I nodded. "If I may make a suggestion? There is a flying field at Armonk, which is only a few miles from Pleasantville. If I may drive up there and get curious?"

"You may. But I doubt if he used a public flying field. He would prefer privacy. So before you go, try this. Take this down."

"Long?"

"Very short."

I got a pad and pencil. Wolfe dictated:

Whoever saw me land in the pasture with my airplane Monday evening, June fifth, please communicate. Am winning a bet and will share.

I said, "Good. Swell. But it might have been a golf links."

Wolfe shook his head. "Still too public, and too much loud objection. Leave it pasture; it will have to be definite.—No, do not phone it. Stop at the *Times* office on your way uptown; leave it, and make sure the answers will reach us. Also—yes, the other papers, morning and evening, with similar proper arrangements. Manuel Kimball is ingenious enough to be annoying; should he see the advertisement it might occur to him to acquire the answers."

I got up. "All right, I'm off."

"Just a moment. Does White Plains come before Armonk?"

"Yes."

"Then on your way see Anderson. Tell him everything except Carlo Maffei and the Argentine. Present it to him; a fine gesture. Also tell him that E. D. Kimball is in imminent and constant danger and should have protection. Kimball of course will deny it and the precaution will be futile; nevertheless, when men undertake to meddle in the affairs of violent persons as you and I do, certain duties are assumed and should not be neglected."

I knew it had to be done, but I said, "I'd just as soon give Anderson a piece of information as tip a subway guard."

"Soon, now," Wolfe replied, "we may be in a position to send him a bill."

Chapter 14

What with stopping to put the ads in and the Friday afternoon summer traffic, by the time I got to the District Attorney's office in White Plains it was nearly four o'clock. I hadn't bothered to telephone ahead to see if Anderson or Derwin would be in because I had to go through White Plains anyhow to get to Armonk.

They were both there. The girl at the desk threw me a smile when I went up to her, and I liked that; when the time comes that they stop remembering you it means that your pan is losing its shine. Instead of asking my name or who I wanted to see, she nodded and pressed down a key on the switchboard. I said, "Who do you think I am, the prodigal son?" She said, "They'll kill you instead of the calf." After she had talked into the phone a couple of seconds one of the doors snapped open and Derwin came out.

He came up to me. "What do you want?"

I grinned. "This is hot. Can you get Ben Cook here in a hurry?" Because I didn't like fits I went right on, "I want to tell Mr. Anderson something. Or you, or both of you."

I never did find out, I don't know to this day, what that White Plains bunch thought they had been doing during the six days that had passed since the autopsy. There was a hint or two, of course; that Friday afternoon Anderson told me that Corbett had spent two days at Holland University. Probably they got hold of a rumor that there was a student there whom Barstow had kept in school an extra hour or some such sizzler. I know they hadn't come within a mile of anything warm. Though it was hard to believe, it was a fact that Anderson didn't even know that Barstow had been using a new bag of golf clubs that had been given to him by his wife as a birthday

present, until I told him. I only got one piece of news that
afternoon; a New York chemist had said definitely that Barstow's blood showed snake venom. It was that report that had
got Anderson and Derwin's minds off of golf clubs and
dwelling fondly on copperheads; and though I hate like the
devil to admit it, it gave me a few bad hours, too. Although it
left the needle unexplained, I had seen odder things than a
needle in a man's stomach accounted for by coincidence.
Copperheads were not unknown in Westchester; what if one
had been visiting the Green Meadow Club that Sunday and bit
Barstow? On the foot or anywhere. It was about good enough
for a headache. The snake venom report hadn't been given to
the newspapers, and it wasn't given to me until after Anderson
and Derwin had my tale, so it didn't cramp my style.

And of course even if the Green Meadow fairway had
been carpeted with copperheads a foot deep, Anderson and
Derwin couldn't get around the fact that Nero Wolfe had told
them exactly what the autopsy would show them.

Derwin took me into Anderson's room. Anderson was
there with another man, not a dick, he looked like a lawyer. I
sat down and hooked my panama on my knee.

Anderson said, "What's on your mind?"

I just simply didn't like that man. I couldn't even have any
fun with him, to speak of, because whatever it was disagreeable about him, his face and his manner, was so deep and
primitive that the only possible way to get any real satisfaction
would have been to haul off and plug him in the nose. Derwin
was different; he certainly wasn't my favorite uncle, but he
would take a lot of kidding.

I said, "Information from Nero Wolfe. Maybe you'd
better call a stenographer."

He had to pass a few remarks first, but I went patient and
forbearing on him. What was the use of thinking up a lot of
snappy comebacks when I couldn't use the one I wanted to? So
pretty soon he saw he wasn't getting anywhere, and called a
stenographer, and I spieled it off. I told about the birthday
present, and the whereabouts of Barstow's golf bag and who
had put it there, and the loan of Kimball's driver on the first
tee. I suggested that they find out all about Kimball's bag,
where he kept it and who had access to it, though I knew that
anyone approaching from that direction would never get
anywhere, for Manuel must have had any number of opportunities. Then I gave them Wolfe's message about protection

for Kimball. I made that strong. I said that Wolfe felt that the responsibility for the safety of a citizen whose life was in jeopardy was a burden for the authorities to assume, and that he would not be answerable, to himself or anyone else, for anything that might happen to E. D. Kimball at any moment.

When I got through Anderson asked questions, and some I answered and some I didn't. He kept it up quite a while, until finally I had to grin at him.

"Mr. Anderson," I said, "you're trying to lure me on."

He was smooth. "But not succeeding, Goodwin. I'll be frank with you. When the autopsy verified Wolfe's prediction, I thought he knew who did it. When the reward was offered and he didn't grab it, I knew he didn't know. We know everything you do now, and a lot more, except the one detail of how Wolfe came to make the prediction in the first place. I'd like to know that, though I don't believe it can be of much value since Wolfe doesn't get anywhere with it. All the same, you might tell me. I'll tell you anything and everything. For instance, this morning snake venom was identified in Barstow's blood."

"Thanks. That saves me the trouble of reading tonight's papers."

"The papers haven't got it. I can tell you a few other things too."

So he did; he mentioned Corbett's trip to the university and a lot of other junk, and wound it up with a lecture on copperheads. Wanting to get on to Armonk, and to be alone to see if the snake venom news sounded hollow when you dropped it on the sidewalk, I thanked him and got up and put on my hat, and he got sore. I didn't bother anymore; I reminded him about protecting E. D. Kimball, and walked out.

Since it was only a few miles out of the way and I didn't know how long it would take me at Armonk, I decided to drop in at the Barstows first. From a booth on Main Street I telephoned; Sarah Barstow was home. Twenty minutes later I was turning into their drive. The same guard was there, and when I stopped he gave me a look and nodded me on. Some people were on the front terrace having tea. I went to the side door, and Small took me to the sun-room at the back, only since it was afternoon the blinds were all up and the glass was in shadow. Small told me that Miss Barstow would join me shortly, and asked if I would have some tea.

I said, "You didn't think that up all alone."

Of course not a flicker. "Miss Barstow told me to offer you tea, sir."

"Sure. She would. A glass of milk would be nice."

In a minute he was back with the milk, and when it was about half gone Sarah Barstow came in. I had told her on the phone it was just a social call, nothing to worry about, and as I got up and looked at her coming toward me, natural and young and human, I thought to myself that if she ever started a clinic for broken hearts I'd be the first in line if I wasn't too busy. I said to her:

"You've had a nap since I saw you last."

She smiled. "I've slept forever. Sit down."

I took my chair and picked up my glass. "Thank you for the milk, Miss Barstow. It's swell milk, too. I'm sorry to call you away from your friends, but it won't take long. I've just been over at Mr. Anderson's office having a chat. I told him about the birthday present and about your night trip to the Tarrytown ferry.—Now wait a minute, you certainly are quick on the trigger. It don't mean a thing, it was just strategy, you know, what generals lose battles with. That junk is all out. There never was any phony driver in your father's bag, when your mother gave it to him or any other time. Nobody ever tried to kill him. He died by an accident."

She was staring at me. I waited to let her digest it. She said, "Then it wasn't murder at all— Nero Wolfe was wrong —but how—"

"I didn't say it wasn't murder. Wolfe wasn't wrong. The accident happened on the first tee. Your father's caddy was off with his bag, and your father borrowed E. D. Kimball's driver. It was that borrowed driver that did it. It was a rotten break, that's all. Nobody wanted to kill him."

She said, "My father—I knew my father—"

I nodded. "Yes, I guess you knew your father all right. That's all I wanted to tell you, Miss Barstow. I didn't like to phone it, because I don't know when Anderson will want to release it. So it's confidential. I didn't want you to find out from him what I had told him and maybe think I had double-crossed you. If he should be so curious that he begins asking you why you go around throwing golf bags in the river, in spite of the fact that that's all washed up, tell him to go to hell. That's why I told you that. The reason I told you about Kimball lending his driver was because I know it can't be any fun lying in bed wondering who murdered your father when you ought to be asleep. Nobody murdered him. But it would be okay to keep that in the family for a while." I got up. "That's all."

She sat still. She looked up at me. "Are you going? I think I'll sit here a little. Thank you, Mr. Goodwin.—You didn't finish your milk."

I picked up the glass and emptied it and went on out. I was thinking that even on a busy day I might find time to drop in at that clinic.

By the time I got to Armonk it was after six o'clock, but the sun was still high and a couple of planes were perched on the field and another one was just landing. There were signs all around, FLY $5, and TRY THE SKY, and other come-ons, painted on the fence and the walls of the wooden hangars. It wasn't much of a field as far as equipment was concerned, that is, it wasn't very elaborate, but the field itself was good-sized and well-kept and flat as a pancake. I parked the roadster off the highway and went through the gate alongside one of the hangars. There was no one around outside except the pilot and two passengers getting out of the plane that had just landed. I went along looking in the doors and in the third hangar found a couple of guys throwing pennies at a crack.

They straightened up and looked at me and I nodded.

"Hello." I grinned. "I hate to interrupt your game, but I'm looking for a map, a bound book of flying maps. Maybe that isn't the technical term for it, but I'm not a flyer."

One of them was just a kid. The other one, a little older, in a mechanic's uniform, shook his head.

"We don't sell maps."

"I don't mean I want to buy one. I'm looking for one, bound in red leather, that my brother left here a week ago Monday. June fifth, it was. You probably remember. He knew I was coming past here today on my way to the Berkshires and asked me to stop and get it. He landed here at your field, in his private plane, around six o'clock that evening, and took off again around ten. He's pretty sure he must have left the map here somewhere."

The mechanic was shaking his head. "He didn't land at this field."

I was surprised. "What? Of course he did. He ought to know what field he landed at."

"Maybe he ought to, but he don't, not if he says he landed

here. There's been no machine here except ours for over a month, except a biplane that came down one morning last week."

"That's funny." I couldn't understand it. "Are you sure? Maybe you weren't here."

"I'm always here, mister. I sleep here. If you ask me, I think your brother had better find his map. I think he needs it."

"It sure looks that way. Are there any other fields around here?"

"Not very close. There's one at Danbury, and one up toward Poughkeepsie."

"Well. This is one on him. Sorry I interrupted your game. I'm much obliged."

"Don't mention it."

I went out and sat in the roadster to decide what to do. The mechanic hadn't talked like a man earning the five-spot that someone had given him to keep his mouth shut; he had just been telling what had happened, or rather what hadn't happened. Armonk was out. Poughkeepsie too; for although Manuel might have made it there in twenty minutes in his plane, he had to have time to get to wherever he had left his car and drive to where he was going to meet Carlo Maffei. He had almost certainly met Maffei near some subway station uptown in New York, and the date had been for seven-thirty. He could never have made it from Poughkeepsie. Danbury, I thought, was barely possible, and I headed the roadster north.

I didn't like to do that at all, for it was June 16, the anniversary of the day little Tommie Williamson had been restored to his parents in Wolfe's office, and Mr. and Mrs. Burke Williamson and Tommie—four years older now—were going to celebrate as usual by dining with Wolfe. Each year they tried to get him to go to their place, but they never succeeded. They were all right, and I liked Tommie, but the point I had in mind was the importance that Fritz attached to that occasion. Of course he knew that Williamson owned a chain of hotels, and I suppose he wanted to show him what a pity it was that hotels never had anything fit to eat. As Saul Panzer would say, lovin' babe, what a feed! One-fifth of that cargo was labeled for my hold, and instead of being there to stow it away where it belonged, at eight o'clock that evening I was unenjoying myself at a fern and palm joint in Danbury with a plate of liver and bacon that had absolutely been fried in differential grease.

Nothing went right in Danbury. After the lubricated liver I went out to the flying field. Nobody knew anything. I waited around, and finally long after dark a man showed up who gave me complete dissatisfaction. He kept records but didn't need to, for he remembered what minute the sun had set everyday since Easter. When I left I was certain that Manuel Kimball had never been near the place; and though it was a grand summer night I didn't particularly enjoy the drive back to New York. It was after midnight when I reached Thirty-fifth Street; the Williamsons had departed and Wolfe had gone to bed.

In the top drawer of my desk was a note in his fine slender writing: *Archie, if you learned nothing, in the morning try the metal-worker advertisement; and if your grace and charm can again entice Miss Fiore, have her here at eleven. N. W.*

I never like to eat late at night unless it seems unavoidable, but I went to the kitchen anyhow for a glass of milk and to look sadly over the remains like a man visiting the graveyard where his sweetheart's bones are resting. Then I went on upstairs and turned in.

I slept late. While I was eating breakfast Fritz told me about the dinner I had missed, but I was only politely interested; yesterday's meals never concern me much. Looking through the newspaper, I turned to the classified ads to see the one I had put in the day before; it was there and I thought it read good. Before I went out I went to the office and cleaned around a little, for it wasn't going to be much of a morning.

One of the various little things that were keeping me doubtful about Manuel Kimball was the fact that the metal-worker ad was keyed at the downtown office. Wouldn't he have been more apt—since even a man plotting murder will not ignore convenience—to use Times Square or 125th Street? But of course that wasn't a real objection, just one of the little things you think about when you're looking around for something to hang a chance on. In any event, I was counting on getting nowhere with that ad.

That's where I got to. To walk into the *Times* downtown classified ad office and try to find out what girl took a particular ad two months before, and what kind of a person handed it in and who called for the replies, was about like asking a Coney Island lifeguard if he remembers the fellow with a bald head who went in bathing on the Fourth of July. I had stopped at the D.A.'s office on the way down and got Purley Stebbins to go with me with his badge, but the only one that did any good was him since I had to buy him a drink. By going over the files I did learn that the ad had appeared in the issue of April 16, and while that spoiled nothing since it fitted in all right, I couldn't even figure that it paid for the drink.

I took Purley back to his temple of justice and went on to Sullivan Street.

Mrs. Ricci wasn't going to let me in. She came to the door herself and put on a scowl as soon as she saw me. I grinned at her and told her I had come to take Anna Fiore for a ride, and I behaved like a gentleman in the face of all her observations until she began shoving the door on me so hard that my foot nearly slipped. Then I got businesslike.

"See here, Mrs. Ricci, wait a minute, you might as well listen while you've still got some breath. Now listen! Anna is in bad, not with us but with the police. Cops. She told us something that could get her in a lot of trouble if the police knew it. They don't know it and we don't want them to know it, but they suspect something. My boss wants to put Anna wise. He's got to. Do you want her to go to jail? Come on now, and cut out the injured womanhood."

She glared at me. "You just lie."

"No. Never. Ask Anna. Trot her out."

"You stay here."

"Right."

She shut the door and I sat down on the top step and lit a cigarette. Since it was Saturday the street was a madhouse again. I got hit on the shin with a ball and my eardrums began to stretch out, but otherwise it was a good show. I had just flipped the butt away when I heard the door open behind me and got up.

Anna came out with her hat and jacket on. Mrs. Ricci, standing behind her on the threshold, said:

"I phoned Miss Maffei. She says you're all right, anyway I don't believe it. If you get Anna into trouble my husband will kill you, her father and mother are dead and she is a good girl, no matter if her head is full of flies."

"Don't you worry, Mrs. Ricci." I grinned at Anna. "Don't you want to go for a ride?"

She nodded, and I led her out to the roadster.

If I ever kill anybody I'm pretty sure it will be a woman. I've seen a lot of stubborn men, a lot of men who knew something I wanted to know and didn't intend to tell me, and in quite a few cases I couldn't make him tell no matter what I tried; but in spite of how stubborn they were they always stayed human. They always gave me a feeling that if only I hit on the right lever I could pry it out of them. But I've seen women that not only wouldn't turn loose; you knew damn well they wouldn't. They can get a look on their faces that would drive you crazy, and I think some of them do it on purpose. The look on a man's face says that he'll die before he'll tell you, and you think you may bust that up; a woman's look says that she would just about as soon tell you as not, only she isn't going to.

I sat and watched Anna Fiore for an hour that morning while Wolfe tried every trick he knew, and if she got away whole it was only because I remembered that you mustn't kill the goose that has the golden egg inside of her even if she won't lay it. Of course I didn't know whether she really had the golden egg and Wolfe didn't either, but there was no other goose we could think of that had any eggs at all.

Anna and I got to Thirty-fifth Street before eleven and were waiting for Wolfe when he came down. He started on her easy, as if all he wanted to do was tell her a story, not to get anything out of her, just to keep her informed. He told her that the man who had sent her the hundred dollars was the one who killed Carlo Maffei; that he was wicked and dangerous; that the man knew that she knew something he didn't want known and that he might therefore kill her; that Miss Maffei was a nice woman; that Carlo Maffei had been a nice man and should not have been killed and that the man who had killed him should be caught and punished.

Looking at Anna's face, I saw we were up against it.

Wolfe went into the subtleties of contract. He explained several times, using different kinds of words, that a contract between two parties was valid only when they both voluntarily agreed to it. She was under no contract of silence with the murderer because no contract had been made; he had merely sent her money and told her what to do. He had even given her an alternative; she could have burned the money if she had wanted to. She could burn it now. Wolfe opened the drawer of his desk and took out five new twenty-dollar bills and spread them out in front of her.

"You can burn them now, Miss Fiore. It would be sacrilege, and I would have to leave the room, but Mr. Archie

will help you. Burn them, and you may have these to take
their place. You understand, I will give you these—here, I lay
them on the desk. You still have the money?"

She nodded.

"In your stocking?"

She pulled up her skirt and twisted her leg around and
the bump was there.

Wolfe said, "Take it out." She unfastened the top of her
stocking and reached inside and pulled out the twenties and
unfolded them. Then she looked at me and smiled.

"Here," Wolfe said, "here are matches. Here is a tray. I
shall leave the room and Mr. Archie will help you and give you
this new money. Mr. Archie would be very pleased."

Wolfe glanced at me, and I said, "Come on, Anna, I know
you've got a good heart. You know Mr. Maffei was good to you,
and you ought to be good to him. We'll burn it together, huh?"

I made the mistake of reaching out with my hand, just
starting to reach out, and the twenties went back into her sock
like a streak of lightning. I said, "Don't get scared, and don't
be foolish. Nobody will touch your money as long as I'm
around. You can burn it yourself; I won't even help you."

She said to me, "I never will."

I nodded. "You said that before, but you see it's different
now. Now you have to burn it to get this other money."

She shook her head, and what a look she had on her face!
She may not have had much of a mind, but what there was of
it was all made up. She said, "I don't have to. I never will. I
know, Mr. Archie, you think I'm not very bright. I think that
too because everybody says I'm not. But I'm not dumb, I mean
I'm not all dumb. This is my money and I never will burn it. I
won't spend it until I can get married. That's not very dumb."

"You'll never get married if the man kills you the way he
killed Mr. Maffei."

"He won't kill me."

I thought, by heaven, if he doesn't I will.

Wolfe took a new tack. He began trying to trick her. He
asked her questions about her parents, her early life, her
duties and habits at the Riccis', her opinions of this and that.
She seemed relieved and answered pretty well, but she took
her time, especially when he got on to the rooming-house.
And the first time he started to edge up on her, by asking
something about cleaning Carlo Maffei's room, she closed up
like a clam. He started somewhere else and came around by

another way, but the same stone wall shut him off. It was really beautiful of her; I would have admired it if I had had time. Dumb or not, she had it fixed up inside so that something went click when Carlo Maffei's name or anything associated with him was approached and it worked just as well as Wolfe's sagacity worked. He didn't give up. He had taken a quiet casual tone, and knowing his incredible patience and endurance I was thinking that after all there was a chance he might wear her down in a couple of weeks.

The door of the office opened. Fritz was there. He closed the door behind him, and when Wolfe nodded, came over and presented a card on the tray. Wolfe took it and looked at it and I saw his nostrils open a little.

He said, "A pleasant surprise, Archie," and handed the card across the desk and I reached and took it. The card said:

Manuel Kimball

Chapter 15

I stood up.

Wolfe sat a moment silent, his lips pushing out and in, then he said, "Show the gentleman into the front room, Fritz. The hall is so dark I would scarcely recognize his face if I saw him there.—Just a moment. Be sure the blinds are up in the front room; and leave the door to the hall open so there will be plenty of air."

Fritz went out. Wolfe said, his voice a little quieter even than usual, "Thank you, Miss Fiore. You have been very patient and have kept within your rights. Would you mind if Mr. Archie does not take you home? He has work to do. Mr. Fritz is an excellent driver. Archie, will you take Miss Fiore to the kitchen and arrange with Fritz? You might then accompany her to the entrance."

I nodded. "I get you. Come on, Anna."

She started, too loud, "Can't Mr. Archie—"

"Don't talk. I'll take you home some other day. Come on."

I got her into the kitchen, and explained to Fritz the pleasure that awaited him. I don't think I had ever really felt sorry for Anna until I saw that Fritz didn't blush when I told him to take her home. That was terrible. But I left the feeling sorry for later; while Fritz was getting off his apron and his coat and hat on, I was figuring how to handle it.

I said, "Look here, Anna, let's have some fun. You said something about getting married, and that made me wonder what kind of a man you'd like to marry. There's a man sitting in the front room now, I'll bet he's just the kind. Very good-looking. As we go out we'll stop and look through the door at him, and then I'll go outside with you and you will tell me if he's the kind. Will you do that?"

Anna said, "I know the kind—"

"All right. Don't talk. I don't want him to hear your voice, so he won't know we're looking at him. Ready, Fritz?"

We went out. Fritz had followed instructions and left the door open between the hall and the front room, and I steered Anna to the left of the hall so she wouldn't be too close to the door. Manuel Kimball was in there, a good view, in an armchair, with one knee hanging over the other. Having heard our steps he was looking in our direction, but it was so dark in the hall he couldn't see much. I had a hand on Anna's elbow and my eyes on her face as she looked in at Kimball. I let her look a couple of seconds and then eased her toward the entrance where Fritz was holding the door open for us. Outside, I closed the door behind me.

"Is that the kind you like, Anna?"

"No. Mr. Archie, if I tell you—"

"Some other day. That's the girl. So long.—It won't matter if lunch is late, Fritz, I've an idea we may be late too, and there'll be no guest."

I ducked back in, and went past the open front room door to the office. Wolfe hadn't moved. I said, "She never saw him before. Or if she did, she could give Lynn Fontanne a furlong start and lope in ahead of her." He inclined his head. I asked, "Shall I bring him in?" He inclined his head again.

I went directly through to the front room, by the connecting door. Manuel Kimball got up from his chair and faced around and bowed. I said, "Sorry to keep you waiting. We had a young lady client who thinks we can bring back her husband just by whistling to him, and it's not that easy. Come this way." Wolfe didn't feel formal enough to get up, but he kept his hands laced on his belly. As I led Manuel toward him he said, "How do you do, Mr. Kimball. You will forgive me for not rising, I am not rude, merely unwieldy. Be seated."

I couldn't see any signs that Manuel Kimball was suffering with agitation, but he did look concentrated. His black eyes seemed smaller than when I had seen him before, and concerned with something too important to permit of darting around everywhere to see what they could see. He was wiry and neat in a lightweight, finely tailored suit, with a yellow bow tie and yellow gloves in his pocket. He wasn't bothering with me. After he got into the chair which was still warm from Anna Fiore, his eyes went to Wolfe and stayed there.

Wolfe asked, "Will you have some beer?"

He nodded his head. "Thank you."

I took the hint. In the kitchen I got a couple of bottles from the ice-box and a glass from the shelf and fixed up a tray. I made it snappy because I didn't want to miss anything. I went back with the tray and put it on Wolfe's desk, and then sat down at my desk and pulled some papers out of a drawer and got things fixed up. Manuel Kimball was talking.

". . . told me of his visit to your office yesterday. My father and I are on a completely confidential basis. He told me everything you said to him. Why did you say what you did?"

"Well." Wolfe pulled out his drawer to get the opener, removed the cap from a bottle and dropped it into the drawer, and filled a glass. He watched the foam a moment, then turned back to Manuel. "In the first place, Mr. Kimball, you say that your father repeated everything to you that I told him. You can hardly know that. So let us be properly selective. Your tone is minatory. What specifically do you wish to berate me for? What did I say to your father that you would rather I had left unsaid?"

Manuel smiled, and got colder. "Don't try to twist my words, Mr. Wolfe. I am not expressing my preferences, I am asking you to account for statements that seem to me unwarranted. I have that right, as the son of a man who is getting old. I have never before seen my father frightened, but you have frightened him. You told him that Barstow was killed as a result of borrowing my father's golf driver."

"I did, indeed."

"You admit it. I trust that your man there taking this down will include your confession. What you told my father is criminal nonsense. I have never believed the tale of the poisoned needle as regarded Barstow; I believe it less now. What right have you to invent such absurdities and distress, first the whole Barstow family, now my father, with them? Probably it is actionable, my lawyer will know about that. Certainly it is unjustifiable and it must be stopped."

"I don't know." Wolfe appeared to be considering; as for me, I was handing it to Manuel for being cute enough to get what I was doing in the first five minutes; not many had done that. Wolfe downed a glass of beer and wiped his lips. "I really don't know. If it is actionable at all, I suppose it could only be through a complaint of libel from the murdered. I don't suppose you had that in mind?"

"I have only one thing in mind." Manuel's eyes were even smaller. "That it has got to stop."

"But, Mr. Kimball," Wolfe protested. "Give me a chance. You accused me of inventing absurdities. I have invented nothing. The invention, and a most remarkable and original one, even brilliant—and I am careful of words—was another's; only the discovery was mine. If the inventor were to say to me what you have said, I would put him down for a commendably modest man. No, sir, I did not invent that golf driver."

"And no one else did. Where is it?"

"Alas." Wolfe turned a hand palm up. "I have yet to see it."

"What proof is there that it ever existed?"

"The needle that it propelled into Barstow's belly."

"Bah. Why from a golf driver? Why on the first tee?"

"The wasp came from nowhere, and synchronized."

"No good, Mr. Wolfe." Manuel's intent little black eyes were scornful. "It's what I said, criminal nonsense. If you have no better proof than that, I repeat, I have a right to demand that you retract. I do so. I have this morning called on Mr. Anderson, the District Attorney at White Plains. He agrees with me. I demand that you see my father and retract and apologize; likewise the Barstows if you have told them. I have reason to suspect that you have."

Wolfe shook his head slowly from side to side. After a moment he said regretfully, "It's too bad, Mr. Kimball."

"It is. But you caught the crow, now you can eat it."

"No. You misunderstand me. I mean it's too bad that you are dealing with me. I am perhaps the only man on this hemisphere whom your courage and wit cannot defeat, and by incredibly bad luck you find yourself confronted by me. I am

sorry; but just as you have assumed a task suitable for your
abilities, I have found one congenial for mine. You will forgive
me for wheeling onto your flank, since you have made it
impossible for me to meet you frontally. I hardly suppose that
you expected your direct attack to gain its feigned objective;
you could hardly have had so poor an opinion of me as that.
Your true objective must have been concealed, and probably it
was the discovery of the nature and extent of the evidence I
have so far acquired. But surely you know that, for how else
could I have foretold the result of the autopsy?—I beg you, let
me finish. Yes, I know when and where and by whom the golf
driver was made, I know where the man who made it is now,
and I know what results to expect from the advertisement
which I inserted in this morning's newspapers and which you
have perhaps seen."

Not a muscle on Manuel's face had stirred, and no change
was perceptible in his tone. His eyes kept straight on Wolfe as
he said, "If you know all that—I doubt if you do—is that not
information for the District Attorney?"

"Yes. Do you want me to give it to him?"

"I? I want? Of course, if you have it."

"Good." Wolfe wiggled a finger at him. "I'll tell you what
you do, Mr. Kimball. Do me a favor. On your way home this
afternoon stop at Mr. Anderson's office; tell him what information I have and suggest that he send for it. Now—I am sorry
—it is past my lunch hour. May I offer you a compliment? If
almost anyone else I have known were in your position I would
try to detain him longer on the chance of learning something.
With you, I feel that eating my lunch will be more profitable."

Manuel was on his feet. "I should tell you, I am going
from here to my lawyer. You will hear from him."

Wolfe nodded. "Certainly your best move. Obvious, but
still the best. Your father would wonder if you did not."

Manuel Kimball turned and went. I got up and started
after him for the courtesy of the house, but he was out of the
front door before I made it.

I went back to Wolfe. He was leaning back with his eyes
closed. I asked loud enough to wake him up, "Did that guy
come here to find out if he'd have to go ahead and kill his
father during the weekend?"

He sighed. His eyes opened and he shook his head.
"Lunch, Archie."

"It won't be ready for ten minutes. Fritz only got back at one."

"The anchovies and celery will divert us."

So we went to the dining-room.

Right there, at that point, the Barstow-Kimball case went dead. At least Wolfe went dead, and that was the case as far as I was concerned. It wasn't a relapse, he just closed up. While plenty went into him during lunch, of course nothing came out; and when the meal was finished he went to the office and sat. I sat at my desk and caught up with a few things, but there wasn't much to do, and I kept glancing at Wolfe wondering when he would open up. Although his eyes were closed he must have felt my glances, for all of a sudden he looked at me and said:

"Confound it, Archie, cannot paper be made not to rattle?"

I got up. "All right, I'll beat it. But damn it, where? Have you lost your tongue?"

"Anywhere. Go for a walk."

"And return?"

"Any time. It doesn't matter. Dinner."

"Are you waiting for Manuel to bump off his old man?"

"Go, Archie."

It seemed to me that he was rubbing it in, since it was already three-thirty and in another half hour he would himself have left to go up to the plant-rooms. But seeing the mood he was in, I got my hat from the hall and went out.

I went to a movie to think, and the more I thought the more uncomfortable I got. Manuel Kimball's visit and his challenge, for that was what it amounted to, darned near succeeded as far as I was concerned. I had been aware that we weren't quite ready to tell Mrs. Barstow what address to mail the check to, but I hadn't fully realized how awfully empty our bag was. We had found out some things to our own satisfaction, but we had no more proof that there had been a murder than we had had when we started. Let alone who had done it. But that wasn't all; the worst was that there was no place to go from there. Granted that it was Manuel Kimball, how could we tie him up? Find the golf driver. Fat chance. I could see him in his plane flying low over the river or a reservoir, dropping the club out with a chunk of lead wired to the shaft. Trace the poison to him. About the same chance. He had been planning this for years maybe, certainly months; he may even have had the poison with him when he came up with his father from the Argentine; anyway, he could have got it from there at any time—and try and find out. Get him to talk on the telephone with Mrs. Ricci and have her recognize his voice. Sure, that was it; any jury would convict on that without leaving the courtroom.

I sat in a movie three hours without seeing anything that happened on the screen, and all I got was a headache.

I never did know what Wolfe was up to that Saturday afternoon and Sunday. Was he just bumping his head against the wall, as I was? Maybe; he wasn't very sociable. Or was he possibly waiting for Manuel to make a move? But the only move Manuel could have made would have been to kill his father, and then where would we have been? Anderson would have left us out in the cold, and while neither Wolfe nor I would have worn any black for E. D. Kimball we certainly would have done so for the fifty grand. As far as E. D. Kimball was concerned, I figured that by rights he had been killed on June fourth anyway and he might be grateful for two weeks of grace. But Wolfe wasn't waiting for that; I was sure he didn't expect it from what he said about Manuel Sunday afternoon. It was then that he opened up and talked a little, but not to much point. He was being philosophic.

It was raining; it rained all that Sunday. I wrote some letters and went through two Sunday papers and spent a couple of hours on the roof chinning with Horstmann and looking over the plants, but no matter what I did I was in a bad humor. The damn rain never let up once. Not that it would have bothered me if I had had anything to do; I don't notice rain or shine if I'm out in it busy; but monkeying around that dry dark quiet house all day long with that constant patter outside and never a let up didn't help my disposition a bit. I was thankful when something happened around five-thirty that I could get good and sore about.

I was in the office yawning over a magazine when the telephone rang. It took me a few seconds to unwind myself out of the armchair I was in and get across to my desk, and when I got the receiver to my ear I was surprised to hear Wolfe's voice. He was answering from the plant-room phone. He always took calls in the plant-room when I was out, but usually when he knew I was in the house he left them to me. But it was his voice:

"This is Wolfe."

Another voice: "This is Durkin, Mr. Wolfe. Everything is okay. She went to church this morning, and a while ago she came out and went to a candy store and bought an ice-cream cone. She's back in now, I expect for the night."

"Thank you, Fred. You'd better stay there until ten o'clock. Saul will be there in the morning at seven, and you resume at two."

"Yes, sir. Anything else?"

"That's all."

I banged the receiver onto the hook, thinking there was a chance it might crack Wolfe's eardrum.

When he came into the office half an hour afterward I didn't look up, and I was careful to be buried in my magazine enough to make sure it wasn't upside down. I held onto that pose another half hour, turning a page when I thought of it. I was boiling.

Wolfe's voice, finally: "It's raining, Archie."

I didn't look up. "Go to hell. I'm reading."

"Oh no. Surely not, in those fitful gusts. I wish to inquire, would it be a good plan in the morning for you to collect the replies to our advertisement and follow their suggestions?"

I shook my head. "No, sir. The excitement would be too much for me."

Wolfe's cheeks folded up. "I begin to believe, Archie, that a persistent rain distresses you even more acutely than it does me. You are not merely imitating me?"

"No, sir. It's not the rain, you know damn well it isn't." I dropped the magazine on the floor and glared at him. "If the very best way you can think of to catch the cleverest murderer that ever gave me a highball is to start a game of tiddlywinks in Sullivan Street, you might at least have told me so I could remember Durkin in my prayers. Praying is all I'm good for maybe. What's Durkin trying to do, catch Anna hocking the golf stick?"

Wolfe wiggled a finger at me. "Compose yourself, Archie. Why taunt me? Why upbraid me? I am merely a genius, not a god. A genius may discover the hidden secrets and display them; only a god could create new ones. I apologize to you for failing to tell you of Durkin; my mind was occupied; I telephoned him yesterday after you went for a walk. He is not trying to catch Miss Fiore but to protect her. In the house she is probably safe; outside probably not. I do not think Manuel Kimball will proceed to devise means of completing his

enterprise until he is satisfied that there is no danger of his
being called to account for his first attempt, which failed
through no fault of his. It was perfectly conceived and
perfectly executed. As for us, I see no possibility but Miss
Fiore; *clever* is too weak a word for Manuel Kimball; he has his
own genius. I would not ask for a better means of defeating a
rainy Sunday than contemplation of the beauty of his arrangements. He has left us nothing but Miss Fiore, and Durkin's
function is to preserve her."

"*Preserve* is good. Since she might as well be sealed up in
a can."

"I think the can may be opened. We shall try. But that
must wait until we are completely satisfied as to June fifth. By
the way, is Maria Maffei's telephone number in the book?
—Good. Of course, we do not know what Miss Fiore is
guarding so jealously. If it turns out to be trivial and insuffi-
cient, then we must abandon the skirmish and plan a siege. No
man can commit so complicated a deed as a murder and leave
no vulnerable points; the best he can do is render them
inaccessible save to a patience longer than his own and an
ingenuity more inspired. In Manuel Kimball's case those
specifications are—well, considerable. If in fact Miss Fiore is
guarding the jewel that we seek, I earnestly hope that he is not
aware of it; if he is, she is as good as dead."

"With Durkin protecting her?"

"We cannot protect from lightning, we can only observe it
strike. I have explained that to Fred. If Manuel Kimball kills
that girl we shall have him. But I think he will not. Remember
the circumstances under which he sent her the hundred
dollars. At that time he could not have supposed that she knew
anything that could connect him with Barstow, or he would
not have made so inadequate a gesture. He knew only her first
name. Probably Carlo Maffei had mentioned it, and had said
enough of her character and of some small discovery she had
made to suggest to Manuel Kimball, after he had killed Maffei,
to risk a hundred dollars on the chance of additional safety
without the possibility of added danger. If that surmise is
correct, and if Miss Fiore knows nothing beyond what Kimball
was aware that she knew, we are in for a siege. Saul Panzer will
go to South America; I warned him yesterday on the telephone
to be in readiness. Your program, already in my mind, will be
elaborate and tiresome. It would be a pity, but we would have
no just grievance against Manuel Kimball. It was only by his ill

fortune, and my unwarranted pertinacity in asking Miss Fiore a trivial question a second time, that the first piece of his puzzle was discovered."

Wolfe stopped. I got up and stretched. "All I have to say is, he's a dirty spiggoty."

"No, Archie, Mr. Manuel Kimball is an Argentinian."

"Spiggoty to me. I want a glass of milk. Can I bring you some beer?"

He said no, and I went to the kitchen.

I felt better. There were times when Wolfe's awful self-assurance gave me a touch of a dash of a suggestion of a pain in the neck, but there were other times when it was as good as a flock of pure and beautiful maidens smoothing my brow. This was one of the latter. After I had finished with a sufficient quantity of milk and cookies I went out to a movie and didn't miss a scene. When I went home it was still raining.

But Monday morning was beautiful. I got out early. Even in New York the washed air was so fresh and sweet in the sunlight that it somehow dissolved all the motor exhausts and the other million smells sneaking out of windows and doors and alleys and elevator lids, and made it a pleasure to breathe. I stepped on it. By half past eight I was out of Bronx Park and turning into the Parkway.

I had collected more than twenty answers to the ad and had gone through them. About half of them were phony; chiselers trying to horn in or poor fish trying to be funny. Some others were honest enough but off of my beat; apparently June fifth had been a good day for landing in pastures with airplanes. Three of them not only looked good but fitted together; it seemed that they had all seen the same plane land in a meadow somewhere a couple of miles east of Hawthorne. That was too good to be true.

But it wasn't. A mile out of Hawthorne, following the directions in the letter, I left the highway and turned into an uphill dirt road with the ruts left washed out and stony by the rain. After a while the road got so narrow and doubtful that it looked as if it might play out any minute, and I stopped at a house and asked where the Carters lived. On up. I went on.

The Carter residence, on top of the hill, was about ready to fall down. It hadn't been painted since the war, and the grass was weeds. But the dog that got up to meet me was friendly and happy, and the wash on the line looked clean in the sunshine. I found Mrs. Carter around back, getting the rest of the wash through. She was skinny and active, with a tooth gone in front.

"Mrs. T. A. Carter?"

"Yes, sir."

"I've come to see you about your reply to an ad I put in Saturday's paper. About my landing with my airplane. Your letter is quite complete. You saw me land?"

She nodded. "I sure did. I didn't see the ad though, Minnie Vawter saw it and I had told her about the airplane and she remembered it and brought the ad up Saturday afternoon. It was lucky I had told her about it. Sure I saw you land."

"I wouldn't have supposed you could see me from here."

"Sure, look. This is a pretty high hill." She led me across the yard and through a clump of sumacs. "See that view? My husband says that view's worth a million dollars. See the reservoir, like a lake?" She pointed. "That field down there's where you landed. I wondered what was up, I thought you'd broke something. I've seen plenty of airplanes in the air, but I never saw one land before."

I nodded. "That's it all right. Thanks to the completeness of your letter, there's not much I need to ask you. You saw me land at ten minutes past six, and saw me get out and walk south across the meadow, toward the road. You came into the house then to look at the dinner on the stove, and saw me no more. At twilight my plane was still there; you went to bed at half past nine, and in the morning it was gone."

"That's right. I thought it would be better to put it all in the letter, because—"

"Correct. I imagine you are usually correct, Mrs. Carter. Your description of my plane is better than I could do myself. And from such a distance; you have good eyes. By the way, could you tell me who lives in that house down there, the white one?"

"Sure. Miss Wellman. She's an artist from New York. It was Art Barrett, the man that works for her, that drove you to Hawthorne."

"Oh. Of course. Yes, that's the place. I'm much obliged to you, Mrs. Carter, you're going to help me win my bet. It was a question of how many people saw me."

I decided to give her a five-spot. The Lord knows she needed it, judging from appearances; and she had sewed Manuel Kimball up tighter than a bag of bran. I don't know how sure Wolfe had been of Manuel up to that point, but I do know that he postponed the works for Anna Fiore until after June fifth was settled. I hadn't been sure at all. I never did like my feelings as well as Wolfe liked his; they often got me talking big, but they always left me uneasy until I got satisfactory facts to tuck them in with. So I figured that Mrs. Carter's handout was cheap at five bucks. Manuel Kimball was settled with us. To get enough to settle him with a jury was another matter, but as far as we were concerned he was all set. Mrs. Carter got her hand all around the five dollar bill and started toward the house, remarking that the wash wouldn't finish itself.

I stood a minute looking down at the meadow far below. That was where Manuel Kimball had landed and left his plane; across that field he had walked to the white house and asked a man there to drive him to Hawthorne; at Hawthorne, which was only a few miles from his home, he had either had his own car waiting or had rented one at a garage; he had driven to New York, stopping probably at White Plains to telephone Carlo Maffei and arrange a meeting. He was already screwed up, and alarmed, because Maffei had abandoned the trip to Europe; and when he met him that evening at seven-thirty and Maffei produced the clipping he had cut from the *Times* that morning and began to talk about how hard it was to keep his mouth shut about golf drivers, that was plenty for Manuel. With Maffei in the car with him, he drove to some secluded nook and found an opportunity to sink a knife five inches into Carlo's back at the point where the heart was waiting for it. Leaving the knife there to hold the blood in, he drove around the countryside until he found the sort of spot he needed, dragged Maffei's body out of the car and carried it into a thicket, returned to the car and drove to Hawthorne, where he got a taxi to take him back to the white house that was there in the valley below me. If he needed help taking off in the plane, Art Barrett and the taxi driver were both handy. Around ten o'clock he landed on his own private lighted field, and told Skinner that it was really more fun flying at night than in the daytime.

There was nothing wrong with that, except possibly one thing: it was giving Carlo Maffei credit for a lot of activity between his ears to suppose that reading that piece about Barstow's death was enough to put him wise. But I laid that away; there was no knowing what might have happened before to make Maffei suspicious, and the mere oddity of the

outlandish contraption he had been paid so well to construct
had certainly made him wonder.

I decided not to tackle Art Barrett. I couldn't very well
present myself as the aviator as I had with Mrs. Carter, since
he had driven Manuel to Hawthorne, and there was nothing
he could tell me that would be worth the trouble of doping out
an approach. For the present I had enough. There would be
time for that later, if we needed him for a case. The other two
replies to the ad could wait too. I was itching to get back to
Thirty-fifth Street, remembering that Wolfe had promised to
use a can opener on Anna Fiore if I succeeded in pulling
Manuel Kimball down out of the clouds for the evening of
June fifth.

I stopped at the clothesline for a good-bye to Mrs. Carter,
got the roadster turned around by inching back and forth
between the boulders that lined the narrow road, and floated
off downhill toward the highway.

I discovered I was singing, and I asked myself, why all the
elation? All I had found was the proof that we were on a spoke
and not on the rim; we still had to get to the hub, and we were
just as far away from that as we had been before. I went on
singing anyhow, rolling along the Parkway; and at Fordham
Road I stopped and telephoned Wolfe what I had got. He was
already down from the plant-rooms, and when I halted at
Thirty-sixth Street for a red light Tiffany's whistle was blowing
noon.

I left the roadster in front. Wolfe was in the office. He was
seated at his desk, and Fritz was bringing in a tray with a glass
and two bottles of beer.

Wolfe said, "Good morning, Friend Goodwin."

"What?" I stared. "Oh, I get you." I had left my hat on. I
went to the hall and tossed it on a hook and came back. I sat
down and grinned. "I wouldn't go sour now even for Emily
Post. Didn't I tell you Manuel Kimball was just a dirty
spiggoty? Of course it was your ad that did it."

Wolfe didn't look as if he was on my boat; he didn't seem
interested. But he nodded, and said, "You found the pasture."

"I found everything. A woman that saw him land and
knows just which parts of his plane are red and which blue,
and a man that drove him to Hawthorne—everything we could
ask for."

"Well." He wasn't looking at me.

"Well! What are you trying to do, get me sore again? What's the matter—"

The palm of his hand coming up from the chair arm stopped me. "Easy, Archie. Your discovery is worthy of celebration, but you must humor me by postponing it. Your explosive return chanced unfortunately to interrupt an interesting telephone call I was about to make. I was reaching for the book when you entered; possibly you can save me that effort. Do you happen to know the Barstow number?"

"Sure. Something's up, huh? Do you want it?"

"Get it, please, and listen in. Miss Sarah Barstow."

I went to my desk, glanced at the book to make sure of the number, and called. In a moment Small's voice was in my ear. I asked to speak to Miss Barstow, and after a little wait she was on the wire and I nodded to Wolfe. He took off his receiver. I kept mine at my ear.

He said, "Miss Barstow?—This is Nero Wolfe—Good morning. I am taking the liberty of calling to inquire if the orchids reached you safely.—No, orchids.—I beg your pardon?—Oh. It is a mistake apparently. Did you not do me the honor of sending me a note this morning requesting me to send you some orchids?—You sent no note?—No, no, it is quite all right.—A mistake of some sort, I am sorry.—Goodbye."

We hung up. Wolfe leaned back in his chair. I put on a grin.

"You're getting old, sir. In the younger set we don't send the girls orchids until they ask for them."

Wolfe's cheeks stayed put. His lips were pushing out and in, and I watched him. His hand started for the drawer to get the opener for a bottle, but he pulled his hand back again without touching the drawer.

He said, "Archie, you have heard me say that I am an actor. I am afraid I have a weakness for dramatic statement. It would be foolish not to indulge it when a good opportunity is offered. There is death in this room."

I suppose I must have involuntarily glanced around, for he went on, "Not a corpse; I mean not death accomplished but death waiting. Waiting only for me perhaps, or for all of us; I don't know. It is here. While I was upstairs this morning with the plants Fritz came up with a note—this note."

He reached in his pocket and took out a piece of paper and handed it to me. I read it:

Dear Mr. Wolfe,—
   *Last week, at your house, Mr. Goodwin kindly
presented me with two orchids, remarkably beautiful. I am daring to be cheeky enough to ask if you can
send me six or eight more of them? They were so
lovely. The messenger will wait for them, if you do
decide to be generous. I shall be so grateful!*
                               Sarah Barstow

I said, "It don't sound like her."

"Perhaps not. You know her better than I do. I of course
remembered the Brassocattlaelias Truffautianas in her hand
when she came downstairs with you. Theodore and I cut a
dozen and boxed them, and Fritz took them down. When I
came to the office at eleven o'clock and sat at my desk there
was a smell of a stranger in the air. I am too sensitive to
strangers, that is why I keep these layers over my nerves. I
knew of course the stranger who had called, but I was
uncomfortable. I sent for Fritz. He told me that the young
man who had brought the note and waited for the orchids had
had with him a fiber box, an oblong box with a handle. On
departing he had taken the box with him; Fritz saw it in his
hand as he left the house. But for at least ten minutes the
young man was alone in the front room; the door between that
room and the office was unlocked; the door from the hall to the
office was closed."

Wolfe sighed. "Alas, Miss Barstow did not write the
note."

I was on my feet and going toward him, saying, "You get
out of here." He shook his head. "Come on," I demanded, "I
can jump and you can't. Damn it, come on, quick! I'm used to
playing with bombs. Fritz! Fritz!" Fritz came running. "Fill up
the sink with water. To the top. Mr. Wolfe, for God's sake get
out of here, it may go off any second. I'll find it."

I heard Fritz back in the kitchen starting the water. Wolfe
wouldn't budge, and the Lord knows I couldn't budge him. He
shook his head and wiggled a finger at me.

"Archie, please.—Stop that! Don't touch anything. There
is no bomb. They tick or they sizzle, and I have good ears and
have listened. Besides, Mr. Kimball has not had time since his
call to construct a good one, and he would use no other. It is

not a bomb.—I beg you, no trepidation; drama, but not trepidation. I have reflected, and I have felt. Consider: when Mr. Kimball was in this room he saw me make no movement worthy the name but one. He saw me open the drawer of my desk and put my hand in it. If that suggests nothing to you, I am sure it did to him. We shall see."

I jumped at him, for I thought he was going to open the drawer, but he waved me back; he was merely getting ready to leave his chair. He said, "Get my red thorn walking stick. —Confound it, will you do as I say?"

I ran to the hall and got the stick from the stand and ran back. Wolfe was moving around the desk. He came clear around to the side opposite his chair, and reached over for the tray and pulled it across to him, with the glass and bottles still on it.

"Now," he said, "please do it this way.—No, first close the door to the hall." I went and closed the door and returned. "Thank you. Grasp the stick by its other end. Reach across the desk and catch the tip of the handle on the lower edge of the drawer-front. Push, and the drawer will open.—Wait. Open it, if you can, quite slowly; and be ready to free the stick quickly should it occur to you to use it for any other purpose. Proceed."

I proceeded. The tip of the handle's curve caught nicely under the edge of the drawer, but on account of the angle I had to keep the drawer wouldn't start. I tried to push so as to open the drawer gradually, but I had to push harder, and suddenly the drawer popped out half a foot and I nearly dropped the stick. I lifted up to get the stick loose, and yelled:

"Look out!"

Wolfe had got a beer bottle in each hand, by the neck, and he brought one of them crashing onto the desk but missed the thing that had come out of the drawer. It was coming fast and its head was nearly to the edge of the desk where we were while its tail was still in the drawer. I had got the stick loose and was pounding at its head but it kept slashing around and I couldn't hit it, and the desk was covered with beer and the pieces of the broken bottle. I was ready to jump back and was grabbing Wolfe to pull him back with me when he came down with the second bottle right square on the ugly head and smashed it flat as a piece of tripe. The long brown body writhed all over the desk, but it was done for.

The second bottle had busted too, and we were splattered

all over. Wolfe stepped back and pulled out his handkerchief and began to wipe his face. I held on to the stick.

"*Nom de Dieu!*"

It was Fritz, horrified.

Wolfe nodded. "Yes. Fritz, here's a mess for you. I'm sorry. Get things."

Chapter 16

I tried it again. "*Fair-duh-lahnss?*"

Wolfe nodded. "Somewhat better. Still too much *n* and not enough nose. You are not a born linguist, Archie. Your defect is probably not mechanical. To pronounce French properly you must have within you a deep antipathy, not to say scorn, for some of the most sacred of the Anglo-Saxon prejudices. In some manner you manage without that scorn, I do not quite know how. Yes, fer-de-lance. *Bothrops atrox.* Except for the bushmaster, it is the most dreaded of all the vipers."

Fritz had cleaned up the mess, with my help, and served lunch, and we had eaten. When the snake had finished writhing I had stretched it out on the kitchen floor and measured it: six feet, three inches. At the middle it was almost as thick as my wrist. It was a dirty yellowish brown, and even dead it looked damn mean. After measuring it I stood up and, poking at it with the yardstick, wondered what to do with it —observing to Wolfe, standing near, that I couldn't just stuff it in the garbage pail. Should I take it and throw it in the river?

Wolfe's cheeks folded. "No, Archie, that would be a pity. Get a carton and excelsior from the basement, pack it nicely, and address it to Mr. Manuel Kimball. Fritz can take it to the post office. It will relieve Mr. Kimball's mind."

That had been done, and it hadn't spoiled my lunch. Now we were back in the office, waiting for Maria Maffei, whom Wolfe had telephoned after receiving my call from Fordham Road.

I said, "It comes from South America."

Wolfe was leaning back in his chair content, with half-shut eyes. He was not at all displeased that it had been his blow that had killed it, though he had expressed regret for the beer. He murmured, "It does. It is a crotalid, and one of the few snakes that will strike without challenge or warning. Only last week I was looking at a picture of it, in one of the books you procured for me. It is abundant throughout South America."

"They found snake venom in Barstow."

"Yes. That could have been suspected when the analysis was found difficult. The needle must have been well smeared. These considerations, Archie, will become of moment if Anna Fiore fails us and we must have recourse to a siege. Many things will be discoverable with sufficient patience and—well, abandonment of reserve. Is there somewhere on the Kimball estate a pit where Manuel has carried rats to his fer-de-lance? Did he extract the venom himself by teasing its bite into the pulp of a banana? Unlikely. Has he an Argentine friend who sent the poison to him? More likely. The young man—dark and handsome, Fritz says—who brought the note not from Miss Barstow, and who is admirably deft with vipers, will he be found to be on duller days an usher in a Hundred and Sixteenth Street movie theater? Or a seaman on a South American boat, providentially arrived at the port of New York only yesterday? Difficult questions, but each has its answer, if it comes to a siege. It is likely that Manuel Kimball arranged some time ago for the journey of the fer-de-lance, as a second string to his bow; thinking that if the contrivance designed by man should for any reason fail it would be well to give nature's own mechanism a chance. Then, when it arrived, there was a more urgent need for it; vengeance stepped back for safety. And now, to this moment at least, he has neither."

"Maybe. But he just barely missed getting one, and he may get the other any minute."

Wolfe wiggled a finger at me. "Faulty, Archie, inexcusably faulty. Vengeance will continue to wait. Mr. Manuel Kimball is not a creature of impulse. Should circumstances render him suddenly desperate he would act with desperation, but even then not impulsively.—But Miss Maffei is due in half an hour, and you should know the arrangements before she arrives. Your notebook."

I got at my desk, and he dictated twenty minutes without stopping. After the first two minutes I put on a grin, and kept it on till the end. It was beautiful, it was without a flaw, and it covered every detail. He had even allowed for Maria Maffei's refusal or her inability to persuade Anna; in that case the action was approximately the same, but the characters were shifted around; I was to take it with Anna. He had telephoned Burke Williamson and arranged for a clear stage for us, and Saul Panzer was to call at the office at six o'clock for the sedan and his instructions. When he had finished dictating it was all so clear that there were few questions for me to ask. I asked those few, and ran back over the pages. He was leaning back in his chair, full of beer, pretending he wasn't pleased with himself.

I said, "All right, I admit it, you're a genius. This will get it if she's got it."

He nodded without concern.

Maria Maffei arrived on the dot. I was waiting for her on my toes and got to the door before Fritz was out of the kitchen. She was dressed in black, and if I had met her on the street I doubt if I would have known her, she looked so worn out. I was so full of Wolfe's program that I had a grin ready for her, but I killed it in time. She wasn't having any grins. After I saw her I didn't feel like grinning anyway; it sobered me up to see what the death of a brother might do to a woman. She was ten years older and the bright life in her eyes was gone.

I took her to the office and moved a chair in front of Wolfe for her and went to my desk.

She exchanged greetings with Wolfe and said, "I suppose you want money."

"Money for what?" Wolfe asked.

"For finding my brother Carlo. You didn't find him. Neither did the police. Some boys found him. I won't pay you any money."

"You might." Wolfe sighed. "I hadn't thought of that, Miss Maffei. I'm sorry you suggested it. It arouses me to sordid considerations. But for the moment let us forget it; you owe me nothing. Forget it. But let me ask you—I am sorry if it is painful, but it is necessary—you saw your brother's body?"

Her eyes were dull on him, but I saw that I had been wrong: the life in them was not gone, it had merely sunk within, waiting back there as if in ambush. She said quietly, "I saw him."

"You saw perhaps the hole in his back. The hole made by the knife of the man who killed him."

"I saw it."

"Good. And if there was a chance of my discovering the man who used that knife and bringing him to punishment, and needed your help, would you help me?"

In the dull eyes a gleam came and went. Maria Maffei said, "I would pay you money for that, Mr. Wolfe."

"I suspect you would. But we shall forget that for the present. It is another kind of assistance I require. Since you are intelligent enough to make reasonable assumptions, and therefore to be made uncomfortable when only reasonable ones are available, I had better explain to you. The man who murdered your brother is sought by me, and by others, for another act he committed. An act more sensational and not less deplorable. I know who he is, but your help is needed—"

"You know? Tell me!" Maria Maffei had jerked forward in her chair, and this time the gleam in her eyes stayed.

Wolfe wiggled a finger at her. "Easy, Miss Maffei. I am afraid you must delegate your vengeance. Remember that those of us who are both civilized and prudent commit our murders only under the complicated rules which permit us to avoid personal responsibility. Let us get on. You can help. You must trust me. Your friend Fanny's husband, Mr. Durkin, will tell you that I am to be trusted; besides, he will also help. I wish to speak of Miss Anna Fiore, the girl who works at the rooming house where your brother lived. You know her?"

"Of course I know her."

"Does she like you and trust you?"

"I don't know. She is a girl who hides her flowers."

"If any? A tender way of putting it; thank you. Could you go in my automobile this evening, with a driver, and persuade Miss Fiore to take a long ride with you; give her a good excuse, so she would go willingly?"

Maria Maffei looked at him; after a moment she nodded. "She would go. It would be a strange thing, I would have to think—"

"You will have time for that. I prefer to leave it to your wit to invent the excuse; you will use it better if it is your own. But that is all that will be left to you; one of my men will drive the car; in all the rest you must carefully and precisely follow my instructions. Or rather, Mr. Goodwin's instructions. Archie, if you please." Wolfe put his hands on the edge of the desk and shoved his chair back, and got himself up. "You will forgive me for leaving you, Miss Maffei, it is the hour for my plants.

Perhaps when you and Mr. Goodwin have finished you would like him to bring you up to see them."

He left us.

I didn't take Maria Maffei upstairs to see the orchids that day; it was nearly five o'clock when I had finished with her, and I had something else to do. She didn't balk at all, but it took a lot of explaining, and then I went over the details three times to make sure she wouldn't get excited and ball it up. We decided it would be better for her to make a preliminary call on Anna and get it arranged, so I took her out and put her in a taxi and saw her headed for Sullivan Street.

Then I started on my own details. I had to get the knife and the masks and the guns ready, and arrange with the garage for hiring a car, since we couldn't take a chance on Anna recognizing the roadster, and get hold of Bill Gore and Orrie Cather. I had suggested them, and Wolfe said okay. He had already told Durkin to report at seven o'clock.

I got it all done, but without any time to spare. At six-thirty I ate a hurry-up dinner in the kitchen, while Wolfe was in the office with Saul Panzer. On his way out Saul looked in at the kitchen to make a face at me, as if his ugly mug wasn't good enough without any embroidery. He called in to me, "Enjoy it, Arch, it may be your last meal, you're not dealing with a quitter this night!"

I had my mouth full, so I only said, "Shrivel, shrimp."

Bill Gore and Durkin were there on time, and Orrie wasn't late enough to matter. I gave them the story, and rehearsed Orrie several times because a lot depended on him. We hadn't been together on anything for over two years, and it seemed like old times to see him again twisting his thin lips and looking around for a place to squirt his tobacco juice.

Wolfe was still in at his dinner when we got away a little before eight o'clock. The garage had given me a black Buick sedan, and it had four wheels and an engine but it wasn't the roadster. Orrie got in front with me and Bill Gore and Durkin in the back. I thought to myself that it was too bad it was only a set-up, because with those three birds I would have contracted to stop anything from a Jersey bus to a truck of hooch. Orrie said I should have hung a sign on the radiator, *Highwaymen's Special*. I grinned, but only with my mouth. I knew everything had to go exactly right and it was up to me, and what Wolfe had said about Anna Fiore was true: her mental vision was limited, but within its limits she might see things that a broader vision would miss entirely.

I went up the west side and got onto the Sawmill River Road. The Williamson place was in the back country east of Tarrytown, on a secondary road; I knew the way as well as I knew Thirty-fifth Street on account of my trips there four years before. I had expected to make it by nine-thirty but traffic up to Yonkers had held me up a little, and it was a few minutes later than that and I had the lights on when I turned into the drive where I had once picked Mrs. Williamson up in a faint and carried her to the pond to throw water on her.

I drove on up to the house, about a third of a mile, and left the three in the car and went and rang the doorbell. Tanzer, the butler, remembered me and we shook hands. I told him I wouldn't go in, I just wanted to speak to his boss a minute. Burke Williamson came right away; he shook hands too and said he was sorry they had missed me Friday night. I said I was sorry too.

"I'm a little late, Mr. Williamson, I came on up just to make sure that everything's set. No loose servants out hunting lightning bugs? Can we go ahead?"

"Everything's arranged." He laughed. "No one will disturb your sinister plot. Of course we're all itching with curiosity. I don't suppose we could get behind a bush and watch?"

I shook my head. "You'd better stay in the house, if you don't mind. I won't see you again, I've got to make a quick getaway. Wolfe will phone you tomorrow, I expect, to thank you."

"He needn't bother. I'll never do enough to make Nero Wolfe owe me any thanks."

I went back to the car and turned it around and started back down the drive. I had the spot picked out, about halfway down, a full three hundred yards from the public road, where high shrubbery was on both sides with trees just beyond and it would be good and dark. There the drive was narrow enough so that I could block it with the sedan without bothering to swing it crosswise.

I got the sedan into position and turned off the lights and we all got out. It was nearly ten o'clock and our prey was due at a quarter past. I passed around the guns and gave Orrie the knife, and then handed out the masks and we put them on. We were a hard-looking bunch and I couldn't help grinning at

Orrie's wisecracks, though to tell the truth I was pretty much keyed up. The thing had to go absolutely right. I went over it again with them. They had it pat, and we scattered into the bushes. It was plenty dark. They began calling back and forth to one another, and pretty soon I told them to shut up so I could listen.

After a couple of minutes the sound came up from below of Wolfe's sedan going into second on the grade. I couldn't see the lights on account of the bushes, but soon I did. They got brighter, and then I saw the car. It buzzed along, getting close, and when the driver saw my sedan right ahead it slowed down. I left the bushes on a run, jumped to the running board of Wolfe's sedan just as it came to a stop, and shoved my gun into the face of Saul Panzer in the driver's seat.

The others were with me. Bill Gore was on my side, on the running board, sticking his gun through the open window; Orrie, with Durkin behind him, was opening the other tonneau door. Maria Maffei was screaming. There was no sound from Anna.

Orrie said, "Get out of there quick. Come on, do you want me to put a hole in you?"

Anna came out and stood on the ground by the running board. Bill Gore went in and got Maria Maffei and hauled her out. Orrie growled, "Shut your trap, you." He called to me, "If that driver grunts let him have it. Turn out the lights."

Bill Gore said, "I've got her purse, it's fat."

"Which one?"

"This one."

"All right, keep it, and keep her trap shut. If she yells rap her one." Orrie turned to Durkin. "Here, hold this one while I put a light on her."

Durkin moved behind Anna and gripped her arms, and Orrie put a flashlight on her face. She looked pale and her lips were clamped tight; she hadn't let out a chirp. Orrie held his light right against her and his masked face was just behind it. He said, "It's you all right. By God, I've got you. So you will tell people about Carlo Maffei cutting out newspaper clippings and talking on the phone and everything you ought to forget. Will you? You won't any more. The knife that was good enough for Carlo Maffei is good enough for you. Tell him hello for me."

He pulled out the long sticker and waved it and it gleamed in the light of the flash. He was too damn good. Maria

Maffei yelled and jumped for him and nearly got away from Bill Gore. Bill, who weighed two hundred and no fat, got all around her. Durkin was pulling Anna Fiore back away from the knife and saying to Orrie, "None of that! Cut it! You said you wouldn't. None of that!" Orrie stopped waving the knife and put the light on Anna again.

"All right." He made it sound bloodthirsty. "Where's your purse? I'll get you later. Come on, don't stand there shaking your head. Where's your purse? Where's that hundred dollars I sent you? No?—Hold her, I'll frisk her for it."

He started for her stocking, and Anna was a wildcat. She busted loose from Durkin and let out a squawk that must have reached to White Plains. Orrie grabbed for her and tore her sleeve half off; Durkin was on her again, and when she saw she couldn't get away she put on a kicking and biting exhibition that made me glad I was leaving that to the help. Durkin finally got her snug, with an arm wrapped around her pinning her arms and his other hand holding her head back, but Orrie never did get his hand inside her stocking, he had to tear it right off. I saw the getaway would have to be quick or we'd have to tie her up, so I had Saul back his car along the edge of the drive so I could get by with mine. Durkin came carrying Anna Fiore, still kicking and trying to bite him, and shoved her into the tonneau; Orrie was with him, growling at her, "You kept my money, did you? You wouldn't burn it, huh? Next time you'll keep your mouth shut."

I ran to the Buick and started the engine and rolled alongside. The others piled in. As we started off Maria Maffei was yelling at us, but I didn't hear Anna's voice. I twisted around the curves of the drive as fast as was practicable, and as soon as I had turned into the public road I stepped on it.

Bill Gore in the back seat was laughing about ready to choke. I got to the Sawmill River Road and turned south, and eased down to forty. Orrie, beside me, wasn't saying anything. I asked him:

"You got the money?"

"Yeah, I got it." He didn't sound very sweet. "I think I'll keep it until I find out if Nero Wolfe carries workmen's compensation insurance."

"Why, did she get you?"

"She bit me twice. That lassie didn't think any more of that hundred bucks than I do of my right eye. If you'd told me

I had to subdue a tiger with my bare hands I'd have remembered I had a date."

Bill Gore started laughing again.

I thought it had been pretty well staged. Wolfe couldn't ask better than that. The only thing I had been afraid of was that Anna would get such a scare thrown into her that she would fold up for good, but now that didn't seem likely. I was glad Wolfe had thought of using Maria Maffei and she had been ready for the job, for I wouldn't have cared a bit about driving Anna Fiore back to town with her empty sock. The only question now was, what did she have and how soon would we get it? Would Wolfe's program carry through to the end as he had outlined it, and if it did what kind of a climax would she hand us?

Anyhow, my next move was to get back to the office without delay, so I didn't take time to distribute my passengers where they belonged. I dropped Bill Gore off at Nineteenth Street and took Durkin and Orrie on downtown and left them at the Times Square subway station. Since it wouldn't do to leave the Buick out in front, I drove to the garage and delivered it, and walked home.

I hadn't cared much for the notion Manuel Kimball had got about the sort of present that would be appropriate for Nero Wolfe, and on leaving I had told Fritz to put the bolt on as soon as we got out, so now I had to ring him up to let me in. It was nearly midnight, but he came to the first ring.

Wolfe was in the office, eating cookies and marking items in Hoehn's catalog. I went in and stood, waiting for him to look up. He did so at length, and said, "On time."

I nodded. "And not on my shield, but Orrie Cather is, nearly. She bit him. She bit Durkin too. She was a holy terror. Your play went off swell. They ought to be here soon; I'm going up and dress for the next act. Can I have a glass of milk?"

Wolfe said, "Good," and turned back to his catalog.

I took the milk upstairs with me to my room, and sipped it in between while I was getting undressed and putting on my pajamas. This part of the stunt seemed to me pretty fussy, but I didn't mind because it gave me a chance to doll up in the dressing gown Wolfe had given me a couple of years before which I hadn't had on more than about once. I lit a cigarette and finished the milk, then put on the dressing gown and gave it the once over in the mirror. While I was doing that I heard a car drive up and stop outside, and I moved closer to the open window and heard Saul Panzer's voice, and then Maria Maffei's. I sat down and lit another cigarette.

I sat there nearly half an hour. I heard Fritz letting them in, and their voices in the hall as they passed on their way to the office, and then all I got was silence. I waited so long that I was beginning to wonder whether it wasn't working right, or Wolfe was finishing his charade without me. Then there were footsteps in the hall, and in a minute on the stairs, and Fritz was at my door saying that Wolfe wanted me in the office. I waited a little, long enough to get awake and into my dressing gown, as if I had been asleep, and ruffled up my hair, and went down.

Wolfe was seated at his desk. Maria Maffei was in a chair in front of him and Anna in one against the wall. Anna was a sight, with one sleeve nearly off, a leg bare, her face dirty and her hair all over.

I stared. "Miss Maffei! Anna! Did they set the dogs on you?"

Wolfe wiggled a finger at me. "Archie. I'm sorry to have to disturb you. Miss Maffei and Miss Fiore have been subjected to violence. They were driving into the country, to visit Miss Maffei's sister, when they were set upon by brigands. Their car was stopped; they were treated with discourtesy, and robbed. Miss Maffei's purse was taken, and her rings. Miss Fiore was despoiled of the money which she has shown to us and which she so hardly earned."

"No!" I said. "Anna! They didn't take that money!"

Anna's eyes were on me. I met them all right, but after a second I thought it would do to turn back to Wolfe.

Anna said, "*He* took it."

Wolfe nodded. "Miss Fiore got the impression that the man who took her money was the one who had sent it to her. I have advised her and Miss Maffei to go to the police at once, but they do not fancy that suggestion. Miss Maffei mistrusts the police on principle. Miss Fiore seems to have conceived the idea that we, more especially you, are more likely to be of help. Of course you are not at the moment properly dressed to go out in search of robbers, and the scene is thirty miles off, but Miss Fiore asked for you. Does anything occur to you?"

"Well," I said. "This is awful. It's terrible. And me upstairs sound asleep. I wish you had got me to drive you to the country, Anna; if you had this wouldn't have happened, I don't care who it was that tried to get your money. I don't believe it could have been the man who sent it to you; that man kills people; he would have killed you."

Anna's eyes were going back and forth between Wolfe and me, but I no longer thought there might me suspicion in them; she was only stunned, overwhelmed by her unimaginable loss. She said, "He wanted to kill me. I bit him."

"Good for you. You see, Anna, what happens when you try to act decent with a bad man. If you had burned that money the other day when I wanted you to, and told us what you know about things, now you would have Mr. Wolfe's money. Now you can't burn the money because you haven't got it, and the only way you could get it back would be if I could catch him. Remember, he's the man who killed Carlo Maffei. And look what he did to you! Tore your dress and pulled off your stockings—did he hurt you?"

Anna shook her head. "He didn't hurt me. Could you catch him?"

"I could try. I could if I knew where to look."

"Would you give it back to me?"

"Your money? I sure would."

Anna looked down at her bare leg, and her hand slid slowly under the hem of her skirt and rested on the spot where the twenties had been. Maria Maffei started to speak, but Wolfe wiggled her into silence. Anna was still looking at her leg when she said, "I've got to undress."

I was slow; Wolfe got it at once. He spoke: "Ah. Certainly, Archie: the lights in the front room. Miss Maffei, if you will accompany Miss Fiore?"

I went to the front room and turned the lights on, and closed the windows and the curtains. Anna and Miss Maffei had followed me in and stood there waiting for me to leave; as I went out I gave Anna a friendly grin; she looked pale but her eyes were brighter than I had ever seen them. In the office I closed the door behind me. Wolfe was sitting up in his chair, not leaning back; there was nothing to remark on the drowsy patient hemisphere of his face, but his forearms extended along the arms of the chair and the forefinger of his right hand was moving so that its tip described a little circle over and over on the polished wood. For Wolfe that was going pretty far in the way of agitation.

I sat down. Faint sounds of movements and voices came from the front room. They were taking long enough. I said, "This is a swell toga you gave me."

Wolfe looked at me, sighed, and let his eyes go half shut again.

When the door opened I sprang up. Anna came through in front, clutching a piece of paper in her hand; her torn sleeve had been pinned together and her hair fingered back. She came up to me and stuck the paper at me and mumbled, "Mr. Archie." I wanted to pat her on the shoulder but I saw she was sure to cry if I did, so I just nodded and she went back to her chair and Maria Maffei to hers. The paper was a fat little manila envelope. I turned to Wolfe's desk to hand it to him, but he nodded to me to open it. It wasn't sealed. I pulled out the contents and spread them on the desk.

There was quite a collection. Wolfe and I took our time inspecting it. Item, the Barstow death clipping that Carlo Maffei had cut from the *Times* on June fifth. Item, a series of drawings on separate little sheets, exact and fine, with two springs and a trigger and a lot of complications; the shape of one was the head of a golf driver. Item, a clipping from a Sunday Rotogravure, a photograph of Manuel Kimball standing by his airplane, and a caption with his name commenting on the popularity of aviation among the Westchester younger set. At the bottom was written in pencil, *The man I made the golf club for. See drawings. May 26, 1933. Carlo Maffei.* Item, a ten-dollar bill. It was a gold note, and there was pencil-writing on it too, the signatures of four people: Sarah Barstow, Peter Oliver Barstow, Lawrence Barstow, and Manuel Kimball. The signatures had been written with a broad-pointed soft pencil and covered half of one side of the bill.

I looked it all over a second time and then murmured at Wolfe, "Lovin' babe."

He said, "I tolerate that from Saul Panzer, Archie, I will not from you. Not even as a tribute to this extraordinary display. Poor Carlo Maffei! To combine the foresight that assembled this with the foolhardiness that took him to his fatal rendezvous! We alone profit by the foresight, he pays for the foolhardiness himself—a contemptible bargain.—Miss Maffei, you have lost your purse but gained the means of stilling the ferment of your blood; the murderer of your brother is known and the weapon for his punishment is at hand.—Miss Fiore, you will get your money back. Mr. Archie will get it and return it, I promise you. He will do it soon, for I can guess how little promises mean to you; the fierce flame of reality is your only warmth and light; the reality of twenty-dollar bills. Soon,

Miss Fiore. Please tell me: when did Mr. Maffei give you all this?"

Anna talked. Not what you could call voluble, but willingly enough to Wolfe's questions. He got every detail and had me take it down. She had actually seen the driver. For many days Carlo Maffei had forbidden her to enter his room when he was there working, and had kept his closet locked; but one day during his absence the closet door had opened to her trial only to disclose nothing to her curiosity more uncommon than a golf club evidently in process of construction. On Maffei's return, finding that the driver was not placed as he had left it, he had been sufficiently disturbed to inform her that if she ever mentioned the golf club he would cut her tongue out. That was all she knew about it. The envelope had been given to her on June fifth, the day Maffei disappeared. Around seven o'clock, just after he had answered the telephone call, she had gone upstairs for something and he had called her into his room and given her the envelope. He had told her that he would ask her to return it in the morning, but that if he did not come back that night and nothing was heard from him Anna was to deliver the envelope to his sister.

When Anna told that Maria Maffei got active. She jumped up and started toward the girl. I went after her, but Wolfe's voice like a whip beat me to it:

"Miss Maffei!" He wiggled his finger. "To your chair.—Be seated, I say!—Thank you. Your brother was already dead. Save your fury. After pulling Miss Fiore's hair you would, I suppose, inquire why she did not give you the envelope. That appears to me obvious; perhaps I can save her the embarrassment of replying. I do not know whether your brother told her not to look into the envelope; in any any event, she looked. She saw the ten dollar bill; it was in her possession.—Miss Fiore, before Carlo Maffei gave you that envelope, what was the largest sum you ever had?"

Anna said, "I don't know."

I asked her, "Did you ever have ten dollars before?"

"No, Mr. Archie."

"Five dollars?"

She shook her head. "Mrs. Ricci gives me a dollar every week."

"Swell. And you buy your shoes and clothes?"

"Of course I do."

I threw up my hands. Wolfe said, "Miss Maffei, you or I

might likewise be tempted by a kingdom, only its boundaries would not be so modest. She probably struggled, and by another sunrise might have won and delivered the envelope to you intact; but that morning's mail brought her another envelope, and this time it was not merely a kingdom, it was a glorious world. She lost; or perhaps it is somewhere down as a victory; we cannot know. At any rate her struggle is over.— And now, Miss Maffei, do this and make no mistake: take Miss Fiore home with you and keep her there. Your driver is waiting outside for you. You can explain to your employer that your niece has come for a visit. Explain as you please, but keep Miss Fiore safe until I tell you that the danger is past. Under no circumstances is she to go to the street.— Miss Fiore, you hear?"

"I will do what Mr. Archie says."

"Good. Archie, you will accompany them and explain the requirements. It will be only a day or so."

I nodded and went upstairs to put the dressing gown away for another year and get some clothes on.

Chapter 17

When I got back after escorting Anna and Maria Maffei to the apartment on Park Avenue where Maria Maffei was housekeeper, the office was dark and Wolfe had gone upstairs. There was a note for me: *Archie, learn from Miss Barstow her excuse for mutilating United States currency. N. W.* I knew that would be it. I went on up to the hay, but out of respect to Manuel Kimball I stepped to the rear of the upper hall to look for a line of light under Wolfe's door. There wasn't any. I called out:

"Are you all in one bed?"

Wolfe's voice came, "Confound it, don't badger me!"

"Yes, sir. Is the switch on?"

"It is."

I went to my own room and the bed I was ready for; it was after two o'clock.

In the morning there was a drizzle, but I didn't mind. I took my time at breakfast, and told Fritz to keep the bolt on while I was gone, and then with a light raincoat and a rubber hat went whistling along on my way to the garage. One thing that gave me joy was an item in the morning paper which said that the White Plains authorities were on the verge of being satisfied that the death of Peter Oliver Barstow had resulted from an accidental snake bite and that various other details of the tragedy not connected with that theory could all be explained by coincidence. It would have been fun to call up Harry Foster at the *Gazette* and let him know how safe it would be to stick pins in Anderson's chair for him to sit on, but I couldn't risk it because I didn't know what Wolfe's plans were in that direction. Another source of joy was the completeness of the briefcase which Anna Fiore had been carrying around all the time pinned to whatever she wore underneath. When I considered that it must have been there that first day I had called at Sullivan Street with Maria Maffei and I hadn't been keen enough to smell it, I felt like kicking myself. But maybe it was just as well. If the envelope had been delivered to Maria Maffei there was no telling what might have happened.

I telephoned the Barstow place from uptown, and when I got there around nine-thirty Sarah Barstow was expecting me. In the four days since I had last seen her she had made some changes in her color scheme; her cheeks would have made good pinching; her shoulders sat straight with all the sag gone. I got up from my seat in the sun-room, a drizzle-room that day, when she came in, and she came over and shook hands. She told me her mother was well again, and this time Dr. Bradford said more likely than not she was well for good. Then she asked if I wanted a glass of milk!

I grinned. "I guess not, thanks. As I told you on the phone, Miss Barstow, this time it's a business call. Remember, the last time I said it was social? Today, business." I pulled an envelope from my pocket and got out the ten dollar bill and handed it to her. "Nero Wolfe put it this way: what excuse did you have for mutilating United States currency?"

She looked at it puzzled for a second, then smiled, and then a shadow went over her face, the shadow of her dead father. "Where did you ever—where did you get it?"

"Oh, a hoarder turned it in. But how did those names get on there? Did you write yours?"

She nodded. "Yes, we all did. I think I told you—didn't I? —That one day last summer Larry and Manuel Kimball played a match of tennis and my father and I acted as umpire and linesman. They had a bet on it, and Larry paid Mr. Kimball with a ten dollar bill and Mr. Kimball wanted us to write our names on it as a souvenir. We were sitting—on the side terrace—"

"And Manuel Kimball took the bill?"

"Of course. He won it."

"And this is it?"

"Certainly, there are our signatures.—Mr. Goodwin, I suppose it's just vulgar curiosity, but where did you ever get it?"

I took the bill and replaced it carefully in the envelope —not Carlo Maffei's envelope, a patent one with a clip on it so the signatures wouldn't rub any more than they had already —and put it in my pocket.

"I'm sorry, Miss Barstow. Since it's just vulgar curiosity you can wait. Not long, I hope. And may I say without offense, you're looking swell. I was thinking when you came in, I'd like to pinch your cheeks."

"What!" She stared, then she laughed. "*That's* a compliment."

"It sure is. If you know how many cheeks there are I wouldn't bother to pinch. Good day, Miss Barstow."

We shook hands while she still laughed.

Headed south again through the drizzle, I considered that the ten-dollar bill clinched it. The other three items in Carlo Maffei's envelope were good evidence, but this was something that no one but Manuel Kimball could have had, and it had got to Carlo Maffei. How, I wondered. Well: Manuel Kimball had kept it in his wallet as a souvenir. His payments of money, one or more, to Maffei for making the driver, had been made not in a well-lighted room but in places dark enough to defeat the idle curiosity of observers; and in the darkness the souvenir had been included in a payment. Probably Manuel had later discovered his carelessness and demanded the souvenir back, and Maffei had claimed it had been spent unnoticed. That might have aroused Manuel's early suspicions of Maffei, and certainly it accounted for Maffei's recognition of the significance of the death, and its manner, of Peter Oliver Barstow; for that name, and two other Barstow names, had been signed on the ten-dollar bill he was preserving.

Yes, Manuel Kimball would live long enough to be sorry he had won that tennis match.

At White Plains, on a last-minute decision, I slowed down and turned off the Parkway. It looked to me as if it was all over and the only thing left was a brief call at the District Attorney's office to explain the facts of life to him; and in that case there was no point in my driving through the rain all the way down to Thirty-fifth Street and clear back again. So I found a telephone booth and called Wolfe and told him what I had learned from Sarah Barstow, and asked him what next. He told me to come on home. I mentioned that I was right there in White Plains with plenty of time and inclination to do any errands he might have in mind. He said, "Come home. Your errand will be here waiting for you."

I got back onto the Parkway.

It was a little after eleven when I arrived. I couldn't park right in front of the house as usual, because another car was there, a big black limousine. After turning off my engine I sat for a minute staring at the limousine, particularly at the official plate hanging alongside the license plate. I allowed myself the pleasure of a beautiful grin, and I got out and just for fun went to the front of the limousine and spoke to the chauffeur.

"Mr. Anderson is in the house?"

He looked at me a couple of seconds before he could make up his mind to nod. I turned and ran up the steps with the grin still on.

Anderson was with Wolfe in the office. When I went in I pretended not to see him; I went across to Wolfe's desk and took the envelope out of my pocket and handed it to him. "Okay," I said, "I've written the date of the match on the envelope." He nodded and told me to put it in the safe. I opened the heavy door and took my time about finding the drawer where the rest of Anna's briefcase was stowed away. Then I turned, and let my eyes fall on the visitor and looked surprised.

"Oh," I said, "it's you! Good morning, Mr. Anderson."

He mumbled back at me.

"If you ever get your notebook, Archie, we shall proceed." Wolfe was using his drawly voice, and when I heard it I knew that one lawyer was in for a lot of irritation. "No, not at your desk, pull a chair around and be one of us.—Good. I have just been explaining to Mr. Anderson that the ingenious theory of the Barstow case which he is trying to embrace is an

offense to truth and an outrage on justice, and since I cherish
the one and am on speaking terms with the other, it is my duty
to demonstrate to him its inadequacy. I shall be glad of your
support. Mr. Anderson is a little put out at the urgency of my
invitation to him to call, but as I was just remarking to him, I
think we should be grateful that the telephone permits the
arrangement on short notice of these little informal confer-
ences.—On reflection, Mr. Anderson, I'm sure you will
agree."

Anderson's neck was swelling. There was never anything
very lovely about him, but now he was trying to keep his
meanness down because he knew he had to, and it kept
choking him trying to come up. His face was red and his neck
bulged. He said to Wolfe, "You can tell your man to put his
notebook away. You're a bigger ass than I thought you were,
Wolfe, if you imagine you can put over this sort of thing."

"Take it down, Archie." Wolfe's drawl was swell. "It is
irrelevant, being merely an opinion, but get it down.—Mr.
Anderson, I see that you misapprehend the situation; I had not
supposed you were so obtuse. I gave you a free choice of
alternatives on the telephone, and you chose to come here.
Being here, in my house, you will permit me to direct the
activity of its inmates; should you become annoyed beyond
endurance, you may depart without ceremony or restraint.
Should you depart, the procedure will be as I have indicated:
within twenty-four hours Mr. Goodwin will drive in my car to
your office in White Plains. Behind him, in another car, will
be an assortment of newspaper reporters; beside him will be
the murderer of Peter Oliver Barstow and Carlo Maffei; in his
pocket will be the indubitable proof of the murderer's guilt. I
was minded to proceed—"

Anderson broke in, "Carlo Maffei? Who the devil is that?"

"Was, Mr. Anderson. Not is. Carlo Maffei was an Italian
craftsman who was murdered in your county on Monday
evening, June fifth—stabbed in the back. Surely the case is in
your office."

"What if it is? What has that got to do with Barstow?"

"They were murdered by the same man."

Anderson stared. "By God, Wolfe, I think you're crazy."

"I'm afraid not." Wolfe sighed. "There are times when I
would welcome such a conclusion as an escape from life's
meaner responsibilities—what Mr. Goodwin would call an out

—but the contrary evidence is overwhelming.—But to our business. Have you your checkbook with you?"

"Ah." Anderson's lips twisted. "What if I have?"

"It will make it more convenient for you to draw a check to my order for ten thousand dollars."

Anderson said nothing. He put his eyes straight into Wolfe's and kept them there, and Wolfe met him. Wolfe sighed. Finally Anderson said, smooth:

"It might make it convenient, but not very reasonable. You are not a hijacker, are you?"

"Oh, no." Wolfe's cheeks folded up. "I assure you, no. I have the romantic temperament, but physically I'm not built for it. You do not grasp the situation? Let me explain. In a way, it goes four years back, to the forgetfulness you displayed in the Goldsmith case. I regretted that at the time, and resolved that on some proper occasion you should be reminded of it. I now remind you. Two weeks ago I came in possession of information which presented an opportunity to extend you a favor. I wished to extend it; but with the Goldsmith case in my memory and doubtless, so I thought, in yours also, it seemed likely that delicacy of feeling would prevent you from accepting a favor from me. So I offered to sell you the information for a proper sum; that of course was what the proffer of a wager amounted to; the proof that you understood it so was furnished by your counter-offer to Mr. Goodwin of a sum so paltry that I shall not mention it."

Anderson said, "I offered a substantial fee."

"Mr. Anderson! Please. Don't drag us into absurdities." Wolfe leaned back and laced his fingers on his belly. "Mr. Goodwin and I have discovered the murderer and have acquired proof of his guilt; not plausible proof, jury proof. That brings us to the present. The murderer, of course, is not my property, he belongs to the sovereign State of New York. Even the information I possess is not my property; if I do not communicate it to the State I am liable to penalties. But I can choose my method. First: you will now give me your personal check for ten thousand dollars, this afternoon Mr. Goodwin will go to your bank and have it certified, and tomorrow morning he will conduct you to the murderer, point him to you, and deliver the proof of his guilt—all in a properly diffident and unostentatious manner. Or, second: we shall proceed to organize the parade to your office as I have described it: the prisoner, the press, and the proof, with a complete absence of diffidence. Take your choice, sir. Though you may find it hard to believe, it is of little concern to me, for while it would give me pleasure to receive your check, I have a great fondness for parades."

Wolfe stopped. Anderson looked at him, silent and smooth, calculating. Wolfe pressed the button on his desk and, when Fritz appeared, ordered beer. Every chance I got to look up from my notebook, I stared at Anderson; I could see it made him sore, and I stared all I could.

Anderson asked, "How do I know your proof is any good?"

"My word, sir. It is as good as my judgment. I pledge both."

"There is no possible doubt?"

"Anything is possible. There is no room for doubt in the minds of a jury."

Anderson twisted his lips around. Fritz brought the beer, and Wolfe opened a bottle and filled a glass.

Anderson said, "Ten thousand dollars is out of the question. Five thousand."

"Pfui! You would dicker? Contemptible. Let it be the parade." Wolfe picked up his glass of beer and gulped it.

"Give me the proof and tell me the murderer and you can have the check the minute I've got him."

Wolfe wiped his lips, and sighed. "Mr. Anderson, one of us has to trust the other. Do not compel me to advance reasons for the preference I have indicated."

Anderson began to put up an argument. He was tough, no doubt about that, he was no softy. Of course he didn't have any real reasons or persuasions, but he had plenty of words. When he stopped Wolfe just shook his head. Anderson went on, and then again, but all he got was the same reply. I took it all down, and I had to admit there wasn't any whine in it. He was fighting with damn poor ammunition, but he wasn't whining.

He wrote the check in a fold he took from his pocket, holding it on his knee, with his fountain pen. He wrote it like a good bookkeeper, precisely and carefully, without haste, and then with the same preciseness filled in the spaces on the stub before he tore the check off and laid it on Wolfe's desk. Wolfe gave me a nod and I reached over and picked up the check and looked it over. I was relieved to see it was on a New York bank; that would save me a trip to White Plains before three o'clock.

Anderson got up. "I hope you never regret this, Wolfe. Now, when and where?"

Wolfe said, "I shall telephone."

"When?"

"Within twenty-four hours. Probably within twelve. I can get you at any time, at your office or your home?"

Anderson said, "Yes," turned on the word, and left. I got up and went to the hall and watched him out. Then I went back to the office and leaned the check up against a paperweight and blew a kiss at it.

Wolfe was whistling; that is, his lips were rounded into the proper position and air was going in and out, but there was no sound. I loved seeing him do that; it never happened when anybody was there but me, not even Fritz. He told me once that it meant he was surrendering to his emotions.

I put my notebook away and stuck the check in my pocket and pulled the chairs back where they belonged. After a little Wolfe said, "Archie, four years is a long time."

"Yes, sir. And ten grand is a lot of money. It's nearly an hour till lunch; I'll run down to the bank now and get their scrawl on it."

"It is raining. I thought of you this morning, adventuring beyond the city. Call for a messenger."

"Good Lord, no. I wouldn't miss the fun of having this certified for a gallon of milk."

Wolfe leaned back, murmured, "Intrepid," and closed his eyes.

I got back in time to bust the tape at lunch.

I figured, naturally, that the hour had struck, but to my surprise Wolfe seemed to have notions of leisure. He was in no hurry about anything. He took his time at the table, with two long cups of coffee at the end, and after lunch he went to the office and reposed in his chair without appearing to have anything of importance on his mind. I fussed around. After a while he roused himself enough to give me some directions: first, type out Anna Fiore's statement completely and chronologically; second, have photostatic copies made, rush, of the contents of Carlo Maffei's envelope; third, go to the Park Avenue apartment and return Maria Maffei's purse to her and have Anna Fiore sign the statement in duplicate before witnesses; and fourth, check with Horstmann the shipment of pseudo-bulbs which had arrived the preceding day on the *Cortez*.

I asked him, "Maybe you're forgetting something?" He shook his head, faintly so as not to disturb his comfort, and I let it slide. I was curious but not worried, for I could tell by the look on his face that he was adding something up to the right answer.

For the rest of the afternoon I was busy. I went out first, to a studio down on Sixth Avenue, to get them started on the photostats, and I made sure that they understood that if the originals were lost or injured they had better use the fire escape when they heard me coming. Then back to the office, to type Anna's statement. I fixed it up in swell shape and it took quite a while. When I went out to the roadster again the rain had stopped and it was brightening up, but the pavements were still wet. I had telephoned the apartment where Maria Maffei worked, and when I got there she was expecting me. I would hardly have known her. In a neat well-cut house-keeper's dress, black, with a little black thing across the top of her hair, she looked elegant, and her manner was as Park Avenue as the doorman at the Pierre. Well, I thought, they're all different in the bathtub from what they're like at Schrafft's. I was almost afraid to hand her her purse, it seemed vulgar. But she took it. Then she led me to a room away off, and there was Anna Fiore sitting looking out of a window. I read the statement to her, and she signed it, and Maria Maffei and I signed as witnesses.

Anna said next to nothing with her tongue, but her eyes kept asking me one question all the time, from the minute I entered the room. When I got up to go I answered it. I patted her on the shoulder and said, "Soon, Anna. I'll get your money real soon, and bring it right to you. Don't you worry."

She just nodded and said, "Mr. Archie."

After I got the photostats from the studio I saw no point in leaving the roadster out ready for action if there wasn't going to be any, so I garaged it and walked home. Until dinner time I was busy checking up the *Cortez* shipment and writing letters to the shippers about the casualties. Wolfe was pottering around most of the time while I was upstairs with Horstmann, but at six o'clock he left us and Horstmann and I went on checking.

It was after eight o'clock by the time dinner was over. I was getting the fidgets. Seven years with Nero Wolfe had taught me not to bite my nails waiting for the world to come to an end, but there were times when I was convinced that an

eccentric was a man who ought to have his nose pulled. That
evening he kept the radio going all through dinner. As soon as
it was over and he nodded to Fritz to pull his chair back, I got
up and said:

"I guess I won't sit in the office and watch you yawn. I'll
try a movie."

Wolfe said, "Good. No man should neglect his cultural
side."

"What!" I exploded. "You mean—damn it all, you would
let me go and sit in a movie while maybe Manuel Kimball is
finishing his packing for a nice little trip to his native land?
Then I can go to the Argentine and buy a horse and ride all
over the damn pampa, whatever that is, looking for him? Do
you think all it takes to catch a murderer is to sit in your damn
office and let your genius work? That maybe most of it, but it
also takes a pair of eyes and a pair of legs and sometimes a gun
or two. And the best thing you can think of is to tell me to go to
a movie, while you—"

He showed me the palm of his hand to stop me. Fritz had
pulled his chair back and he was up, a mountain on its feet.
"Archie," he said. "Spare me. A typical man of violence; the
placidity of a hummingbird. I did not suggest the movie, you
did. Even were Manuel Kimball a man to tremble at shadows,
there has been no shadow to disturb him. Why should Manuel
Kimball take a trip, to his native land or anywhere else? There
is nothing he is less likely to take at this moment, I should say.
If it will set your mind at rest, I can tell you that he is at his
home, but not packing for a trip. I was speaking to him on the
telephone only two hours ago.—Fritz, the buzzer, attend the
front door, please.—He will receive another telephone call
from me in the morning at eight o'clock, and I assure you he
will wait for it."

"I hope he does." I wasn't satisfied. "I tell you, monkeying
around at this stage is dangerous. You've done your part, a part
no other living man could do, and now it's simple but it's damn
important. I just go there and wrap myself around him, and
stay wrapped until you tell Anderson to go and get him. Why
not?"

Wolfe shook his head. "No, Archie. I understand your
contention: that a point arrives when finesse must retire and
leave the coup de grâce for naked force. I understand it, and I
deny it vehemently.—But come; guests are arriving; will you

stop in the office a moment before you proceed to your entertainment?"

He turned and went to the office, and I followed him, wondering what the devil kind of a charade he was getting up. Whatever it was, I didn't like it.

Fritz had gone to the door, and the guests had been shown into the office ahead of us. I had no definite ideas as to who it might be, but certainly I didn't expect that bunch. I stared around at them. It was Fred Durkin and Bill Gore and Orrie Cather. My first thought was that Wolfe had got the funny notion that I needed all that army to subdue the fer-de-lance, as I had decided to call Manuel Kimball instead of the spiggoty, but of course Wolfe knew me too well for that. I tossed a nod around to them, and grinned when I saw a gauze bandage on Orrie's left wrist. Anna Fiore had got under his skin all right.

After Wolfe got into his chair he asked me to get a pencil and a large piece of paper and make a rough map of the Kimball estate. With the guests there I asked no questions; I did as he said. I told him that I was acquainted with the ground only immediately around the house and the landing field, and he said that would do. While I made the map, sitting at my desk, Wolfe was telling Orrie how to get the sedan from the garage at six-thirty in the morning, and instructing the other two to meet him there at that hour.

I took the map to Wolfe at his desk. He looked it over a minute and said, "Good. Now tell me, if you were sending three men to that place to make sure that Manuel Kimball did not leave without being seen, and to follow him if seen, how would you dispose of them?"

I asked, "Under cover?"

"No. Exposed would do."

"How long?"

"Three hours."

I considered a minute. "Easy. Durkin on the highway, across from the entrance to the drive, with the sedan backed into a gate so it could start quick either way. Bill Gore in the bushes—about here—where he could cover all approaches to the house except the back. Orrie on top of a hill back here, about a third of a mile off, with field glasses, and a motorcycle down on the road. But they might as well stay home and play pinochle, since they can't fly."

Wolfe's cheeks folded. "Saul Panzer can. The clouds will

have eyes. Thank you, Archie. That is all. We will not keep you longer from your entertainment."

I knew from his tone that I was to go, but I didn't want to. If there had to be a charade I wanted to help make it up. I said, "The movies have all been closed. Raided by the Society for the Suppression of Vice."

Wolfe said, "Then try a harlot's den. When gathering eggs you must look in every nest."

Bill Gore snickered. I gave Wolfe as dirty a look as I could manage, and went to the hall for my hat.

Chapter 18

I was awake Wednesday morning before seven o'clock, but I didn't get up. I watched the sun slanting against the windows, and listened to the noises from the street and the boats and ferries on the river, and figured that since Bill and Fred and Orrie had been instructed to meet at the garage at six-thirty they must already be as far as the Grand Concourse. My part hadn't been handed to me. When I had got home the night before Wolfe had gone up to bed, and there had been no note for me.

I finally tumbled out and shaved and dressed, taking my time, and went downstairs. Fritz was in the kitchen, buzzing around contented. I passed him some kind of a cutting remark, but realizing that it wasn't fair to take it out on him I made up for it by eating an extra egg and reading aloud to him a piece from the morning paper about a vampire bat that had had a baby in the zoo. Fritz came from the part of Switzerland where they talk French. He had a paper of his own every morning, but it was in French and it never seemed very likely to me that there was much in it. I was always surprised when I saw a word in it that meant anything up-to-date; for instance, the word Barstow which had been prominent in the headlines for a week.

I was starting the second cup of coffee when the phone rang. I went to the office and got the receiver to my ear, but

Wolfe had answered from his room. I listened. It was Orrie
Cather reporting that they had arrived and that everything was
set. That was all. I went back to my coffee in the kitchen.

After a third cup and a cigarette I moseyed into the office.
Sooner or later, I thought, genius will impart its secrets;
sooner or later, compose yourself; just straighten things
around and dust off the desk and fill the fountain pen and
make everything nice for teacher. Sooner or later, honey—you
damn fool. I wasn't getting the fidgets, I had them. A couple of
times I took off the receiver and listened, but I didn't catch
Wolfe making any calls. I got the mail and put it on his desk,
and opened the safe. I pulled out the drawer where the Maffei
stuff was just to make sure it hadn't walked off. The envelope
into which I had put the photostats felt thin, and I took them
out. One set was gone. I had had two sets made, and only one
was there. That gave me my first hint about Wolfe's charade,
but I didn't follow it up very far, because as I was sticking the
envelope back into the drawer Fritz came in and said that
Wolfe wanted to see me in his room.

I went up. His door was open. He was up and dressed all
but his coat; the sleeves of his yellow shirt—he used two fresh
shirts every day, always canary yellow—looked like enormous
floating sheeps' bladders as he stood at his mirror brushing his
hair. I caught his eyes in the mirror, and he winked at me! I
was so astonished that I suppose my mouth fell open.

He put the brush down and turned to me. "Good
morning, Archie. You have breakfast?—Good. It is pleasant to
see the sun again, after yesterday's gray unceasing trickle. Get
the Maffei documents from the safe. By all means take a gun.
Proceed to White Plains and get Mr. Anderson at his office
—he will be awaiting you—and drive him to the Kimball
estate. Show him Manuel Kimball; point, if necessary. When
Manuel Kimball has been apprehended deliver the documents
to Mr. Anderson. Return here, and you will find that Fritz will
have prepared one of your favorite dishes for lunch."

I said, "Okay. But why all the mystery—"

"Comments later, Archie. Save them, please. I am due
upstairs in ten minutes and I have yet to enjoy my chocolate."

I said, "I hope you choke on it," and turned and left him.

With the Carlo Maffei stuff and Anna's statement on my
breast and a thirty-eight, loaded this time, on my hip, I walked
to the garage. It was warm and sunny, June twenty-first, the
day for the sun to start back south. It was a good day for the

finale of the fer-de-lance, I thought, the longest one of th
year. I filled up with gas and oil and water, made it cross tow
to Park Avenue, and turned north. As I passed the marbl
front of the Manhattan Trust Company I saluted; that wa
where I had had Anderson's check certified. Going north o
the Parkway at that hour of the morning there was plenty o
room, but I kept my speedometer at forty or under; Wolfe ha
told Anderson this would be unostentatious, and besides,
wasn't in the mood for repartee with a motor cop. I was prett
well on edge. I always am like that when I'm really on my wa
for a man; there never seems to be quite enough air for me;
breathe quicker and everything I touch—the steering whee
for instance—seems to be alive with blood going in it. I don
like the feeling much but I always have it.

Anderson was waiting for me. In his office the girl at th
desk tossed me a nod and got busy on the phone. In a minut
Anderson came out. There were two men with him, carryin
their hats and looking powerful. One of them was H. F
Corbett; the other was new to me. Anderson stopped to sa
something to the girl at the desk, then came over to me.

"Well?" he said.

I grinned. "I'm ready if you are. Hello, Corbett. Yo
going along?"

Anderson said, "I'm taking two men. You know what th
job is. Is that enough?"

I nodded. "All we'll need 'em for is to hold my ha
anyway. Let's go." The third guy opened the door and we file
out.

Anderson came with me in the roadster; the other tw
followed us in a closed car, official, but I noticed it wasn
Anderson's limousine. Going down Main Street all the traff
cops saluted my passenger, and I grinned considering ho
surprised they would have been if they had known how muc
the District Attorney was paying for that little taxi ride.
opened her up as soon as I got onto the highway, and rolle
over the hills, up and down, so fast that Anderson looked
me. He didn't know but what the speed was part of th
program, so I kept going, slowing down only at the poin
where I had to make a turn and needed to make sure th
Corbett, trailing along behind, had caught it. It took ju
twenty-five minutes from the White Plains courthouse to th
entrance to the Kimball drive; the clock on my dash sai
ten-forty as I slowed up to turn in.

Durkin was there, across the road, sitting on the running board of the sedan which had been backed in as I had suggested. I waved at him but didn't stop. Anderson asked, "That Wolfe's man?" I nodded and swept into the drive. I had gone about a hundred feet when Anderson said, "Stop!" I pushed the pedals down, shifted into neutral, and pulled the hand brake.

Anderson said, "This is E. D. Kimball's place. You've got to show me right here."

I shook my head. "Nothing doing. You know Nero Wolfe, and that'll do for you. I'm obeying orders. Do I go on?"

Corbett's car had stopped right behind us. Anderson was looking at me, his mouth twisted with uncertainty. I had my ears open, straining, not for Anderson's reply, but for what I was taking for the sound of an airplane. Even if I had been willing to get out and look up I couldn't, on account of trees. But it was an airplane, sure. I shifted and started forward on the jump.

Anderson said, "By God, Goodwin, I hope you know what you're risking. If I had known—"

I stopped him, "Shut up!"

I pulled up at the house and ran over and rang the bell. In a minute the door was opened by the fat butler.

"I'd like to speak to Mr. Manuel Kimball."

"Yes, sir, Mr. Goodwin? He is expecting you. He told me to ask you to go to the hangar and wait for him there."

"Isn't he there?"

The butler hesitated, and he certainly looked worried. "I believe he intended to go aloft in his plane."

I nodded and ran back to the car. Corbett had got out and walked to the roadster and was talking with Anderson. As I got in Anderson turned to me and started, "Look here, Goodwin—"

"Did you hear me say shut up? I'm busy. Look out, Corbett."

I shot forward onto the back drive and headed for the graveled road that led to the hangar. On that, out from under the trees, the sound of the airplane was louder. I made the gravel fly, and whirled to a stop on the concrete platform in front of the hangar. The mechanic, Skinner, was standing there in the wide open door. I jumped out and went over to him.

"Mr. Manuel Kimball?"

Skinner pointed up, and I looked. It was Manuel Kimball's plane, high, but not too high for me to see the red and blue. It seemed to make a lot of noise, and the next second I saw why, when I caught sight of another plane circling in from the west, higher than Manuel's and going faster. It was helping with the noise. Both planes were circling, dark and beautiful in the sun. I brought my head down to sneeze.

Skinner said, "He's got company this morning."

"So I see. Who is it?"

"I don't know. I saw it first a little after eight o'clock and it's been fooling around up there ever since. It's a Burton twin-motor, it's got a swell dip."

I remember Wolfe saying the clouds would have eyes. There weren't any clouds, but no doubt about the eyes.

I asked, "What time did Mr. Kimball go up?"

"A little after ten. They came out around nine-thirty, but the second seat wasn't ready and I had to fix the straps."

I knew what it meant as soon as he said it, but I asked him anyhow. I said, "Oh, is there someone with him?"

"Yes, sir, his father. The old gentleman's having a ride. It's only his third time up. He nearly backed out when the seat wasn't ready, but we got him in."

I looked up at the airplanes again. Manuel Kimball and his father having a ride together, up there in the sun, the wind and the roar. No conversation probably, just a morning ride.

I started toward the roadster, to speak to Anderson. Corbett had left his car and came to meet me. I stopped to listen to him: "Well, we've come to your party, where's your guest of honor?"

I brushed past him and went on to the roadster. Seeing no point in giving the mechanic an earful, I lowered my voice. "You'll have to wait, Mr. Anderson. Barstow's murderer is taking an airplane ride. I'm sorry you won't get him on time but you'll get him."

Anderson said, "Get in here. I want a showdown."

I shook my head. Maybe it was just contrariness, but I was set on carrying it out exactly as Wolfe had ordered. "That's not next on the program." Corbett had come up, around on the other side of the roadster, and now he stuck his face in at the window and said to Anderson, "If he's got anything you want I'd be glad to get it for you."

I had my mouth open to invite him formally when I heard my name called. I turned. Skinner had left the hangar and was

approaching me; in one hand he had a golf driver and in the
other an envelope. I stared at him. He was saying, "I forgot.
You're Mr. Goodwin? Mr. Kimball left these for you."

I got to him and grabbed. The driver! I looked at it, but
there was nothing to see; in outward appearance it was just a
golf club. But of course it was it. Lovin' babe! I tucked it
under my arm and looked at the envelope; on the outside was
written, *Mr. Nero Wolfe*. It was unsealed, and I pulled out the
contents, and had in my hand the set of photostats I had
missed from the safe. They were fastened with a paper clip,
and slipped under the clip was a piece of paper on which I
read: *Thank you, Nero Wolfe. In appreciation of your courtesy
I am leaving a small gift for you. Manuel Kimball.* I looked up
at the sky. The red and blue airplane of the leading character
in Wolfe's charade was still there, higher I thought, circling,
with the other plane above. I put the photostats back into the
envelope.

Corbett was in front of me. "Here, I'll take that."

"Oh no. Thanks, I can manage."

He sprang like a cat and I wasn't expecting it. It was neat.
He got the envelope with one hand and the driver with the
other. He started for the roadster. Two jumps put me in front
of him, and he stopped. I wasn't monkeying. I said, "Look out,
here it comes," and plugged him on the jaw with plenty
behind it. He wobbled and dropped his loot, and I let him get
his hands up, and then feinted with my left and plugged him
again. That time he went down. His boy friend came running
up, and Skinner from his side. I turned to meet the boy friend,
but Anderson's voice, with more snap in it than I knew he had,
came from the roadster:

"Curry! Lay off! Cut it!"

Curry stopped. I stepped back. Corbett got up, glaring
wild. Anderson again: "Corbett, you too! Lay off!"

I said, "Not on my account, Mr. Anderson. If they want to
play snatch and run I'll take them both on. They need to be
taught a little respect for private property."

I stooped to pick up the driver and the envelope. It was
while I was bent over, reaching down, that I heard Skinner's
yell.

"Good God! He's lost it!"

For an instant I imagined he meant I had lost the driver,
and I thought he was crazy. Then as I straightened up and
glanced at him and saw where he was looking, I jerked my

eyes and my head up. It was Manuel Kimball's plane directly
overhead, a thousand feet up. It was twisting and whirling as if
it had lost its senses, and coming down. It seemed to be
jerking and coiling back and forth, it didn't look as if it was
falling straight, but I suppose it was. It was right above us
—faster—I stared with my mouth open—

"Look out!" Skinner was shouting. "For God's sake!"

We ran for the hangar door. Anderson was out of the
roadster and with us. We got inside the door and turned in
time to see the crash. Black lightning split the air. A giant
report, not thunderous like a big gun, an instantaneous
ear-splitting snap. Pieces flew; splinters lay at our feet. It had
landed at the edge of the concrete platform, not ten yards from
Corbett's car. We jumped out and ran for the wreckage,
Skinner calling, "Look out for an explosion!"

What I saw first wasn't pretty. The only way I knew it had
been E. D. Kimball was that it was mixed up with a strap in
the position of the back seat and Skinner had said that the old
gentleman had gone up for a ride. Apparently it had landed in
such a way that the front seat had got a different kind of a
blow, for Manuel Kimball could have been recognized by
anybody. His face was still together and even pretty well in
shape. Skinner and I got him loose while the others worked at
the old gentleman. We carried them away from there and
inside the hangar and put them on some canvas on the floor.

Skinner said, "You'd better move your cars. An explosion
might come yet." I said, "When I move my car I'll keep on
moving it. Now's a good time. Mr. Anderson. You may
remember that Nero Wolfe promised I would be diffident.
That's me." I pulled the documents from my pocket and
handed them to him. "Here's your proof. And there's your
man on the floor, the one with the face."

I picked up Manuel Kimball's envelope and the golf
driver from the floor where I had dropped them, and beat it. It
took me maybe four seconds to get the roadster started and out
of there and shooting down the road.

At the entrance, turning onto the highway, I stopped long
enough to call to Durkin, "Call your playmates and come on
home. The show's over."

I got to White Plains in twenty-two minutes. The roadster
never did run nicer. I telephoned Wolfe at the same drugstore where two weeks before I had phoned him that Anderson
had gone to the Adirondacks and I had only Derwin to bet

with. He answered right off, and I gave him the story, brief but complete.

He said, "Good. I hope I haven't offended you, Archie. I thought it best that your mind should not be cluttered with the lesser details. Fritz is preparing to please your palate.—By the way, where is White Plains? Would it be convenient for you to stop on your way at Scarsdale? Gluekner has telephoned me that he has succeeded in hybridizing a Dendrobium Melpomene with a Findlayanum and offers me a seedling."

Chapter 19

It certainly didn't look like much. It was a sick-looking pale blue, and was so small you could get it in an ordinary envelope without folding it. It looked even smaller than it was because the writing in the blank spaces was tall and scrawly; but it was writing with character in it. That, I guessed, was Sarah Barstow. The signature below, Ellen Barstow, was quite different—fine and precise. It was Saturday morning, and the check had come in the first mail; I was giving it a last fond look as I handed it in at the teller's window. I had phoned Wolfe upstairs that a Barstow envelope was there and he had told me to go ahead and open it and deposit the check.

At eleven o'clock Wolfe entered the office and went to his desk and rang for Fritz and beer. I had the Barstow case expense list all typed out for his inspection, and as soon as he had finished glancing through the scanty mail I handed it to him. He took a pencil and went over it slowly, checking each item. I waited. When I saw him hit the third item from the bottom and stop at it, I swallowed.

Wolfe raised his head. "Archie. We must get a new typewriter."

I just cleared my throat. He went on, "This one is too impulsive. Perhaps you didn't notice: it has inserted an extra cipher before the decimal point in the amount opposite Anna

Fiore's name. I observe that you carelessly included the error in summing up."

I managed a grin. "Oh! Now I get you. I forgot to mention it before. Anna's nest-egg has hatched babies, it's a thousand dollars now. I'm taking it down to her this afternoon."

Wolfe sighed. The beer came, and he opened a bottle and gulped a glass. He put the expense list under the paperweight with the mail and leaned back in his chair. "Tomorrow I shall cut down to five quarts."

My grin felt better. I said, "You don't have to change the subject. I wouldn't make the mistake of calling you generous even if you said to double it; you'd still be getting a bargain. Do you know what Anna will do with it? Buy herself a husband. Look at all the good you're doing."

"Confound it. Don't give her anything. Tell her the money cannot be found."

"No, sir. I'll give her the money and let her dig her own grave. I'm not violent, the way you are, and I don't put myself up as a substitute for fate."

Wolfe opened his eyes. He had been drowsy for three days, and I thought it was about time something woke him up. He murmured, "Do you think you're saying something, Archie?"

"Yes, sir. I'm asking where you got the breezy notion of killing E. D. Kimball."

"Where his son got the notion, you mean?"

"No, you. Don't quibble. You killed him."

Wolfe shook his head. "Wrong, Archie. I quibble? E. D. Kimball was killed by the infant son whom he deserted sitting on the floor among his toys in a pool of his mother's blood.—If you please. Properly speaking, E. D. Kimball was not killed last Wednesday morning, but on Sunday June fourth. Through one of the unfortunate accidents by which blind chance interferes with the natural processes of life and death, Barstow died instead. It is true that I helped to remedy that error. I had Durkin deliver to Manuel Kimball copies of our evidence against him, and I telephoned Manuel Kimball that he was surrounded, on the earth and above the earth. I left it to nature to proceed, having ascertained that E. D. Kimball was at home and would not leave that morning."

I said, "You told me once that I couldn't conceal truth by building a glass house around it. What are you trying it for? You killed him."

Wolfe's cheeks folded. He poured another glass of beer and leaned back again and watched the foam. When nothing was left of it but a thin white rim he looked at me and sighed.

"The trouble is," he murmured, "that as usual you are so engrossed in the fact that you are oblivious to its environment. You stick to it, Archie, like a leech on an udder. Consider the situation that faced me. Manuel had tried to kill his father. By an accident beyond his control the innocent Barstow had been killed instead. Evidence that would convict Manuel of murder was in my possession. How should I use it? Had I been able to afford the luxury of a philosophic attitude, I should of course not have used it at all, but that attitude was beyond my means, it was an affair of business. Put myself up as a substitute for fate? Certainly; we do it constantly; we could avoid it only by complete inaction. I was forced to act. If I had permitted you to get Manuel Kimball, without warning, and deliver him alive to the vengeance of the people of the State of New York, he would have gone to the chair of judicial murder a bitter and defeated man, his heart empty of one deep satisfaction life had offered to it; and his father equally bitter and no less defeated, would have tottered through some few last years with nothing left to trade. If I had brought that about I would have been responsible for it, to myself, and the prospect was not pleasing. Still I had to act. I did so, and incurred a responsibility which is vastly less displeasing. You would encompass the entire complex phenomenon by stating bluntly that I killed E. D. Kimball. Well, Archie. I will take the responsibility for my own actions; I will not also assume the burden of your simplicity. Somehow you must bear it."

I grinned. "Maybe. I don't mean maybe I can bear it, I mean maybe all you've just said. Also, maybe I'm simple. I'm so simple that a simple thought occurred to me as I was walking back from the bank this morning."

"Indeed." Wolfe gulped his glass of beer.

"Yes, sir. It occurred to me that if Manuel Kimball had been arrested and brought to trial you would have had to put on your hat and gloves, leave the house, walk to an automobile, ride clear to White Plains, and sit around a courtroom waiting for your turn to testify. Whereas now, natural processes being what they are, and you having such a good feeling for phenomena, you can just sit and hold your responsibilities on your lap."

"Indeed," Wolfe murmured.

ABOUT THE AUTHOR

REX STOUT, the creator of Nero Wolfe, was born in Noblesville, Indiana, in 1886, the sixth of nine children of John and Lucetta Todhunter Stout, both Quakers. Shortly after his birth, the family moved to Wakarusa, Kansas. He was educated in a country school, but, by the age of nine, was recognized throughout the state as a prodigy in arithmetic. Mr. Stout briefly attended the University of Kansas, but left to enlist in the Navy, and spent the next two years as a warrant officer on board President Theodore Roosevelt's yacht. When he left the Navy in 1908, Rex Stout began to write freelance articles, worked as a sightseeing guide and as an itinerant book-keeper. Later he devised and implemented a school banking system which was installed in four hundred cities and towns throughout the country. In 1927 Mr. Stout retired from the world of finance and, with the proceeds of his banking scheme, left for Paris to write serious fiction. He wrote three novels that received favorable reviews before turning to detective fiction. His first Nero Wolfe novel, *Fer-de-Lance*, appeared in 1934. It was followed by many others, among them, *Too Many Cooks, The Silent Speaker, If Death Ever Slept, The Doorbell Rang* and *Please Pass the Guilt*, which established Nero Wolfe as a leading character on a par with Erle Stanley Gardner's famous protagonist, Perry Mason. During World War II, Rex Stout waged a personal campaign against Nazism as chairman of the War Writers' Board, master of ceremonies of the radio program "Speaking of Liberty" and as a member of several national committees. After the war, he turned his attention to mobilizing public opinion against the wartime use of thermonuclear devices, was an active leader in the Authors' Guild and resumed writing his Nero Wolfe novels. All together, his Nero Wolfe novels have been translated into twenty-two languages and have sold more than forty-five million copies. Rex Stout died in 1975 at the age of eighty-eight. A month before his death, he published his forty-sixth Nero Wolfe novel, *A Family Affair*.

NERO WOLFE

He's not much to look at and he'll never win the hundred yard dash but for sheer genius at unraveling the tangled skeins of crime he has no peer. His outlandish adventures make for some of the best mystery reading in paperback. He's the hero of these superb suspense stories.

BY REX STOUT

THE THRILLING AND MASTERFUL NOVELS OF ROSS MACDONALD

Winner of the Mystery Writers of America Grand Master Award, Ross Macdonald is acknowledged around the world as one of the greatest mystery writers of our time. *The New York Times* has called his books featuring private investigator Lew Archer "the finest series of detective novels ever written by an American."

Now, Bantam Books is reissuing Macdonald's finest work in handsome new paperback editions. Look for these books (a new title will be published every month) wherever paperbacks are sold or use the handy coupon below for ordering:

- ☐ THE GOODBYE LOOK (24192 * $2.95)
- ☐ THE FAR SIDE OF THE DOLLAR (24123 * $2.95)
- ☐ THE ZEBRA-STRIPED HEARSE (23996 * $2.95)
- ☐ MEET ME AT THE MORGUE (24033 * $2.95)
- ☐ THE WAY SOME PEOPLE DIE (23722 * $2.95)
- ☐ THE IVORY GRIN (23804 * $2.95)
- ☐ THE CHILL (24282 * $2.75)
- ☐ THE DROWNING POOL (24135 * $2.75)
- ☐ THE GALTON CASE (22621 * $2.75)
- ☐ THE FERGUSON AFFAIR (13449 * $2.75)
- ☐ THE THREE ROADS (22618 * $2.75)
- ☐ THE DARK TUNNEL (23514 * $2.95)
- ☐ TROUBLE FOLLOWS ME (23516 * $2.95)
- ☐ BLACK MONEY (23498 * $2.95)
- ☐ THE DOOMSTERS (23592 * $2.95)
- ☐ THE NAME IS ARCHER (23650 * $2.95)

Prices and availability subject to change without notice.